Also by Janelle Taylor

Watching Amanda
Dying to Marry
Don't Go Home
Not Without You
Night Moves
In Too Deep

HAUNTING
OLIVIA

JANELLE TAYLOR

ZEBRA BOOKS
Kensington Publishing Corp.

ZEBRA BOOKS are published by

Kensington Publishing Corp.
850 Third Avenue
New York, NY 10022

ISBN 978-0-7394-7519-5

Printed in the United States of America

Chapter 1

The moment Olivia Sedgwick entered the playground, the dream boy and girl flitted through her mind as they always did, the girl's light blond hair bouncing on her thin shoulders as she skipped. The boy, holding a frog, gently cupped it in his hands as he held it out to Olivia before both children faded away.

Visits to the playground always brought the children to mind, their images as real as they were in her dreams, which were more frequent now.

Olivia sat down on a bench near the wrought-iron bars separating the playground from the busy city street, her lunch, a salad in a plastic container, on her lap. Her appetite was gone.

The last time she'd come to this playground, just two days ago, the dream boy, three or four years old, had been marveling over a daddy longlegs making its way up his little arm. The girl, the same age, in a yellow tutu, twirled along a meadow filled with wildflowers, despite it being January in New York City. Like now, the images were fleeting, a moment, maybe two. But they were as vivid as a photograph. Sometimes the boy and girl were very young—but never infants—and sometimes they were older. Like thirteen.

"What you're doing is illegal, you know."

Olivia turned at the unexpected voice of her coworker, Camilla Capshaw. *Glitz* magazine's assistant beauty editor, one of her only friends at the office, waited for a group of moms pushing strollers to pass, then sat down next to Olivia, pulling her own salad from a bag onto her lap.

"Sitting on a bench is illegal?" Olivia asked.

"Entering a playground when you're not accompanied by a kid is illegal," Camilla explained, tossing her shiny, straight dark hair behind her shoulder.

Olivia glanced at her. "Really? We could be arrested for just sitting here?"

Camilla nodded and speared a cucumber. "Don't you remember reading about that woman who got a ticket last year for doing the same thing?"

Olivia shook her head and swiped a cherry tomato from Camilla's salad, her appetite returning. Camilla's presence always made Olivia feel better. "No, but I guess I understand the reasoning behind it. Especially in a city like New York."

"Why would you spend your precious lunch minute watching a bunch of tiny screaming lunatics, anyway?" Camilla asked. "We work with enough screaming lunatics." She sipped from her water bottle. "I've seen you sitting here many times. How can you stand the noise?"

Olivia made a show of glancing at her watch. "We'd better get back to the office. Our lunch minute is up."

Camilla raised an eyebrow. "One day you're

going to tell me all your secrets, Ms. Private. But you're right: if we're a second late for Bitch Face's two o'clock staff meeting, she'll probably fire us."

Their boss was definitely a nightmare to work for, but at least she'd saved Olivia from having to answer Camilla's question.

"Motherhood ruins your life," Camilla whispered into Olivia's ear. "Case in point—your boss."

Olivia followed Camilla's upped chin at her supervisor, Vivian Carl, senior features editor of *Glitz* magazine. Vivian, sitting at the far end—the executive end—of the conference room table, was nine months pregnant, due three days ago, and looked very uncomfortable, both physically and otherwise.

"Vivian, we've reassigned your celebrity interviews for the upcoming months," the editor in chief, Desdemona Fine, announced, without looking at Vivian. "Olivia will now interview Nicole Kidman for our June issue and take over your feature article on the best spas in the country."

Vivian sent Olivia a withering glance, then turned to the editor in chief. "I'm sure I can handle all my work. I'm planning only a three-day maternity leave, and—"

"Moving on to personnel matters," Desdemona interrupted, pushing her poker-straight blond hair behind her shoulder. "As representatives of *Glitz* magazine, one of the most influential and popular beauty and fashion journals in the country, I expect you to dress *appropriately*. For example"—she slid her cold gray gaze on an editorial assistant—"Uggs are out. And *mock* Uggs were never *in*." Additionally, we at *Glitz* magazine do not support the counterfeiting of designer goods." The editorial assistant turned red and slid lower in her chair. "If you are unsure about the image you are projecting as a *Glitz* staffer, please see our fashion director or one of our stylists."

Olivia glanced at *Glitz*'s fashion director, whose cropped blazer was made entirely of sparkling black feathers. Olivia tried not to stare at her hat, a bizarre silver cone that reminded her of an art project for preschoolers.

"Bitch Face chewed me out over the length of my skirt yesterday," Camilla whispered to Olivia as the editor in chief droned on. "An inch higher would completely change your look," Camilla mimicked. "'You really should invest in a full-length mirror, dear.' I hate her guts."

Olivia shot her friend a commiserating smile. "I love the way you dress," she whispered back, taking in Camilla's thrift-store glamour ensemble. The editor in chief often commented that vintage and "send to Goodwill" were not synonymous.

Olivia had worked at *Glitz* for five years and had never been taken to task by the editor in chief.

Because you have a great sense of style, Camilla had once said. *That's all Bitch Face really cares about. And because you have the bucks to buy great clothes. And because you're a Sedgwick. You can do no wrong.*

First of all, Olivia wouldn't say she had a great sense of style. She was attracted to understated, classic clothes in pale, muted shades or black. She hated to stand out. And she didn't have big bucks. As the associate features editor of *Glitz*, Olivia could barely afford the rent on her Manhattan apartment.

It was the *Sedgwick* that gave the impression of

money and glamour and grandeur. Olivia's father, William Sedgwick, who'd passed away only one month ago, had been a regular on *Forbes* magazine's Wealthiest in America list.

In fact, magazines and newspapers provided Olivia with most of her information about her father; the rest came from gossip—which might or might not be true—from her mother.

Olivia hadn't even known that her own father had been dying of cancer.

If he hadn't named Olivia in his will, she had no doubt she would have found out about his death from the *New York Times* obituary section. As it was, she'd learned of his death from his lawyer.

Olivia forced herself to focus on the editor in chief, who was sitting at the head of the long, polished table, still cutting staffers down with a word or even just a glance.

"You're not related to *the* Sedgwicks, are you?" the editor in chief had asked five years ago at Olivia's interview—her fifth and final for the magazine.

The Sedg*wick* Olivia had wanted to correct. But she'd rightly sensed you didn't correct Desdemona Fine, whose real name—according to office gossip—was Mona Fingerman. There was no family of Sedgwicks, past or present. There was William, *the* Sedgwick. And his three daughters, each born of a different mother, none of whom were society page material or remotely well-off, let alone living in luxury.

Olivia's mother berated Olivia on a daily basis for not living up to her name. *You're a Sedgwick! If I had the name, I'd milk it for all it's worth. And it's worth millions.*

Olivia's mother had never married William Sedgwick. She'd famously sued him for millions in child support and had been awarded a very comfortable settlement. Of Olivia's half sisters, only Ivy was a "legitimate" child, only Ivy's mother had been married to William. Briefly of course. According to legend, Dana Sedgwick had gotten a young William dead drunk during a trip to a luxury casino in Las Vegas and sweet-talked him into marrying her at a drive-through wedding chapel. He had the marriage annulled within the week. When anyone asked Dana how long she'd been married to William, she often said they'd had many good years together.

Olivia's mother had had a fling with William. She'd been his flavor of the month twenty-nine years ago, and when Candace Hearn told him she was pregnant with his child, he ended the relationship. She won her settlement and had tried to foist Olivia on her father since the day she was born. William had never been interested. Fatherhood wasn't among his interests or priorities.

Except for the summer she turned sixteen. A summer she never allowed herself to think about.

"Those staffers on the associate level would do well to emulate Olivia Sedgwick's style," Desdemona said, smiling at Olivia.

Olivia felt her cheeks burn. She also felt the eyes of her coworkers and her immediate supervisor, Vivian, narrow on her. Thanks to being Desdemona's pet, most of Olivia's coworkers hated her. Those who took the time to get to know her, like Camilla had, realized that Olivia wasn't the affected snob they thought she was.

"I can handle the Nicole Kidman interview," Vivian said to Desdemona. "It's the cover story, so—"

Desdemona held up a hand. "So *Olivia* will handle

it for you. Do you really think you can represent *Glitz* magazine with leaky tits and baby spit-up on your blouse?"

Vivian burst into tears. Hormonal, I-can't-take-another-minute-of-you tears.

Olivia closed her eyes and shook her head. This was so unfair. Desdemona was so unfair. But instead of threatening the editor in chief with a discrimination suit, Vivian simply sobbed, then ran out of the room. No one would ever back her up anyway. Desdemona was too powerful.

"Waddling doesn't become anyone," Desdemona said under her breath with a tsk-tsk tone, then returned her attention to the meeting minutes.

And Olivia thought Desdemona couldn't possibly get any more vicious.

"Do yourself a very big favor," Camilla whispered to Olivia. "Never get pregnant."

Too late, Olivia thought. Not that she was pregnant right now. But she had been once. A long time ago.

As Olivia settled herself in bed with an article to edit (how many pieces on Botox was *Glitz* going to run?), a boy's face flitted into her mind, a good-looking face with intelligent, kind hazel eyes. This was not the dream boy, though once upon a time he had been Olivia's dream man. Not that Zachary Archer at sixteen had been a man, of course.

Olivia could still see the way Zach's sandy brown hair fell over his forehead. She could still see him so clearly.

It had been so long since that summer—since that

lonely fall and winter and heartbreaking spring—
that thinking of Zach and what she'd gone through
had lost its power to send her to her knees. She had
no idea how she'd managed to get through that time
and then immediately afterward, college, as though
she'd graduated from a regular high school like
every other incoming freshman. Her mother had
used the Sedgwick name and legacy to get her into
her father's alma mater. Olivia would be walking
across campus, forcing herself not to think of Zach,
but his face would appear before her mind's eye and
the pain would whoosh the air of her lungs.

She'd spent her college years either studying or
crying, which didn't allow for friends. And then
after college she'd come home to New York City,
where she'd grown up just off Park Avenue in a
small apartment her mother had managed to buy
with her settlement from William. Her mother had
a contact at *Glitz,* and Olivia, still numb, had come
back to life just a little. Working for a fashion magazine like *Vogue* or *Glitz* had always been her dream.
Olivia's relationship with her mother had improved
in those early months, when Olivia had had something else to think about other than Zach.

Other than the pregnancy. The birth. The news
that had come so cruelly.

"Why isn't it crying?" sixteen-year-old Olivia had
asked the nurse, still unsure whether she'd had a
boy or a girl.

"Because it's dead," the nurse had said flatly. *"Stillborn."*

She'd fainted then and had woken up alone in a
small, airless room. When the nurse's words had
come back to her, she'd gasped and dropped to her

knees and then screamed. The same nurse had come rushing in and told her to "stop making such a racket," that it was the middle of the night.

Her mother was all she'd had after that. Her father couldn't stand the sight of her after that summer. Her sisters had no idea that Olivia had been pregnant and shipped off to a home for unwed mothers hours up the Maine coast. They had no idea that she'd been forced to put the baby up for adoption. Or that the baby hadn't taken a single breath. And so Olivia had distanced herself from her sisters even more. Her mother had been an only child, so there were no aunts, no cousins to turn to. Just Olivia and her memories.

Her father's name had gotten Olivia the job at *Glitz*, and she'd been there ever since. Five years. She'd started as an editorial assistant to Vivian and had been promoted twice. Desdemona had often hinted that Olivia could count on having Vivian's job, too.

Tears burning her eyes, Olivia set the article aside and glanced out the window of her skyscraper apartment building; flurries blew around in the January wind. Despite the warmth of her apartment and her cozy down comforter, she shivered. The idea of stealing her boss's job while Vivian was on maternity leave—a weeklong maternity leave—made her sick to her stomach. Sometimes Olivia thought about leaving *Glitz*, but crazy as it sounded, she liked her job very much; she was suited to it, and she adored Camilla. Despite the bitching and backstabbing, *Glitz* had provided Olivia with work she loved, structure, a life. And with a mother like Candace Hearn, Olivia had learned to tune out bitching. Backstabbing was another story. Her mother might have had a shrill shell, but inside she was something of a marshmallow. Desdemona Fine, on the other hand, was a shrill shell inside and out.

Out of the corner of her eye, Olivia noticed the red light blinking on her answering machine. She'd been so wrapped up in memories and work when she arrived home that she hadn't even thought to check her messages.

She padded out of bed and pressed Play.

"Livvy, dear, it's Mother. I ran into Buffy Carmichael. You remember, Buffy, darling. She chairs so many charity events. Anyway, Buffy mentioned that her son, Walter, is recently separated, and of course I gave Buffy your number, so expect a call, dear. He's very wealthy. She showed me a photo and he's no Orlando Bloom, but at your age you can't afford to be picky about looks—only about income. Bye, dear. Oh—I'd really like you to consider changing your mind about tomorrow. I'd really like to be there when you find out what your father left you in his will. Ta-ta!"

Olivia rolled her eyes at the phone. She'd gotten out of bed for that? And why couldn't her mother talk like a normal person?

At your age . . . Please. Olivia was twenty-nine! Young. And she couldn't care less about a man's looks or income. Once she'd moved back to New York and started working at *Glitz*, Olivia had numbly dated many different men—grad students, CEOs, a plumber (whose pants did not hang down), a chef, a mechanic, a shrink. The list went on and on. She dated. She had sex. And that was about it. She tried— really tried—to fall in love with several of the men she dated; she tried to develop real relationships with them, but a piece of her—the most important piece, the deepest piece—just didn't come out of its hiding place. It had once. With Zach. Maybe you loved like that only once.

She hoped not. She'd last loved like that when she was sixteen. If that was her last hurrah—her *only* hurrah—she was in big trouble.

And no, Mommy Dearest, you can't come with me tomorrow. Tomorrow, Friday, January thirtieth, was the day she was to receive her father's letter from his lawyer. An envelope with her name on it. To Be Opened No Sooner or Later Than January 30.

Olivia had no idea what the date could possibly mean. Why January 30? It was just an arbitrary day, but perhaps it meant something to her father.

Her sister Amanda had already received her inheritance letter a month ago (also on a specific day); it had stated that Amanda would inherit their father's million-dollar brownstone on the Upper West Side—*if* she followed a bunch of ridiculous and arbitrary rules for a month, such as not looking out of certain windows or going in certain rooms. Her father had even arranged for a watchdog to ensure that Amanda followed his rules to the letter—literally. That watchdog ended up becoming Amanda's husband. The happy couple—who donated the brownstone to a children's charity—was now on an extended honeymoon.

Olivia was so happy for Amanda. She was still getting to know Amanda and Ivy, her other sister, who was engaged. *Both my sisters are getting on with their love lives, and I'm stuck getting fixed up by my mother.*

She had no idea what her father had in store for her—or if she'd bother jumping through his hoops. He owned only two other properties: a cottage in Maine and an old inn in New Jersey. He wouldn't leave her the Maine house. Not after what happened there.

The summer she had turned seventeen, Olivia had gone back to her father's cottage for her annual summer vacation with him and her sisters. It had taken so much out of her to agree to the trip. But Zachary hadn't been in town. His family had moved away, she'd heard. No one knew where. She kept hoping she might hear something of what became of him, but no one knew. And no one really cared. Zach Archer, whose father was famous for falling down drunk in the middle of the street during the day, and whose mother was famous for sleeping with other women's husbands for small favors, didn't have much of a chance in Blueberry, Maine, a coastal town of wealthy year-rounders and summer tourists. When Olivia had known him, people liked to shake their heads and say, "That poor kid." Zach had hated that.

Perhaps William left me the New Jersey house, Olivia thought, heading into the bathroom. She'd never thought of her father as "Dad"; she'd always referred to him as her father, or William. She had called him dad just once, thinking it might soften him, make him see inside her, listen to her, but it hadn't.

Anyway, she was sure the bequest would come with some silly rules about doors to open and windows not to raise. Maybe she'd accept the terms of the will and donate the house to a charity close to her heart, as Amanda had done with her inheritance. Olivia would probably have to spend a month at the house—and the idea of spending a month in her father's world made her faintly sick—but she could always commute to Manhattan from New

Jersey. She'd need more time to handle all her boss's work while she was on maternity leave anyway.

Olivia headed into the bathroom, opened the medicine cabinet, and took out the jar of $100-an-ounce cucumber nighttime moisturizer that Camilla had swiped for her from the beauty department's goodie bags (the magazine got so many expensive freebies). She breathed in the fresh scent and looked at herself in the mirror. At times like this, when her face was fresh scrubbed and her hair was down (she liked wearing chignons at work) and her elegant outfits were replaced by an old "Buffy the Vampire Slayer" T-shirt and her comfiest yoga pants, she could still see the sixteen-year-old girl she was before her life changed forever. Before she began spending a part of every day in a playground—sometimes just a few minutes, sometimes hours—just to imagine what her baby might have grown up to be like at every stage, every age.

Chapter 2

What Zachary Archer needed was a guidebook: *How to Deal with Your Thirteen-Year-Old Daughter without Scarring Her—or Yourself—for Life*. Until now, he'd been doing fine as a single parent. More than fine. Great. If he did say so himself. He'd gotten through Kayla's infancy and the terrible twos and the first day of school and her first broken bone and her first crush on a boy.

He'd even gotten through her first menstrual period, through an embarrassing ten-minute analysis of the feminine protection aisle (what the heck were *wings?*) of a drugstore before a grandmotherly type saved him, loading up his basket with brightly colored packages and boxes.

He had no idea *how* he'd gotten through it. A few months ago, Kayla had come running out of the bathroom shrieking, crying, clapping her hands: *"I got it! I got it! I'm not the last of my friends, after all!"* At his perplexed expression, she'd said, *"Duh, Daddy, my period!"*

But you're just a little girl! he'd thought frantically, wondering how his baby had grown up so fast.

His first thought had been to call Marnie, his girl-friend, and ask her to bring over the necessary items and show Kayla how to use them, but before he could even mention Marnie's name, Kayla had screeched, *"If you tell whatshername I'll never tell you anything again! Swearsies you won't tell Marnie! It's my private business!"* By the time he'd returned from Rite Aid, Kayla was locked in the bathroom with a girlfriend and had half yelled, half laughed through the door that she didn't need his help.

He'd gotten through all that. He'd get through her first cigarette. *Repeat, repeat, repeat,* he told him-self as Kayla got into his SUV, a little too okay with having been suspended from school.

First cigarette. Ha. First cigarette he *knew* about.

"You can't ground me, Dad," Kayla said, twirling a long, blond spiral curl around her finger as she stared out her window. "I'm *already* grounded."

At the moment she was actually *thrice* grounded. For purposely pushing a girl at the ice-skating rink, which had resulted in a badly twisted ankle. For telling the six-year-old boy two houses over that she was sending a monster to eat him at night and soon there would be nothing left of him but his finger-nails. (Apparently, the Herman family had suffered through three sleepless nights before little Conner told them why he refused to close his eyes.) And for this tidbit to his girlfriend while he went to pay the check at a "give Marnie a chance lunch": "My dad doesn't love you, you know that, right? He told me it was just a sex thing—whatever that means."

"*Do* you love me?" Marnie had asked later, which was

what had driven him to ground Kayla for *two* weeks instead of the one he'd been planning. Whether or not he loved Marnie wasn't a question he wanted—or was ready—to answer. Or that Marnie would have asked without Kayla's dig.

Which meant that Kayla was grounded for four weeks. Of course, he'd lost track of when the punishments started and ended. And he had no clue where to fit in punishment for being suspended from school. Suspended. Even he himself, the kid from the wrong side of the tracks, the kid from whom bad behavior was *expected,* had never been suspended from school. He let out a deep breath.

In the middle of an important meeting with a potential client, Zach had received a phone call from Blueberry Middle School's assistant principal. *Your daughter has been caught smoking on school property for the second time. She's therefore suspended for one week.* And so he'd postponed his meeting—good thing the client was a parent herself and assured him they'd reschedule—and driven down to the school and sat in a stuffy room with a sullen, defensive Kayla; the gym teacher who'd caught her redhanded in the second-floor girls' bathroom; and the assistant principal, who'd reminded Zach that she'd had to call him in to discuss Kayla's behavior six times since the school year began.

So much for the New Year's resolutions he and Kayla had made a month ago. Getting her to sit down and think about what she wanted from the coming year was hard enough, but she'd actually gotten into it, disappearing into her room, door closed as usual, music blaring. The next morning she said she had made her list but it was private.

"Is one of them for you to try to accept that I'm dating Marnie?" he'd asked.

"No," she'd said, grimacing, her hazel eyes narrowed. "Definitely not."

He'd handed her a plate of scrambled eggs and toast. "Well, share *one* of them."

"Okay," she had said. "I resolve to make a certain boy, who'll go nameless, like me by spring break."

That he wasn't so sure he would get through.

Now, as he pulled out of the school's parking lot, Kayla's triumphant smile over getting out of school for a week turned into a frown. "She thinks she's so great," Kayla said, staring out the window at a blond girl getting into her mother's car. "Just because she's popular. She's only popular because she has big tits."

Oh, God. Zach let out a deep breath and silently counted to ten, willing the powers that be to give him strength to get through the next—what? Five years? Ten?

"Kayla, I'd appreciate it if you'd use the proper words to describe parts of the body," he said. "Your body is something to respect, not to put down."

"Fine, *breasts*," she said.

Why was Kayla so comfortable talking about *tits* with him anyway? Shouldn't she be fidgety and uncomfortable?

He really needed that guidebook.

"Are *you* popular?" he asked, having no idea what he was supposed to say or how best to deal with this new jealousy issue. His instincts told him to be careful with her self-esteem, give her some room with her thoughts, let her express herself without jumping down her throat.

"Who cares about popularity?" she snapped. "It's totally fake. The popular girls aren't even nice—except to boys. At least I'm not a fake."

Nope, fake she was not. What you saw was what you got.

So. She wasn't popular. But she had a couple of friends: two girls from the neighborhood who were her best friends one week, her mortal enemies the next. It had been that way since Zach and Kayla had moved back to Blueberry eight years ago. Right now, Kayla wasn't talking to the girls, who'd dared to tell her that she had big feet.

They drove the few miles to their house, a white colonial that Zach built himself. He pulled into the driveway, hoping all the answers would magically come to him before they got inside.

"Kayla, I know you're a smart girl," he said, as they both got out. "I know you must be aware that smoking causes cancer. That's not some lie parents make up to keep their teenagers from smoking."

She rolled her eyes. "Like I'm going to get cancer. I'm only *thirteen*. And I don't smoke that much. Like one cigarette a day. Two maybe."

"That's too many," he said. "And you could get cancer anytime, Kay. Kids younger than you have cancer. I'm dead serious. And I'm going to tell you right now so there's no misunderstanding. You are not allowed to smoke. If I catch you smoking or if I hear you've been smoking, you will be disciplined. And trust me, you won't like it."

She bit her lip, then pouted, then wrapped a curl around her finger. "So what am I—grounded for a year?"

"I'm taking away your iPOD for a week, Kayla.

And no television for a week. And no going out for a week."

Which meant he'd have to take the week off from work to supervise her.

"What?" she shrieked. "What am I supposed to *do*?"

"Think," he said as they headed inside. "About yourself. You can also do your homework, which I'll make sure you receive each day. And you'll help me clean out the attic. That should take about a week. And you'll write a three-page term paper about the effects of smoking. You can do your research on-line." *With me looking over your shoulder to make sure you're not surfing or IMing your friends.*

She rolled her eyes and let out a few exaggerated deep breaths, then flopped onto the couch and began braiding and unbraiding her baby-fine blond hair.

So like her mother's. Out of nowhere, Olivia came to mind. Forget thinking for a second that Kayla's mother would be better at all this than he was; aside from the fact that Olivia had never been interested in being a mother from day one of Kayla's life, Olivia hadn't been a rabble-rouser like Kayla was. She'd been something of a goody two-shoes. Except for dating him, of course. Until her father found out, anyway.

He quickly shook his head to clear his mind of Olivia Sedgwick. Not that it was easy. There were times—nights when he was alone mostly—that he couldn't stop thinking about her. He was grateful that Kayla looked exactly like him, except for her hair, which was all Olivia's.

"So, since I'm grounded, I can't eat dinner with you and whatshername and the snot, right?" Kayla asked without looking up.

"Kayla, being disrespectful—to me and to Marnie and to her daughter—isn't going to help your case. It's not going to help you, period."

"Do I have to eat with you and them?" she asked, turning to face him, her expression betraying her, as it always did. She wasn't so much angry and petulant as she was just plain upset. Confused. Thirteen. Her dad had been dating for one month and she was now finally old enough not to like it. Not that he was making excuses for his daughter. He knew what he was up against with Kayla.

"Kayla, I wish you'd give Marnie a chance. She really is a good person. And I care about her, okay?"

"Are you in love with her?" she asked, her hazel eyes nervous.

"We've only been dating a month and I'm still getting to know her," he said.

She smiled. "That means no. At school if you just start dating someone at lunch, you know if you're in love by the time the bell rings."

He shook his head but couldn't contain the smile. "I'm making my famous lasagna. Your favorite."

"I'd rather miss it than sit across from that snot," she shot back.

The "snot" was Marnie's thirteen-year-old daughter, Brianna, who *was* a little on the snotty side.

"Kayla, her name is Brianna. And, yes, you're having dinner with us."

She flung her braid over her shoulder and ran into her room.

If only he had that guidebook.

Zach had just pulled the pan of lasagna from the oven when the doorbell rang. "Kayla, can you get that, please?" he called out.

No answer.

"Kayla, the door."

No answer.

He eyed the lasagna. Perfecto. Unlike his daughter's attitude. "Kayla, come out of your room right now."

Her door opened and she poked her head out.

"I asked you to answer the door," he said, his voice, his expression stern.

"I didn't hear you," she said, glancing away as she always did when she was lying.

He set the pan on the stove top and pulled off the oven mitts. "Well, go open the door now before our guests freeze on the porch."

"Or we could just let them do that," she whispered, shooting him a grin and stepping into the hallway.

He sighed inwardly. "Hysterical, Kayla," he whispered back. "You know what else isn't funny? Your T-shirt. Go change. Now."

"What about your big speech last month about accepting me for who I am and my individuality?" she shot back, crossing her arms over her chest, upon which it said "I HATE YOU" in big block letters.

"Go. Change. Now," he said.

"Fine. I'll be who I'm not."

How about a charming, delightful daughter, just for five minutes? he thought, heading to the door as the bell rang again. *I'll take that.*

He opened the door; Marnie and Brianna stood on the porch, each carrying a container. "Finally," Brianna said.

Zach smiled. "Sorry. We were handling hot pans when the bell rang. Come on in."

They stepped inside the small entry room, then slipped out of their coats and boots and hats and gloves. Marnie wore a fitted red fuzzy sweater and sexy jeans. Every time she lifted her arms he got a glimpse of her belly button. Zach was always surprised by how pretty, how sexy Marnie was. Once, she asked him if he thought about her a lot when they weren't together, and he said, of course, *how could he not,* but the truth was he didn't. So when he did see her, the fact that she was so . . . hot always took him by surprise. She was his age—thirty—and had gorgeous long, silky, dark brown hair and dark brown eyes, yet very fair skin. And as they were both single parents (Marnie was divorced; Zach had never been married), they had a lot in common. On the surface, anyway.

Brianna was a budding Marnie. Ten boys had already asked her to the winter dance. If anyone had asked Kayla, she hadn't mentioned it.

"Chocolate cream pie," Marnie said, handing him the container and kissing him on the cheek.

Mmmm . . . She always smelled as delicious as she looked. He realized he was staring at her breasts, which were huge, and he quickly glanced away.

She smiled sensuously at him. "Brianna made her famous garlic bread."

"What is it famous for?" Kayla asked, coming into the foyer, her shirt normal. "Stinking up the house? People's breath?"

"Kayla!" Zach snapped.

Brianna rolled her eyes at Kayla. "You're so immature."

"Okay, you two," Marnie said. "Let's make some predinner rules right now. No name-calling. No insults. Just good food, good conversation, and a good time."

Now both girls rolled their eyes.

Zach refused Marnie and Brianna's offers to help and set Kayla to work instead. "Be good," he whispered as he put Brianna's garlic bread in a basket for Kayla to take into the dining room while he carried the lasagna.

"I have nothing to lose by being bad," she pointed out.

"Be good for me," he said, "because I'm asking you to. Because it would mean a lot to me."

"Fine. I won't ask Brianna if she's tried Clearasil on that giant zit on her chin."

"Kayla, I'm warning you," he said through gritted teeth.

She rolled her eyes for the umpteenth time.

"Yum, something smells delicious!" Marnie said as she and Brianna sat down at the dining room table. "Kayla, did you help cook?"

Kayla opened her mouth to make one of her famous snarky statements, he was sure, but she thought better of it. Good girl. "I'm a terrible cook. Trust me, you wouldn't want to eat anything I made. I can't even boil an egg."

"Boiling an egg is so easy," Brianna said. "You boil the water, then place—"

"Sweetie," Marnie interrupted her daughter, "would you please pass the lasagna?"

"I'm only having a little," Brianna said, scooping a small square onto her plate. "I'm entering the town's beauty contest, and I have only two weeks before I'll be paraded on stage."

"*Inner*-beauty pageant," Marnie corrected. "There's a big difference, Brianna. Inner beauty is what we should all strive for."

"*Inner*-beauty pageant?" Kayla repeated. "Is that some kind of joke?"

Brianna glared at Kayla. "It's not a joke. The pageant is for girls from thirteen to seventeen who possess remarkable inner beauty. Girls who know that real beauty is inside, not just outside."

Marnie nodded. "That's right, Brianna." She turned to Kayla. "I heard that your mother won when she was fifteen."

Zach almost choked on his bite of garlic bread. *Tell me she didn't just say that. Please.*

Kayla stared from Marnie to Zach. "My mother? My mother won the Inner-Beauty Pageant?"

Marnie's cheeks reddened. "I thought you would have . . ." She trailed off. "Mmm, that garlic bread smells heavenly! Sweetie, could you pass me the basket?" she asked Kayla.

"You didn't even know your own mother won the pageant?" Brianna said to Kayla. "How weird is that?"

Kayla threw the basket of garlic bread at Brianna, clocking her on the chest, and then ran upstairs.

Zach closed his eyes for a moment.

"What a freak!" Brianna screamed. "I can't believe her! This shirt is ruined."

Her shirt was the least of what was ruined.

"Brianna Sweetser, apologize right now!" Marnie said. "To Zach and then to Kayla."

"It's all right," Zach said. "It was a reasonable question, Brianna." He could tell that Marnie was hoping he'd elaborate on the subject of Kayla's mother, but he didn't. He'd told Marnie a little about Olivia, that theirs had been a teenaged summer romance, that he'd been a punk kid then and Olivia, who'd won the Inner-Beauty Pageant, had somehow seen something in him.

As for Kayla, he'd prepared an answer for her when she'd first started asking in earnest about her mother.

She was very young when you came along, too young to be a mom, and she wanted you to have the very best life, so she did the responsible thing and gave you to me to take care of.

That wasn't close to what had happened, but it was the only version of events he could bear to tell his daughter.

But weren't you also very young—too young to be a dad? had been Kayla's question. *Why didn't she ever come back? Why? How could she just walk away and never look back?*

Those were questions he couldn't answer. Not at four, when the questions started in earnest. And not now.

As Brianna headed upstairs to knock on Kayla's bedroom door to apologize, Marnie rushed over to him and sat down on his lap. What he wouldn't give for a half hour alone with a naked Marnie, to lose himself inside her, to forget everything, just for a little while. But tonight was going to be about damage control.

He breathed in her sexy perfume as she trailed kisses along his neck.

"Sorry about all that," she whispered. "They're at such a tough age, and Kayla must have so many questions about her mom."

He took a deep breath. "I think we're going to have to make this a short night. I need to get up there and give her some answers."

"You know," she said, pressing her breasts against his chest, "when you're ready, I'd like to have some of those answers too. There's so much about you I don't know, Zach Archer."

At the sound of Brianna's footsteps coming down the stairs, Marnie scooted off his lap, and he missed her warmth and perfume instantly.

"I said I was sorry and really sorry and double sorry, like, three times," Brianna said, "but Kayla told me to go away and wouldn't open the door."

"Sweetie, why don't we pack up two portions of this delicious dinner and eat at home," Marnie said to Brianna. "I think Zach and Kayla need some time alone to talk."

Score one for Marnie. He'd never appreciated her quite so much.

Chapter 3

Olivia darted up in bed, the dream already fading. The boy and girl, standing side by side, staring at her with unreadable expressions, were gone. No matter how she tried to hold their faces in her mind, she could never fully remember them. She'd been having the dream for years, since she'd been pregnant. The boy and girl, around three or four in this dream, never spoke. The girl wore a bathing suit, pink with yellow flowers on the straps. The boy was holding a stuffed cow.

In the dream, Amanda always gently asked them if she could help them, if they wanted something, but they just continued to stare. The boy held out the cow, but just as Olivia reached for it, the dream ended, as it always did.

When she was pregnant, she thought the boy and girl represented her unborn child, since she didn't know the sex. She'd asked, of course, but the nurse had told her she'd be better off not knowing. Mostly Olivia agreed with that one. Knowing would have been too painful.

I wanted you, she always said to the dream children. *I wanted to keep you, I really did.*

But I signed your life away to another family, a family that could take much better care of you than I could at sixteen. A family my mother and father both promised would love you as though you were their own. Olivia remembered how much that comforted her during her pregnancy and the birth.

But then the baby had been stillborn.

A skinny pigeon settled onto the snow-dusted windowsill of Olivia's bedroom, and she forced herself to pay attention to its darting head, its tiny feet. Anything to put her thoughts out of reach. The bird flew away, and she glanced at the clock. It was just after six in the morning. Which left three hours to wonder what she'd find in the envelope she'd pick up today from her father's lawyer.

What would her father bequeath to her? To the daughter who "disappointed" him? Perhaps he wanted to continue punishing her for "running around like a slut with a loser kid."

Her mother had asked her a hundred times what she thought might be in the envelope, as if Olivia could possibly know. "You might have ruined your chances with him because of getting pregnant as a teenager," her mother had ruminated earlier that week. "But the stillbirth probably fixed everything for him. He wouldn't have to think of some grandkid out there who'd one day try to lay claim to his money."

Olivia shook her head. She had some set of parents. As self-serving as two people got. *You're so much nicer than we thought you'd be,* was a refrain she'd heard her entire life upon meeting people who knew her mother and father.

Olivia pulled the covers over her head with a sigh. Whenever she had the dream, usually every few weeks, she had a really crappy day. The last time she'd had the dream, she'd returned home from work to find a message on her answering machine from her father's lawyer, which was how she'd been notified of her father's death. The lawyer had assumed she knew, of course. She hadn't known. She'd come home that evening, pressed Play, heard the words, and the air had gone out of her lungs. And then she'd cried.

Which meant she did care about William Sedgwick. Was affected by him. Despite how hard she'd tried over the years to pretend it didn't matter that her father didn't want to be a father, didn't want to know her or her sisters.

Interestingly, before she'd gotten pregnant, he seemed to favor her over her sisters. She was the golden girl, "the beauty," as he called her, the daughter who had preppy assholes with roman numerals after their names lined up to date her in New York and Maine. The daughter who won the Inner-Beauty Pageant as well as "belonged on the cover of a magazine." But favoring her meant only smiling at her when they passed in the house during the two-week summer vacations she spent in Maine with her sisters. Amanda and Ivy seemed to get nods or absolutely nothing. Olivia didn't even know why he bothered inviting them every summer from the time they were toilet trained. But he did.

I wish my sisters were around today, Olivia thought,

getting out of bed. But Amanda was on her honeymoon and Ivy, a police officer, was on a stakeout in New Jersey. She wasn't exactly looking forward to opening the envelope by her lonesome.

It was just a white envelope, legal size, exactly like Amanda's.

Olivia spent just a few moments in the lawyer's office, signing for the envelope, and then left with it unopened in her purse. She took a taxi to the offices of *Glitz* magazine, then rode up in the elevator to the twenty-second floor, said hello to the receptionist and her coworkers, and headed into the kitchenette for some coffee, as she always did.

"Bitch Face is on the warpath," Camilla whispered to Olivia. "Stay out of her way."

Olivia nodded, pouring a cup of coffee for herself and a cup of decaf for her boss, Vivian. Olivia wanted to have a talk with Vivian, explain that she wasn't angling—

"You little bitch," Vivian screeched at Olivia as the woman suddenly appeared in the doorway of the kitchenette. "You angled for my job and now you've gotten it. Congratulations. I'll send a pitchfork as a gift." Olivia had never seen Vivian so furious.

"Vivian, I have no idea what you're talking about," Olivia said, her heart racing. "Angled for your job?"

"Cut the goody two-shoes crap," Vivian spit out. "Desdemona just fired me. Don't act like you don't know."

Olivia stared at Vivian. "Fired? But"—her eyes

dropped to Vivian's belly—"she can't fire you—
you're—"

Desdemona's assistant appeared in the kitchenette.
"Ah, there you are, Olivia. Desdemona would like to
see you right away."

Vivian stalked away.

"Vivian, wait!" Olivia called, but Vivian didn't
even turn around.

"Desdemona is waiting," clipped the assistant.

Olivia followed the tall, thin woman into Desdemona's huge corner office, which was larger than
Olivia's entire apartment.

"Ah, congratulations, Olivia. You're *Glitz* magazine's new features editor. You'll now be reporting
directly to me. Sit. We need to discuss how you'll
handle the transition. Today is Vivian's last day, and
as her employment has been terminated, you may
move into her office and adopt her Rolodex."

So it really was true. Desdemona had fired a long-
term staffer on the eve of her maternity leave. A
long-term staffer who'd been very good to Olivia
from day one. Vivian had never cared that Olivia's
father was William Sedgwick. She never tried to use
Olivia's supposed connections. And she treated
Olivia the way she treated everyone—with respect
and professionalism.

"Actually, Desdemona," Olivia said, taking a deep
breath, "if you'd taken the time to actually offer me
the position, I would have declined it."

Desdemona glanced up so sharply that her ubiq-
uitous *Glitz* mug of tea spilled on her desk. Her assistant rushed to mop up the mess. "You may go,
Eleanor," she snarled.

"I can't work for someone who'd fire a wonderful person and a top-notch employee when she's nine months pregnant," Olivia said. "I learned everything I know from Vivian. I owe her something."

"You're an idiot," Desdemona said. "You owe her nothing. You don't owe anyone anything. Spineless bleeding hearts don't have a place at *Glitz* anyway. Good day, Olivia. Eleanor will escort you out. You have five minutes to collect your personal possessions under supervision."

As a personnel assistant and Desdemona's assistant watched with eagle eyes, Olivia took only one thing from her desk: a framed photograph of the three Sedgwick sisters taken a month ago at her sister Amanda's wedding. Everything else she left behind.

Olivia sat on the same bench in the same playground she'd visited the day before, this time more intent on the photograph on her lap than on the children playing.

Now that she'd quit *Glitz* (actually, she wasn't sure if she'd resigned or gotten fired), the two other women in the photograph felt like all she had. And she barely had them. They were her sisters, yes, her half sisters. She hadn't grown up with them. She barely knew them. Until last month, the three Sedgwick sisters had rarely spoken. They hadn't been raised to be close, and so in adulthood they'd been wary of each other, a trait their mothers had instilled in them since toddlerhood. Well, Olivia's and Ivy's mothers, anyway. Amanda's mother had been very kind and not the least bit competitive, but she'd passed away years ago.

Olivia glanced at the photo. The three sisters had the same eyes, almond shaped and blue, like their father's, but the similarity ended there. Olivia's hair was blond and straight. Amanda's hair was brown and wavy, and Ivy's was short with an auburn cast.

As the eldest sister, Olivia felt as though she should do something to bring the sisters closer, but what? And how? Amanda now lived in Maine with her new husband and her adorable year-old son, Tommy, from a previous relationship. Ivy lived in New Jersey, almost two hours' driving distance from Manhattan, and her job as a police officer and her wedding plans (she was engaged to be married in March) kept her very busy.

Her cell phone rang. Olivia glanced at the Caller ID. Her mother. For the fourth time this morning.

"Hi, Mom. No, I haven't opened the envelope." She'd almost forgotten all about it.

"What the hell are you waiting for?" her mother yelled in her ear. "Open it!"

"I'm afraid to," she said, surprising herself with her honesty. She rarely felt she could be honest with her mother.

"Honey, there's nothing in there but property or a pile of money. I'm sure your father left you something of equal value to the brownstone he bequeathed to Amanda. Millions!"

"Amanda and Ethan donated the brownstone to a children's charity," Olivia reminded her mother. "Maybe I'll do that with whatever William left me.

Do I really want to inherit anything from a man who couldn't bother being my father?"

"He was your father when it counted, Olivia," her mother snapped. "When you were in trouble, he stepped up."

Her mother never said the actual words: *when you got pregnant.* Nor did she ever mention the home Olivia had been sent to, the lies told to distant relatives and friends and school administration. And the birth—it was as though it had never happened.

"Stepped up or took care of business?" Olivia asked. "He did what was good for himself. He was embarrassed and he 'handled' what he considered a problem."

"Olivia, there's no need to rehash the past. Your father owes you for being an absentee father. Take the money and buy yourself a beautiful apartment. You might even have something left over for your dear mother."

Olivia smiled. She could always count on her mother for honesty, that was for sure.

"Mom, when I open it, I'll call you first thing, okay?"

Having extracted a promise from Olivia to open it today (which she was legally bound to, according to her father's lawyer), her mother harrumphed and hung up. Olivia put her phone and the photograph away and took out the white envelope, turning it over in her hands.

"My ball!"

Olivia glanced up to find an adorable little girl, around four, racing toward her. With her white blond hair, blue eyes, and heart-shaped face, she could be Olivia's own child.

Except that her child, had he or she lived, would now be thirteen. And he or she would have inherited some of Zach's features and coloring. His thick sandy brown hair or his intense hazel eyes. His dimple or his cleft.

She hadn't even had the chance to hold her own baby, see him or her. She'd never know what their baby had looked like. Tightness squeezed her chest and she shut her eyes.

"My ball! Under bench!"

Olivia opened her eyes to find the blond girl almost in tears, pointing under Olivia's bench.

"Don't worry, sweetie," Olivia told her. "I'll get your ball." She kicked it out with her foot and the little girl scooped it up and ran back to her mother, by the slide.

Before she could procrastinate another second, Olivia slit open the envelope. Inside was a letter, just one page, typed and signed by William Sedgwick.

> *Dear Olivia,*
>
> *I bequeath to you my beloved summer cottage in Blueberry, Maine, where you and your sisters spent vacation each summer, albeit just a bit of each summer, as a family. In order to inherit the cottage, you must live in Blueberry for at least one month and you must go into town at least once per day and buy one item each from two different establishments.*
>
> *Upon completion of the thirty-day stay—the house's caretaker will stop by each morning at 8 A.M. for you to sign and date a roll sheet and to collect your receipts—and a tally of your receipts by my*

lawyer, Edwin Harris, you will inherit the cottage and a lump sum of money to be disclosed at that time.

You may pick up keys to the house from Edwin, who has a copy of this letter. Should you not spend thirty days in Blueberry, Maine, or buy one item each from two different town establishments (you'll love the blueberry scones and Rocky Coast coffee at the Blueberry Eat-In Diner), you will forfeit your inheritance, including the cottage and the lump sum of money, which I assure you is generous.

You may not want to go to Blueberry, Olivia. In fact, I'm sure you won't want to. However, if you do go, your every dream will come true. On this you can trust me.

Your father,
William Sedgwick

Olivia crumpled up the letter and tossed it in the garbage can a few feet away. And missed, of course. She picked it up and angrily stuffed it in her pocket. Her dreams? What would William Sedgwick possibly know about her dreams? She spent two weeks a year with him—and of those two weeks, she saw him about two hours a day. During the past thirteen years, she'd rarely seen him. A handful of times, maybe.

Why in the world would he think she would ever go back to Maine, the place where all her dreams were destroyed? Where she fell in love for the first time and where her heart was broken. Where she was banished, hours up the coast on an island to live out her pregnancy alone. Where she gave birth to a baby who hadn't drawn a breath.

She wouldn't step foot in Blueberry, let alone spend a month there.

Her cell phone rang again. Camilla. Thank God it wasn't her mother.

"I guess you've heard," Olivia said, absently watching a mother push her toddler on the baby swings.

"Everyone's heard!" Camilla said. "You're our hero!"

"How much does that pay?" Olivia joked. "I'm out of a job."

"Meet for lunch?" Camilla asked. "My treat. To celebrate your escape from the wicked witch."

Lunch with a friend was exactly what Olivia needed.

The more Olivia talked, the more Camilla's huge brown eyes widened even more.

"Wow," Camilla said, poking at her salad. Salad was all Camilla—and most of the *Glitz* staffers—ever ate. Only one teaspoon of dressing, of course. "I had no idea how much you were keeping inside. Your family, Zach, the pregnancy. Maybe going to Blueberry will give you some closure."

Olivia shrugged and poked at her omelet. "Maybe."

But closure from what? Nothing in Blueberry had been left unresolved. Both her relationship with Zach and the birth of her baby had very clear endings.

"Enough about me," Olivia said. "And *Glitz*. Tell me about you. How's that cute guy you're dating?"

Camilla's entire face lit up. And for the next hour, Olivia was happy to lose herself in Camilla's warm chatter and forget all about lawyers, letters, the State of Maine, her mother, and joblessness.

* * *

After lunch, Olivia headed back home to think. Her phone rang nonstop—her mom—and Olivia let the machine get it. It felt so strange to be aimless at two in the afternoon on a weekday. So after scrubbing her apartment (her tub had never been so sparkling) and making an elaborate chicken dish for dinner, involving sherry and walnuts, and then staring out the window at the gathering dusk, Olivia headed into the bathroom to slather on yet another of Camilla's complementary masks, this time soothing lavender.

In her plush pink bathrobe she flopped down on her bed to wait for the mask to dry and mulled over her sisters' advice. She'd called both Amanda and Ivy after dinner, bringing them up to date on everything— except her own past. *That* she still wasn't ready to share with her sisters.

"Sounds just like the letter I received," Amanda had said. "I don't know, Olivia. Since you're free and clear for a while anyway, you could just go and get it over with and then decide if the cottage and the money are something you want or not. Maybe a month away from it all is exactly what you need."

But Blueberry wasn't "a month away from it all." It *was* "it all."

Ivy had similar advice.

"And one more thing, Olivia," Ivy had said. "Will you be my co–maid of honor with Amanda?"

Olivia had been so touched. "Of course! I'd love to. And thanks so much for asking me."

"I'll have more details on the wedding plans soon. I can't believe I'm getting married in two months!"

Ivy's fiancé was a handsome business student

named Declan. Ivy's mother adored him; he was the friend of a friend of a friend, but William Sedgwick hadn't approved of Declan and let Ivy know it. In fact, she was scheduled to receive her inheritance letter on March 20. Her wedding day. Ivy's mother thought William was up to no good and would send her on a wild goose chase in order to receive her inheritance—anything to get her not to marry Declan.

"I'm planning to open that letter *after* the ceremony," Ivy had said. "I'm not letting William or his crazy letter ruin my wedding day. I'll deal with whatever's in my envelope after I'm a married woman."

But what if William was right about Declan? Olivia had worried silently. *What if there's a good reason he arranged for Ivy's envelope to be opened on her wedding day? What if he knew something?* He certainly ended up doing well enough by Amanda, posthumously setting her up with the man she married.

It was all so confusing. William couldn't have known that Amanda—a daughter he barely knew—would fall in love with Ethan, the man he'd chosen to make sure she followed the instructions in her bequeathal envelope. How could he possibly have known?

Your every dream will come true . . .

I have no dreams, she thought. *I once dreamed of running away with Zach, raising our child, being happy. That was all I ever wanted. What could I possibly want now?*

Once, she wanted to be editor in chief of a women's magazine, but that was less a dream and more pure ambition to make up for the lack of anything else in her life, like love. Like a relationship.

When she gave birth only to know the baby died instead of living and thriving with a family who would take good care of him or her, a huge piece of Olivia died too. The piece that wanted or hoped. The only dreams Olivia had were recurring ones she'd had for thirteen years.

She picked up the phone and called her mother. It was time to tell her mom what her father had conditionally left her—and that she wasn't going to meet the conditions. Her mother was the only person, aside from Camilla now, who knew about her past. She'd understand. And then Olivia could get on with the business of trying to find a new job at a women's magazine—if Desdemona hadn't blackballed her, that was.

"But you must do as your father wants!" her mother screeched. "You have to go to Blueberry!"

"Mom, I did as my father wanted when I was sixteen and confused and scared and abandoned by my boyfriend. I'm not that terrified teenager anymore. I'll do as I want. I'll do what I think is right for me."

"How about doing what's right for me, then?" her mother asked in a low, cracking voice.

"What are you talking about?"

"I involved myself in a moneymaking scheme and it turned out to be a scam," her mother said.

"How much?" Olivia asked, bracing herself.

"A quarter of a million."

"Mom! That was your entire life's savings!"

"I can pay February's bills, but come March, I won't be able to pay the maintenance on the apartment or my bills, and I do have quite a balance on my credit cards. I guess I could sell the apartment and move in with you. If I sell, I could afford to pay my share of your rent. Or perhaps we could look for an inexpensive two bedroom since you won't have much privacy once you move to the pullout couch in the living room."

Olivia closed her eyes and slowly counted to five. She was pretty sure she had the most manipulative mother on the planet. "Do you have any idea what it will do to me to go back to Blueberry? To live in that cottage for a month? Do you have any idea, Mom?"

"No, I don't," she said more gently than Olivia was used to. "Perhaps going will help, though."

"Help what?"

"Help give you some peace, Olivia. Something you haven't had since you were sixteen."

"I doubt I'll find peace in Blueberry, Mom. In fact, I'm sure that's the last thing I'll feel there."

Her mother was silent for a moment. "I'm pretty desperate, Olivia. I'm very sorry, but until I figure out the best way to replenish my accounts, I'm in a terrible pickle."

Ding-ding! I know—it's called getting a job! Something you've never had in your life!

Olivia let out a deep breath. Her mother had been there for her when Olivia was a total wreck; well, she'd been there as best she could, providing a home and a job and structure, a routine she could numbly go about.

Twenty-nine years ago, William Sedgwick had left her mother pregnant and alone, moving on to the next woman without a backward glance. Granted, her mother had taken William to court and won a good settlement, the rest of which she'd now blown, but Olivia never really knew the extent to which William had hurt her mother. Olivia only knew what it felt like to be pregnant and abandoned. So did her mom. Her father had the money; her mother needed it. And Olivia was the middleman.

It was a good thing that Blueberry was a seven-hour drive from New York City. She'd need every one of those hours to prepare mentally and emotionally for the first sight of the highway sign that read, "Welcome to Maine: The Way Life Should Be."

More like the way life should have been.

Chapter 4

According to the posters advertising the Inner-Beauty Pageant all around town, entry forms were available at the post office, the town hall, and the Blueberry Eat-In Diner.

Zach decided on the diner, despite the fact that Kayla was grounded for the foreseeable future. His daughter had a bad habit of slipping most of the healthful breakfasts he made her every morning to their dog, Lucy, but she loved eating breakfast out. Maybe Zach was just a bad cook.

He and Kayla had had a long talk last night, once Marnie and Brianna had left. She didn't want to know anything about her mother; she was in a phase where she hated even the mention of the words *your mother*, but she was very interested in the fact that Olivia had won the Inner-Beauty Pageant.

"Do you think I could win something like that?" Kayla had asked, her eyes tear filled one moment and shooting sparks the next.

"Of course you could," he had said. "That's why I come down so hard on you when you do things that are just plain wrong. You're a good, kind, warm, funny, beautiful person in there," he had said, pointing to the vicinity of her heart.

"But when I get in trouble, doesn't that prove I'm not a good person?" she had asked. "How could I have inner beauty if I'm always getting grounded?"

"Kayla, I know that when you mess up, you know you're messing up. You know you're not doing the right thing. That's part of what inner beauty is. It's knowing. You're thirteen and I've got to give you some leeway for that alone, but not much, honey. Real inner beauty means knowing what the right thing is and doing it. And I know you're more than capable of that."

"If I did enter and I did win—as if—do you think my mother would find out?" she had asked without looking at him, tears pooling in her eyes.

He had squeezed her hand. "I don't know, honey."

Kayla received two cards a year from her mother: one for her birthday and one for Christmas. There was never a personal message, just, "Dear Kayla" and "Your Mother."

Real warm.

Last year, Kayla began ripping them up. All years previous, she opened them eagerly, hoping for an enclosed letter, a photo, a "How are you?" But she was always disappointed. He supposed on some basic level the impersonal cards were better than nothing. Nothing would be much, much worse. The cards were just an eighth of an inch up from nothing, but every year on her birthday and at Christmas, he breathed a sigh of relief at the sight of the card in the mailbox, no return address, just a postmark from New York, New York.

"If I did win and she found out," Kayla had said last night, "she would probably feel really bad about just abandoning me the way she did. She would be, like, 'Wow, I messed up by walking out on Kayla. She's special—she won the Inner-Beauty Pageant just like I did.'"

He had grabbed his daughter into a hug and hadn't even bothered trying to hide the fact that he'd had tears in his eyes. "Kayla Archer, I want to make sure you know one thing: you've been special from the day you were born. You're the most special thing in the world to me. Your mother didn't leave us because you weren't special. She left because she couldn't deal with having a family. That's about *her*—not you."

"I'm still going to show her what she missed out on," Kayla had said, the sparkle back in her eyes. "Can I be ungrounded so I can enter and do whatever stupid stuff I have to do?"

He had smiled. "You're still grounded. But you may enter the contest and you may do all the wonderful things necessary to compete in the pageant. You're in luck that I can take off this week from work. I can go with you everywhere you need to go."

She had frowned, then smiled. "I'm going to beat Brianna by, like, a million points. I have so much more inner beauty than she does."

He had wagged his finger at her. "Those with inner beauty don't say things like that."

She had grinned. "Do they think things like that?"

"Sometimes. If they really can't help it."

"I really can't," she had said.

He'd yanked her braid and off they'd gone to the diner.

Once inside, he found the entry forms available in a manila folder on the community bulletin board.

"I have to write an essay just to enter?" Kayla complained, studying the rules on the application. "I'll fail the application! I won't even get to enter."

"What does the essay have to be about?"

She frowned and shoved the entry form away. "What inner beauty means to me."

Thank you, he directed heavenward. This could not have been a more perfect assignment for Kayla this week.

Their breakfast was served, and Kayla dug into her scrambled eggs and bacon. While he drank his coffee, Zach took a minute to read the flyer and the rules.

The town of Blueberry announces its annual Inner-Beauty Pageant for girls age 13–17 who know beauty is only skin-deep! Open only to year-round residents of Blueberry who attend the Blueberry public or private schools.

Ah. The pageant used to be held in the summer, but the coordinators must have decided that too many out-of-towners with summer homes in Blueberry were taking the pageant away from the girls who lived in Blueberry all year.

The winner would receive $2,500 and a monthly column for a year in the *Maine Daily News* on the subject of inner beauty. Zach remembered Olivia telling him that was why she'd wanted to enter the pageant and win so badly; she thought the columns would help her land her dream job as a magazine writer or editor.

Kayla sipped her orange juice. "Okay, Dad, so what does inner beauty mean to me?"

He smiled. "Why don't we head home so you can spend some time thinking about that."

"Can't you help me?"

"The answer needs to come from you, honey, not me."

She rolled her eyes. "Fine."

By the time Olivia arrived at the cottage, it was pitch dark and late, almost 11:00 P.M. She was grateful for the darkness; she wasn't quite ready for the familiar sights and shops and people and places, particularly places where she and Zach used to go to be alone.

She sat in her car for a moment and stared at the lovely gray shingled house. Even in winter, the cottage was so welcoming. There were quaint touches everywhere, from folk art bird feeders to a decorative wishing well, in which she and her sisters used to pitch pennies. The house would be warm; her father's lawyer had alerted the caretaker that she would be arriving this evening and the woman had promised to turn on the heat and stock the place with some basic necessities.

Tomorrow she'd have to go into town and buy one item from two stores. The charming coastal village was always bustling on Sundays. She wondered if she'd run into anyone she knew, anyone she'd remember or who would remember her.

Olivia grabbed her overnight bag, deciding to leave her suitcases in the trunk until tomorrow. With a deep breath, she opened the door with the key Edwin Harris had given her, and warmth and the foyer light and the scent of pine needles greeted her.

She was surprised to discover brand-new furniture and artwork and knickknacks, down to the switch plate covers. The cottage had always had a nautical theme; William Sedgwick loved boating and the water, but now the cottage was decorated in a folk-country style, much like Olivia's own apartment, with whimsical feminine touches. In the entryway was a console table upon which sat eight figurines of ballet dancers. Olivia had loved ballet as a teenager. It was almost as if William had the place completely redecorated to suit her taste.

She'd learned from Amanda last month that William had known he was dying. He hadn't told his daughters that he'd been diagnosed with late-stage cancer or that he'd suffered a heart attack. He'd been given a certain number of months to live, and the sisters had surmised that he'd decided to get his affairs in order.

But why redecorate the cottage for her? How could he have been so sure she'd accept the terms of the letter?

Questions. She had plenty. But she was exhausted and didn't want to think too deeply about anything, especially about how she felt even being in this house, standing in this living room, where for so many summers she had sat uncomfortably on the sofa, trying to feel as though she belonged here, to these people, to this family—if it could even be called that. And then there had been Zach, and Olivia had understood what the word *family* really meant to some people. Zach had been family.

She glanced around the pretty living room, and despite how little it looked like it used to, Olivia could remember that first day she met Zach, how she'd been sitting in this room with her sisters on the second day of their annual vacation, and there'd

been a fight, something stupid and petty and based
on charged emotions the girls simply didn't know
what to do with. And so she'd gone out for a long
walk along the beach, and there was Zach, a boy
she'd never seen before, angrily throwing rocks into
the ocean.

"Can you spare some?" she'd asked, tossing a shell
as hard as she could into the gorgeous blue water.

He'd whipped around, that delicious tangle of
thick, almost curly hair shielding his eyes. He had
brushed back a lock from his forehead, and she
had stopped in her tracks, just stopped breathing
for a moment. His eyes had held hers in a way she'd
never experienced. A green-gray hazel, intense,
penetrating, expressive, those eyes were strangely
familiar, though she'd never seen the guy before.

This is what it feels like to fall in love, she had
thought crazily. *You meet someone, and before you even
hear his voice, before you even know his name, know him,
you're enamored.* It made no sense, but that was how
she had felt. As though she *did* know him. Inside
and out.

"What are you so ticked off about?" he had asked,
raising an eyebrow at her. "What could possibly
ruin your day?"

"What is that supposed to mean?" she had asked,
hands on hips.

"I've seen you around," he had said, squinting in
the sunlight. "You're a summer kid. You come every
summer, litter up the beach for a week, then go
back to your ritzy house in Connecticut or wherever.
Like you've ever had a problem."

"Judgmental, much?" she had shot back. "How about
the fact that my father sees me and my half sisters two

weeks a year and then can't even bother spending any of those weeks with us. How about my sisters don't seem to like me for no reason at all. How about I come here year after year, and it's always the same thing: my expectations get totally blown."

"I know about that," he had said, skimming a rock into the water. "Though I stopped expecting anything when I was about six, maybe seven. However old you are when you realize your parents aren't these magical, perfect people."

"I'd settle for halfway decent," she had said, dropping down onto the sand and tucking her knees under her chin.

He had eyed her. "Yeah, me too."

They had sat there on the beach, for a half hour, talking, throwing rocks, talking, throwing more rocks. They had sifted sand between their fingers. She had learned that he lived on the "other side" of Blueberry, in what was practically a shack next to a used-parts lot. His father was an alcoholic.

"And supposedly my mother puts food on the table and pays our bills by selling her body," he had said, his face twisting. He had squeezed his eyes shut and kicked the sand. "I don't know if that's true. I hope it's not."

"Me too," she had said, her heart squeezing in her chest.

"Everyone thinks it is," he had said. "So what's the difference anyway."

Olivia had turned to face him. "It doesn't matter what everyone else thinks. It matters what you believe in there"—she had pointed at his head—"and in here," she had said, patting his chest.

He had glanced at her, then down at where her

hand rested on his worn blue T-shirt. He had nodded, then looked back out at the ocean. "Thanks."

She had nodded too, for want of knowing what else to say.

"I'm Zach. Zach Archer."

"Olivia Sedgwick," she had said. "So how old are you? I'm sixteen."

"I'm seventeen. For another six months. One more year of high school and then I'm outta here."

"Where are you going to go?" she had asked.

"Anywhere. New York City. Boston. San Francisco. Chicago. I'm going to try everywhere and see where feels like home."

"That's a good idea," she had said, wanting him to find happiness but not wanting him to go anywhere without her.

He had looked at her then as though he could read her thoughts. "I wish I didn't have to leave right now, but I have to go to work."

"Where do you work?"

"Back room of a supermarket," he had said. "Opening boxes, shelving. One day, though, I'm going to be an architect. I'm going to build skyscrapers." He had glanced down. "That probably sounds pretty stupid to you. Like I'm ever going from shelving boxes of Cheerios to designing glass towers."

"I have no doubt you will, Zach," she had said. "You sound determined. That's what it takes."

He had smiled at her for the first time. A smile that completely stole her heart. "Meet me here later?"

"What time?" she'd asked, grinning.

A much older Olivia smiled at the memory. She sat down on the plush sofa, recalling how in that moment, that question, they both knew they would be together. That something special had begun. They'd met that night at nine-thirty, once it was dark enough and late enough for Olivia to sneak out of the cottage. Her father never had anything to do with the girls after dinner, which was the only time he spent with them. They met on the beach, and hand in hand they walked for an hour, talking, kissing, falling very much in love.

Olivia sighed, barely able to remember that girl she used to be. She closed her eyes, forcing away the memories, memories of a time *before*. Before she was pregnant. Before Zach abandoned her. A time when, for a few precious days, she was happier than she'd ever been.

Olivia yawned and headed for the bedroom that had been hers as a girl. The cottage had five bedrooms, one for each girl, one for William, and one for the sour-faced housekeeper.

Olivia opened the door and gasped. The room hadn't been changed. Nothing had been changed. But that's bizarre, she thought. Why would William redecorate down to the knickknacks and leave this room exactly as it was?

It was a pink room. A pink girlie-girl's room. A four-poster bed dominated, its fluffy pink down comforter so inviting. As she sat on the edge of the bed, she thought she saw something dart past the door.

She got up and peered out the doorway. Yes. There. A little girl! She had her back to Olivia, and she was flying a kite, a kite in the shape of a cat. The girl was laughing and running down the hall.

"Wait!" Olivia called.

The girl turned around, smiled, and then ran—

right through the wall at the end of the hallway. She was gone.

Olivia opened and closed her eyes. She was imagining the girl, that was all. She'd driven so many hours and it was late. And she was back here in this house. Her mind was telling her it was time to go to bed.

After washing her face and brushing her teeth and changing into comfortable yoga pants and a tank top, Olivia slid under the comforter.

The running girl was the girl from her dreams, she realized. But where was the boy? She'd never dreamed of just the girl before. Why had she seen only the girl running through the house?

She darted up. *Because the baby was a girl,* she knew suddenly. *I gave birth to a girl.* She knew this with startling clarity. *Yeah, right,* she thought, dropping back down onto the soft pillows. *I know absolutely nothing.*

Olivia darted up in bed again, her heart pounding. She glanced at the clock on the bedside table. It was just after two in the morning. She had the dream again. And again, there was no boy.

Chapter 5

Buzz! Buzzzz!

Someone was pressing on the doorbell. No—
pounding on the doorbell.

Olivia glanced at the alarm clock. How had she
slept until eight o'clock? She rarely slept past six.
She got out of bed and put on her warm terry
bathrobe as she slid her feet into her favorite sheep-
skin slippers, a good-bye gift from Camilla for chilly
Maine mornings.

Buzz! Buzzzz!

"I'm coming!" Olivia called out, wondering who
could possibly be at the door so early on a Sunday
morning. Who knew she was here, anyway?

Ah, she thought, running to the front door. The
caretaker. The letter from her father indicated that
the house's caretaker would stop by every morning
at eight to ensure she was there and to collect her
receipts.

I'm definitely here, she thought, looking around the
living room in the bright light of day. *I can't believe
it, but I am definitely here.*

Buzz!

Olivia opened the door. This was the caretaker? A very attractive redhead in her early forties stood on the doorstep, wearing a cropped hot pink down jacket, jeans that form fit her sexy figure, and a scowl.

"Let me make one thing clear," the woman said, tossing her mane of ringlets behind her shoulders. "When I come tomorrow morning to collect your receipts, I will ring the bell once. If you don't answer in a minute or two, I will leave and you'll forfeit your inheritance. So I wouldn't take ten minutes again to answer the damned door if I were you."

"Good morning to you, too," Olivia said. If she weren't so used to rudeness from working at *Glitz,* she would have been too shocked to speak.

"I've been retained by William Sedgwick's attorney to take roll each morning at eight o'clock. You will need to sign this form and date it. Today is day one. Tomorrow, I will begin collecting your receipts. You must purchase one item from two different establishments in town for a minimum of two items per day. A cup of coffee counts. So does a cashmere sweater from Johanna's, which happens to be the store I own and operate."

"Is your name Johanna?"

"Ooh, you're a smart one," the woman said, turning to leave.

"Excuse me," Olivia said sharply. "Any reason why you're such a bitch?"

The woman whipped around, clearly surprised. "Maybe it's because I don't like greedy opportunists. You broke your father's heart when you were a slutty teenager, then estranged yourself from him for years. Now you're here to collect your inheritance? Sickening."

Now Olivia *was* too shocked to speak. She took a moment to regain her composure. "Let me make one thing clear, Johanna. You have no idea what you're talking about. Nothing you said is true. And I don't appreciate your coming here and throwing ugly false statements at me."

"You should be thinking about what your father would have appreciated," Johanna said, continuing down the path.

"Just what was your relationship to William Sedgwick?" Olivia called.

The woman opened the white gate and let herself out onto the sidewalk. "I was his fiancée."

Olivia gasped. His fiancée? This was the first she'd heard of a fiancée.

"We were planning a summer wedding," the woman said, her voice cracking.

"I'm very sorry for your loss," Olivia said. She had no idea what else to say at the moment.

"Oh, I'm sure you're not," Johanna tossed back. "My loss is your very lucrative gain." She wiped away at tears under her eyes and hurried away.

Good Lord, Olivia thought.

Her father had a fiancée. Strange. Olivia's sister Amanda had told Olivia and Ivy that she'd met two of William's "girlfriends" last month. One woman had turned out to be an opportunist much like Johanna made out Olivia to be. But the other had seemed genuinely grief stricken over William's loss and had said they too were engaged.

A woman in every port, perhaps. Olivia had no idea what to think about her father's romances. She knew absolutely nothing about how he conducted his life. She only knew that he had a flavor-of-the-month way of looking at relationships.

She closed the door against the morning chill. It was forty-two degrees, according to the adorable thermometer attached to a bird feeder in the yard. Warm for the start of February in Maine.

If Johanna is my first introduction to Blueberry, what else is awaiting me in town? she wondered as she headed into the kitchen to make a pot of coffee. What if William was some sort of local hero? He spent every summer in Blueberry, hunting or just to relax. He probably had a lot of friends. Friends who wouldn't take kindly to the daughter who'd been the "slutty teenager" who'd broken his heart.

The strong coffee began brewing. Olivia breathed in the delicious aroma, then headed into the bathroom for a shower.

I wish Amanda were around, she thought as she slipped under the pounding hot spray, which felt absolutely wonderful. Amanda and her new husband, Ethan, lived just an hour or so north, but the newlyweds were still on their European honeymoon and wouldn't be back for a couple of weeks.

She suddenly felt very much alone.

Olivia decided to walk the half mile to the town center. She bundled up in her down coat, hat, and mittens; took a deep breath; and headed out.

The houses were the same, beautiful old Victorians and stately Colonials, and many shingled cottages that were really mansions like her father's, reminiscent of those on Cape Cod. Even in winter, with a light coating of snow on the ground, Blueberry was beautiful and charming. As she approached town, she could see the stores had changed. There was now a gourmet eatery called Ollie's Organic Everything and an adorable retro diner with fifties decor and an inviting-looking coffee lounge with free "wi-fi" service. One-of-a-kind shops lined the half-mile stretch of Blueberry Hill Boulevard, including Johanna's Cashmere Emporium. In the window was a pair of sexy pink cashmere panties. Somehow Olivia doubted they would be comfortable.

She headed into the coffee lounge. The cozy place was furnished with overstuffed couches and chairs, all of which were taken by people sipping coffee drinks, reading newspapers or books, or talking. Olivia glanced around to see if she recognized anyone—or if anyone recognized her. No one.

She purchased a small black coffee (she was unemployed, after all), careful to tuck her receipt into her purse. Then she headed down Blueberry Hill Boulevard and stopped at the General Store, where she bought three postcards: two for her sisters, one for her mom.

Now that she had her two items, all she wanted was to go back to the cottage. One hour in Blueberry was enough for her at the moment. She turned around, trying not to look at the village green, a quaint square in the center of the boulevard, with its gazebo and playground set. Next to it, the town hall—

Olivia froze and sucked in her breath. Running from the town hall to the gazebo was the girl from her dream. Olivia blinked. No, it wasn't the same girl. They simply had similar coloring, like Olivia's.

And of course, the smiling, running girl was much older, twelve, thirteen maybe.

Like my child would have been, Olivia thought for a moment.

She watched the girl race into the gazebo, carrying a pink folder. A man sitting on one of the benches turned around, scooped her up, and swung her, as if congratulating her.

As the man turned, Olivia gasped.

Zachary Archer. Zach Archer all grown up. A man. He stood at least 500 feet away, but she was sure it was him. As she stared, he met her gaze and staggered backward for a moment. He said something to the girl, who then sat down in the gazebo and began looking through the folder.

He stomped over to Olivia, his expression contemptuous. "What are *you* doing here? It's not like it's her birthday. Oh, wait a minute—you don't care about her birthdays, do you? Just a card every year and a check."

Whoa. *What?*

She stared at him, unable to process that he was standing in front of her, let alone what he was saying.

"Birthday?" she repeated, looking from him to the girl sitting in the gazebo. "What are you talking about?"

He looked at her as though she had four heads. "What are *you* talking about. Her *birthday.* What part of the word don't you understand?"

"What birthday?" she asked. "*Whose* birthday?"

He rolled his eyes. "Why are you here? You suddenly want to know your daughter after thirteen years?"

My daughter? She glanced at the girl, the girl with hair exactly like hers.

"Our baby was stillborn," she said in such a low voice that she wasn't sure she even said the words aloud.

His eyes glinted. "I don't know what game you're playing, Olivia, but you'd better tell me the rules right now. I decide how to handle this. Got that?"

Handle what?

He shook his head. "Your father hands over our newborn daughter and a check for twenty-five thousand dollars, not a word from you, and suddenly you're standing five hundred feet away from her. We do this my way."

Olivia's hand trembled, and her foam cup of coffee dropped to the ground, splattering onto the fine layer of white snow. Her legs trembled and then gave out. She dropped to the ground, barely registering that her knees were soaking in coffee. Zach immediately helped her up. "Our baby was stillborn," she repeated slowly.

He stared at her. "Is that the lie you told everyone in order to live with yourself for walking away like you did?"

She glanced up at him, unable to speak.

"I was told our baby was dead," Olivia said, every breath difficult to latch onto. "The doctor said so. The nurse said so. My father said it was for the best. So did my mother. Our baby was stillborn."

Zach stared at her. "*Our baby* is sitting right there."

There was no processing what Zach was saying. It simply could not be true. She glanced at the blond girl and then at Zach. She opened her mouth to speak, but there were no words.

"Daddy, I'm freezing!" the girl shouted at the top

of her lungs. "And I have to get started on my inner-beauty essay!"

Olivia's legs threatened to buckle again. She closed her eyes, the girl's words echoing in her mind. *Inner Beauty essay . . .* Olivia had written an essay on inner beauty for the pageant the summer before she'd met Zach.

"One sec," he called back. He turned to Olivia. "Are you staying at the cottage?"

She nodded, her gaze going back to the girl.

"Meet me at Barker's Lounge tonight. Do you remember where it is? On the outskirts of town. We'll have privacy there."

"You could just come by the cottage, if you want," she offered.

He shook his head. "I'd rather we met in a neutral place. Seven o'clock?"

She nodded, and he turned and walked away toward the gazebo.

Look back, she willed his retreating figure. *Look back so I'll know this wasn't all a figment of my imagination.*

He didn't look back.

Olivia felt her legs threaten to give out again, and she rushed over to the gazebo and sat down just as her legs *would* have given out.

Your father hands over our newborn daughter and a check for twenty-five thousand dollars. . . .

Just a card every year and a check . . .

Our baby is sitting right there . . .

Olivia covered her face with her hands. A scream rose and died in her throat.

It couldn't possibly be true. It couldn't.

Her father's face floated into her mind. And she knew it absolutely *could* be true.

Olivia glanced over to the parking lot in front of the town hall. An attractive woman was standing by the window of Zach's shiny red truck. She traced a finger down his cheek, then slid her tongue along his ear. Girlfriend? Wife? Olivia hadn't noticed whether Zach wore a wedding ring.

She forced herself up. She had to get back to the cottage, to a telephone. There was only one person alive who would know—or admit to—the truth.

Her mother.

"So who was that hot babe?" Kayla asked as Zach pulled out of the town hall parking lot.

His fingers were shaking on the steering wheel. He steadied them, forcing himself to pull it together. "You mean Marnie?"

"Duh, Daddy. *No.* The blond woman."

He hadn't been confused by who she'd meant. He just wasn't ready to answer the question.

What the hell? What the hell was Olivia Sedgwick doing in Blueberry?

"She's someone I used to know a long time ago," Zach finally said, glancing over at Kayla.

He suddenly realized that Kayla had Olivia's cheekbones. Olivia's heart-shaped face. Olivia's long, slender fingers. He'd only had one photograph of Olivia, from when she was sixteen, and he never allowed himself to look at it. When Kayla asked him, as a five-year-old, if he had any photos of her mother, he gave her the picture and told her to be very careful with it, that it was the only one.

For months she slept with it under her pillow. And then she told him that she wanted to put it away, like her mother: away. He tried to get Kayla to open up about her feelings over the years, paid for some expensive therapy, but Kayla never wanted to talk about her mother. *There's nothing to say,* was her refrain.

Zach had no idea where Kayla had put the picture, but he'd bet anything she had it tucked safe somewhere in her room. Anyway, all he'd had of Olivia over these years was his memory of her, and he'd forgotten those little details, like the shape of her face. He only knew that when he looked at Kayla, he was reminded of Olivia.

"She's so pretty," Kayla said. "I wish I looked like that."

You do, he thought. *You look more like me, but your mother is everywhere in your face. And the hair, of course.*

"Was she an ex-girlfriend?" Kayla asked, wiggling her eyebrows at him. At his nod, Kayla giggled. "Well, she's a total klutz. First she drops her coffee and then she wipes out on the snow right into it." She laughed, then opened her pink Inner-Beauty Pageant folder and began reading.

He took a deep breath. *Thank you,* he sent heavenward. He wasn't ready for questions. He wouldn't lie to his daughter about who Olivia was, but he needed time to think, needed time to figure out what to say and how.

He needed to talk to Olivia and find out what the hell she was doing in Blueberry. What her intentions were.

Our baby was stillborn. . . .

What was that all about? Had her father really told her the baby she'd given birth to had been born dead? That seemed beyond even William

Sedgwick's lack of decency. Or maybe not. And what about the doctor and nurses? Had they been paid off?

Or was Olivia playing some kind of game with him? He'd find out in a few hours. Of that much he was damned sure.

Out of breath from running back to the cottage, Olivia dropped down on the sofa in the living room and stared at the phone. One telephone call stood between her and the truth.

She picked up the phone. Her hand trembled, and she silently counted to ten. Then twenty.

She dialed. Her mother answered on the first ring.

"Hello, Candace Hearn speaking."

Olivia hesitated.

"Hello?" her mom repeated.

"Mom, it's me," she said, standing up and pacing the room. "I'm going to get straight to the point. I need you to tell me the truth."

"The truth about what, dear?"

Olivia stopped. "About my baby."

There was silence for a moment. "Your baby? Olivia, I'm not sure I'm follow—"

No. Her mother was not going to pull one of her famous "I have no idea what you're talking about" routines, her voice all feigned innocence. "I just ran into Zach Archer. And, according to him, our *daughter.*"

Now it was her mother's turn to suck in her breath. "What do you mean 'our daughter'? What are you talking about?"

Olivia began pacing again. "Damn it, Mom. No lies! Tell me the truth right now!"

"Olivia, I have no idea what—"

"Mother, was I lied to? Did my baby live?"

"No!" her mother insisted. "The baby was still-born. The doctor said so. That rude nurse, as well. I have a copy of the death certificate."

Olivia closed her eyes and shook her head. "Could William have paid off the doctor? Could the death certificate have been forged?"

"Olivia, my God, I just don't know. Why would he do such a thing? Why would he arrange to have the baby supposedly be born dead when you were giving it up for adoption anyway?"

Yes, why? That made no sense. In either case, she would not have been going home with a baby.

"Olivia, what do you mean you saw Zach Archer and your daughter?"

Olivia took a deep breath. "I mean, he's here in Blueberry and he told me that our child is alive and well. She was with him, though not within earshot of our conversation."

"I don't understand any of this!" her mother said. "Your father handled the adoption, said that he knew a top-notch lawyer, that the baby would go to a wonderful family." She let out a breath. "Oh, God, Olivia. What did your father do?" She was silent for a moment. "I'm flying up. You need my sup—"

"No, Mom," Olivia interrupted. "I appreciate that you want to help, but if this girl is my daughter, if Zach is telling the truth, then I'm going to need to proceed alone and with the utmost caution."

That was an understatement.

Chapter 6

Olivia pulled up to Barker's Lounge at a few minutes to seven. There were several cars in the lot. She glanced around for the pickup she'd seen Zach driving. It didn't look like he was here yet.

She headed inside and sat at one of the round tables in the back. She'd expected the place to be more of a bar, but it was a charming grill, with a blackboard menu dominating the wall behind the long, wooden bar. A jukebox softly played a Johnny Cash song, and an attractive couple played pool at the table at the far end. A few people were seated at the bar, none of whom Olivia recognized.

She glanced up at the blackboard menu, her stomach growling at the words *hamburger, mac and cheese, fish and chips, chef salad*. She hadn't eaten a thing all day. She wasn't sure she'd be able to here, either.

She glanced at the door every few seconds while tearing the napkin on her lap to shreds. Finally, the door opened. And there was Zach, his cheeks slightly pink from the cold, a green wool scarf wrapped round his neck.

God, he was handsome.

He came over and sat down. "This is crazy," he said, shaking his head. "What the hell are you doing in Blueberry all of a sudden? What is this story about being told our baby was stillborn? What the hell is going on, Olivia?"

Slow down, Zach. You've got to slow down. "It's good to see you," she said. And it was. So good.

"Forget the niceties, Olivia," he snapped. "I just want answers to my questions. What are you doing here? What do you want?"

A barmaid came over. They both ordered coffee.

"There's a five-dollar minimum per person for the tables," the barmaid said. "Menu's up there," she added, gesturing at the blackboard.

Zach shook his head. "We'll each have a hamburger and fries." He turned to Olivia. "Unless you're suddenly a vegetarian."

"I still love hamburgers and French fries," she said, surprised that he remembered her old addiction. In the brief time they'd had together in Blueberry, they'd always eaten hamburgers and fries, ordering them from the greasy spoon diner and bringing their lunch to the deserted area of the beach.

"I want answers, Olivia," he said, his hazel eyes narrowed.

"My father died last month," she told him. "At the reading of his will, I was told I would receive a letter to open on January thirtieth. The letter stated that I would inherit the cottage and an undisclosed sum of money if I lived in Blueberry for one month and bought a couple of things each day from town."

Zach unwound his scarf from his neck, but he didn't take off his heavy brown leather jacket. "Am I supposed to offer condolences for the loss of your father? I have no idea if you two suddenly became father and daughter after I last spoke to you."

She shook her head. "My relationship with my father never changed. If anything, it became more nonexistent than it was."

"I assume you're more interested in the 'undisclosed sum of money' than in the cottage," he said. "But then again, I thought I knew you once and I found out how wrong I was, so what the hell do I know about you?"

The slap stung, surprising her. But she cautioned herself against getting too emotional. "Zach, I don't think *either* of us knew anything thirteen years ago. I think my father lied to both of us. I have no idea what he told you about me. All I know is that he told me my baby was stillborn. The doctor confirmed it. I believed that my baby was born dead until you said otherwise this morning." She took a deep breath. "I called my mother when I got back to the cottage, and she swears she was told the same thing. My father was handling the adoption—"

Zach stared at her. "What adoption?"

"He browbeat me into agreeing to it. He kept telling me that you abandoned me when I told you I was pregnant and that you took off. That I'd be penniless and living on the street. That I'd be found an unfit and terrible mother by the courts and that my baby would be taken away from me and put into foster care. He told me all this and worse every hour until I signed the papers."

Zach stared at her. "But I didn't abandon you,

Olivia. I was told that you 'wanted nothing to do with a punk like me.' That when I got you pregnant you realized what a mess I was making of your life. Your father told me he'd put the baby up for adoption or that I could have sole custody. I chose the baby."

Olivia gasped. "How could he have done this? Why would he deny me my own child all these years?"

He stared at her. "Start from the beginning," he said, finally taking off his coat. "Tell me everything. From the moment you found out you were pregnant. Don't leave anything out."

The waitress brought their burgers and fries, and Olivia was grateful for the reprieve to prepare herself for telling a story she never allowed herself to think about.

"Tell me, Olivia," he said. "I have a right to know everything."

She nodded. "I found out I was pregnant a month after I returned home to New York. I called you the day I took the pregnancy test. It was a Sunday morning, and my mother was sleeping. I took the phone into the bathroom, staring at the pink line on the stick of the pregnancy test."

"And I immediately suggested we run away together," Zach said.

Her heart squeezed in her chest. "I know." She would never, ever forget those words, his first reaction. "But my mother overheard part of our conversation and she stormed in and grabbed the phone out of my hand and hung it up."

"I'd assumed you hung up on me," he said, shaking

his head. "That it was your answer to my idea of running away together."

"Zach," Olivia said, "I loved you. How could you think I'd hang up on you?" She leaned back against her chair and stared up at the ceiling.

In that month between leaving Maine and learning she was pregnant, she and Zach spoke every day. Her mother, curious about the long-distance bill, never asked if it was a boy or girl; all that mattered to her mother was that she'd made a good friend from the wealthy community. She and Zach spoke for just a few minutes every day, but sometimes for as long as twenty minutes, and always about how much they missed each other, how incredible their connection was, how they wished they could just run away together, start over from scratch, but how hard that would be at their age. They would wait until Olivia turned eighteen, and then they'd be together. That was the plan. Neither doubted their love. But then she'd gotten pregnant, and as hard as it would be to run off together and take care of a baby, Zach had been willing.

Just finish the story, she ordered herself.

"My mother flipped out," she continued. "Over and over she said, 'How could you have been so stupid!' and then she called my father, screaming at him that he'd let such a thing happen on 'his watch.' A moment later, she hung up with a 'Your dad will handle this.' Five minutes later, the phone rang. My father had made some calls, and I was being sent way up the coast of Maine to a home for pregnant teenagers. The baby would be adopted by a good family, I was told. It's for the best, my mother said before dropping me off at the home."

"The best for *you*," Olivia had wanted to scream. Olivia's pregnancy was an embarrassment to Candace, even though no one knew about it. And the best for her father, who wanted nothing to do with his own daughter, let alone a "problem."

To everyone else, Olivia was in a Swiss boarding school.

"I tried to call you back," she said. "In the middle of the night. But a recording came on and said the phone had been disconnected."

"I remember that," he said. "The phone was always getting disconnected every few months. My parents never paid the bill." Now it was Zach's turn to lean back against his chair and expel a breath. "I was so frustrated that I couldn't get in touch with you. I tried to find you, but you were impossible to find. I went to New York to look for you, at your school, at shops around your house. I even waited on your doorstep to talk to your mother, but she refused to talk to me, refused to tell me anything."

"I didn't know that," Olivia said, in such a low voice she barely heard it herself. "I tried, too, Zach. I couldn't reach you by phone, so I wrote letters. And they were all returned unopened and marked 'Return to Sender.'"

His mouth dropped open. "My mother . . . or father. Clearly, your father got to them. Paid them off. Paid them off to disconnect the phone most likely."

They sat in silence for a moment. Olivia was emotionally exhausted and they hadn't even gotten up to the birth yet.

"What was the home for pregnant teenagers like?" Zach asked.

Olivia could see the building, a mile down a dirt driveway and surrounded by nothing but trees and the ocean, as though she'd just been driven there for the first time. She'd never forget how unwelcoming the brick building had looked. Like a detention center, a juvenile hall.

She shrugged. "It was what it was. No one was particularly kind there, but we were cared for physically. We were given prenatal vitamins and prenatal checkups and nutritious meals. I made a few friends there, but none of the girls really wanted to talk much; no one could bear to talk about how they really felt about being there or giving up their babies for adoption." She took a deep breath. "I went into labor and I was so scared," Olivia said, staring at her lap. "And then the baby was born and taken away. I didn't even get to see her, Zach."

"And you were told she was stillborn?" he asked, his expression incredulous.

She nodded. "By the doctor. By the nurse."

"An employee of your father's arrived at my house with a baby in his arms," Zach said, "a check for twenty-five thousand dollars, and a bus ticket to Boston. I was told you never wanted to see me again, that you thought I was pathetic trash who'd almost ruined your life. And then he handed over the baby, who looked just like me."

Olivia gasped and stared at Zach. "Why? Why, why, why would my father do that? Why would he lie and tell me the baby was born dead?" The tears came then, rushing down her cheeks.

Zach reached across the table for her hand, and she was so surprised that she glanced up at him. "I don't know, Olivia. If there's an 'at least,' though, at least he gave me the baby. I have no idea why he didn't give the baby up for adoption, as you'd been told was the plan."

She looked at him. "It must have been so hard. Seventeen years old and taking care of a newborn. All alone, no help."

He nodded and slipped his hand away. "It *was* hard. But I had the money, and you bet I used it. I needed it. I found support in Boston, a center for fathers in my position. I accepted all the help I was offered. And I worked my ass off so that I could go to college. Thank God I had a good babysitter, a retired nurse whose own grandchildren lived far away. She took good care of Kayla while I was in school and worked."

"Kayla. Her name is Kayla?"

He nodded.

It was all she could do not to burst into tears. "My middle name is Kaye," she whispered.

"I know," he said.

Again, they sat in silence for a few moments.

"What did you tell her about me?" she asked.

"I've told her the only truth I knew: that her mother was very young when she was born and needed to get her life together and one day, perhaps, she would come back."

Olivia nodded.

"The sole reason I moved back to Blueberry was so that you would be able to find us if you ever did come," Zach said.

"Where do you live now?"

"I built on the water, at the end of Spider's Cove. Do you remember all that wild brush and that sad weeping willow? I got rid of most of the brush, but the weeping willow is in my front yard."

"I always loved that tree," she said, so many memories hitting her at once. She and Zach had sat under that tree just twice, sharing French fries, sharing stories.

"Zach, will you tell Kayla about me? That I'm here?"

"I need to sleep on all this," he said. "Kayla is going through a tough time." He mentioned the suspension. The recent questions about Olivia and the pageant.

"I can't quite process that this is my daughter we're talking about. My child."

"*My* child," Zach snapped, as he stood up.

She glanced up at him.

He threw a twenty on the table, then put on his coat. "I need to think, Olivia. Until I call you, you're not to go within two feet of Kayla. Do we have an agreement?"

She nodded, and in an instant, he was gone.

Olivia drove home, her fingers white on the steering wheel. She was relieved to be finally back at the cottage, where she could collapse and not think about Zach. About Kayla. About everything she'd learned and still couldn't wrap her mind around.

She turned her key in the lock of the front door but was surprised that it wasn't locked. She distinctly remembered locking the door behind her; it had offered her a few extra seconds before leaving the safety of the cottage to go meet Zach. Had Johanna, the caretaker, been by? Did she have a key?

Huh. In everything that had happened today, Olivia had forgotten all about Johanna. Anyway, why would Johanna come by in the evening? Olivia had been told the caretaker would stop by every morning at eight. And Johanna had said the same thing this morning.

She stood outside on the porch, the cold night air slapping at her cheeks. She wasn't sure about going in. *This isn't New York City,* she told herself. *You're perfectly safe. And you probably just left the door unlocked.*

But she knew she hadn't.

She opened the door and peered in. And then gasped. The collection of beautiful figurines that had been on the console table in the entryway was smashed on the floor. And on the mirror above the table, someone had scrawled with a marker: "Go away. No one wants you here."

Her heart hammering, Olivia turned and ran for her car.

Chapter 7

What the—

As Zach pulled up to his house, he saw Olivia sitting on the steps. She jumped up and raced over to the car.

"Someone was in the cottage," she said in a panicky rush, her shoulders trembling. "The entryway is trashed and there is a note scrawled on the mirror."

He got out of the car and walked her up to the steps, gesturing for her to sit down. "Someone broke in? Or did you leave the door open?"

"I definitely locked the door."

"What does the note say?" he asked.

She took a deep breath. "Go away. No one wants you here."

He stared at her. "That's insane. Who'd do that? You've been here for a day."

She shrugged. "It makes no sense."

"Let me go in and tell the sitter I'll need her to stay a bit longer," he said. "Then I'll call the police and have them meet us over at the cottage."

She nodded, but as he headed up the steps, she looked panicked.

He hesitated for just a moment, surprised by the urge to hold her, comfort her. "I'll be right back."

"Okay."

Inside, the house was quiet, except for the television, which he could barely hear in the family room. He found Mrs. McGill, the grandmother of five who lived a few houses away, sitting on the sofa, Kayla sitting on the floor in front her, Mrs. McGill French braiding Kayla's hair. A Harry Potter movie was on, but Kayla was fast asleep, lightly snoring.

"She just nodded off," Mrs. McGill said.

"Would you mind staying for another couple of hours?" he asked. "I'll carry Kayla up to bed, but there's something I need to tend to in town."

"No problem," she said. "Take your time."

Zach scooped up his daughter, who weighed next to nothing, and breathed in the scent of her strawberry shampoo as he carried her up the stairs to her room. She looked so peaceful, hardly like the rabble-rouser she was.

He glanced at the French braid. Olivia had once worn her hair like that.

He settled Kayla in bed and tucked her beloved Winnie the Pooh under her arm. She hugged it and turned over. He pulled the blanket up and kissed her on the forehead.

On his way back downstairs, he called the police on his cell phone. Outside, Olivia was pacing in front of the door. "The police will meet us at the cottage," he told her. "I'll drive us over. You can leave your car here."

Silently she got into his pickup, hardly looking

like she belonged in a pickup truck. Olivia Sedgwick was Jaguar material.

"I guess I should have just gone to the police sta-
tion myself," Olivia said, staring out the windshield.
"I'm sorry I bothered you. Not five minutes earlier
you asked me not to come near Kayla, and what did
I do? Drove straight to your house. I'm sorry, Zach.
I just wasn't thinking."

"It's okay," he said, glancing at her.

The cottage was only a couple of miles from Zach's
house. They drove in silence, and when they pulled
up to the house, the police were already there.

"Miss Sedgwick?" a uniformed officer asked.

She nodded.

"The lock wasn't broken," he said. "Whoever
broke in used a key.

"A key?" she repeated. "But who else would have
a key?"

"You tell me," the officer said.

"Well, I just arrived today," Olivia told him. "I inherited the cottage from my father, William Sedgwick. There's a caretaker, but I don't know if she
has a key."

"Who's the caretaker?" Zach asked.

"A woman named Johanna," Olivia said. "She
stopped by this morning. But she rang the doorbell."

"Redhead?" the officer asked. "Owns the sweater
store on Blueberry Boulevard?"

Olivia nodded.

Another officer came out of the house. "Well, whoever it was didn't leave a calling card. Usually, people
who do this kind of immature nonsense are dumb
enough to leave a clue."

"We'll be in touch if we uncover anything, Miss

Sedgwick," the first officer said. "In the meantime, I suggest you change the locks."

As the officer drove away, another car drove up.

Marnie. Now what was she doing here?

"That's the woman you were with earlier today," Olivia whispered.

Zach said nothing as Marnie got out of her car. She wore tight jeans, high-heeled boots, and a cropped white down jacket.

"I heard from my cousin on the force that there was a break-in at the Sedgwick cottage and that William Sedgwick's daughter was staying there," Marnie said, rushing up to them. "Zach, what are you doing here?"

"I'm an old friend of Olivia's," he told her. He introduced them, then said, "We were catching up at Barker's, and she came home to the break-in, so she drove over to the house."

He noticed the change in Marnie's expression. His girlfriend's gaze was all over Olivia. "Ah, I see," Marnie said. "Well, I figured I'd stop by and see if you were all right, Olivia. You're welcome to stay with me tonight if you don't feel comfortable staying here."

"Thanks so much," Olivia said. "But there's a dead-bolt on the front door, so I'll feel safe inside. I'll have a locksmith come change the locks first thing in the morning."

Marnie nodded. "That's a good idea. Well, I'd better get back to Brianna."

"Thanks for coming out," Olivia said. "That was very thoughtful of you."

"No problem," Marnie said, leaning over to kiss Zach. Her lips lingered. Zach stepped back, and he didn't miss the look Marnie gave him. "See you tomorrow," she added before jogging back to her car.

"You're sure you'll be okay here alone?" Zach asked Olivia, whose gaze was on Marnie's back.

She turned to him. "I'll be fine. Thanks again for being there for me, Zach."

It was all he could do to take his eyes off her. She was so damned beautiful, so damned *Olivia*. "Well, then, good-bye again," he said and began walking to his truck, his feet like lead.

As he pulled the pickup into his driveway, Zach saw Marnie's car idling in his usual spot by the door. He parked on the far side and turned off the lights. Had she been waiting to see how long it would take him to get home? Waiting to see if he'd gone inside Olivia's house or if he'd come straight home?

Before he could even turn off the ignition, she got inside the warm, dark truck. She took off her little puffy white coat. She wore nothing underneath. He stared at her breasts, huge and full and milky white, their rose-tipped nipples hard. He couldn't help himself; he reached out, teasing the nipples between his fingers, wanting them in his mouth.

And after shimmying off her jeans and a tiny white thong, she reached over to undo his belt buckle and unzip his jeans, pulling what was now his rock-hard erection out of his underwear. She kneeled length-wise along the seat, her perfect ass up in the air as she wrapped her lips around the head of his shaft, then teased him with her tongue and sucked on him hard.

He groaned and closed his eyes, unable to tell her

no, that he had so much on his mind, that he needed some time to think, some time to himself. As her mouth went up and down on him, all thoughts were obliterated, and he was damned grateful for that at the moment. She licked and sucked, her silky dark hair teasing his thighs and stomach.

He grabbed onto her hair and groaned again, and she kissed her way up his stomach, then sat back against the passenger side door, staring at him, her legs spread open. She reached for her coat on the floor and pulled a little pink bottle from one of the pockets. She poured some of its contents onto her hand and then reached between her legs and rubbed herself, the fragrant smell of strawberries filling the truck. She then took his face between her hands and pulled his head down between her legs, her nails scratching his back. He tasted the sweet, sticky strawberry oil she'd rubbed on, licking and darting his tongue until she arched her back and writhed. He teased her clitoris until she almost came; Marnie liked them to come together during intercourse.

"I can't take anymore," she whispered into his ear, her tongue and breath almost his undoing. She sat up and settled him back in the driver's seat and then straddled him, kissing him, tasting herself. "I want you in me now."

He was an inch away from entering her, but she held aloft, torturing him with her breasts against his mouth. She sucked two of his fingers, her gaze on his, and then put his fingers inside her. She moaned and he suckled hard on both of her breasts as she finally slid onto him, her back against the steering wheel. She rocked up and down against him, then turned around so that he could take her from behind. Somewhere in the dimmest recesses of his mind, he hoped those huge breasts didn't honk the horn. He wrapped his hands around them, squeezing, kneading her nipples, and then grabbed her hips and rocked her up and down on top of him until her breathy moans and screams came so fast that he couldn't contain himself anymore.

She slid off him, put on her jeans and coat, and whispered into his ear, "Anytime you need more of that, you just come see me." And then she headed back to her own car and drove off, leaving him to watch her red taillights as he caught his breath.

Olivia woke before six, surprised that she'd managed to fall asleep at all. When she'd gone inside last night, she'd swept up the smashed figurines and Windexed the mirror and then checked the deadbolt four times before going to bed.

And then she'd lain there.

Thinking about Zach. Thinking about Kayla. Thinking about being sixteen. Wondering what the hell gave her father the right to play with her life that way. And Zach's.

She'd been so furious that she'd jumped out of bed, planning to leave in the dead of night. And then she remembered. She was someone's mother.

I am someone's mother. She'd run into the bathroom to stare at herself in the mirror, as though she might have changed since yesterday. *I have a daughter,* she'd told her reflection. But she looked and felt like the same old Olivia she always was. Except for the questions, so many of them. And thoughts coming to her and at her from every direction. What was her daughter like? What was Kayla's world? Who *was* she?

All these years. Thirteen years. A baby had become a toddler, a preschooler, and had probably started asking questions that young, around three years old. Where is my mother? Why don't I have a mother like everyone else?

As a kid Olivia had spent stupid hours on self-pity, upset that her own father didn't really love her, didn't want to know her. And for all these years, her own little girl had grown up into a teenager thinking that her mother had abandoned her.

She'd thought herself sick, literally throwing up right into the little plastic-lined wicker trash can next to her bed.

How dare her father have done this. How could he? How could anyone have done what he did? Why tell her the baby *died*? Why let her go through the pregnancy and birth only to let her think her baby had been born dead?

She'd closed her eyes against the questions and gotten up to recheck the doors and windows one last time and then slipped into bed, wondering what Zach was doing. Wondering if Marnie had followed him home. Wondering if they were making love right now.

The thought of Zach having sex with another woman almost made her sick again and she'd vowed to close her eyes and go to sleep. She'd set the alarm so that Johanna wouldn't surprise her again. This time, Olivia would be ready for her.

Ha. Now that it was morning, she didn't feel ready for anything. She pulled the blankets up to her chin and glanced out the window at the gray winter morning. She shivered, then realized the cold blast up her spine had more to do with the welcome note she'd received last night *and* Marnie than the weather. Zach's girlfriend, if that's what she was, had been polite, and it was nice of her to offer to let Olivia stay at her home, but years of working at *Glitz* had clued in Olivia to the word *guarded*. Olivia had immediately sensed Marnie's sense of self-preservation. The woman had come because she'd either heard or seen with her own eyes that Zach had been dining earlier with Olivia at the bar and grill. Olivia had felt Marnie sizing her up, determining how nervous, how ready to fight she needed to be.

All that from a two-minute meeting. But five years of watching *Glitz* staffers lie with straight faces and then stab coworkers in the back had taught Olivia a thing or two about people when they felt threatened.

As she headed into the bathroom for a long, hot shower, she thought about that kiss Marnie had given Zach. Perhaps Marnie knew about their past relationship, although it hadn't sounded that way. Perhaps Marnie was responsible for the vandalism. A *"keep away from my man"* kind of thing.

Olivia wondered if Marnie was a mother figure to Kayla. On one hand, Olivia hoped Kayla *did* have a mother figure in her life. On the other, she had no idea how in the world she was going to inch her way into her daughter's life as "mom" when she'd missed out on thirteen years. When Kayla had grown up believing her mother hadn't wanted her. Didn't want her.

The shower helped. Olivia stood naked on the fluffy

bath mat and reached for a towel, then shrieked as she saw someone dart past the window. She grabbed the towel and wrapped it around herself, then ran to the window and stared out—nothing but bare trees and evergreens. The bathroom window looked out onto nothing but forest, and the trees were so close to the house on that part of the property that there was no need for blinds on the window.

It could have been just a tree branch that had blown across the window, she thought. Or maybe whoever had left the note and destroyed her foyer was skulking around outside. Getting an eyeful. The cottage had been empty for a while; it was possible that teenagers had been breaking in to hang out in the house; perhaps they didn't like that *their* place had been usurped. If only it was teenagers. She liked that idea a lot better than some nameless, faceless adult hell-bent on scaring her away. Or worse.

As she dried her hair and put on a little make-up, just some mascara and lip gloss, she made a mental note to make window blinds one of her purchases in town for today.

Olivia was dressed and on her second cup of coffee when the doorbell rang at exactly eight o'clock. Johanna was punctual.

Olivia took a deep breath and opened the door. Johanna stood on the porch, glaring at her.

"The next time you make accusations against someone to the police, have some proof," Johanna snapped. "And I don't like finding dead rats on the porch when I arrive at the butt crack of dawn in the dead of winter. If this is your little way of communicating, I suggest you grow the hell up."

"What are you talk—" Olivia began, but then glanced down at Johanna's feet, where a dead rat lay.

Oh, God. Did a rat just up and die on her front porch? Doubtful. Had Johanna been the skulker she'd seen dart past her window? Or was the timing a coincidence?

"Johanna, I realize you don't know me, but you can rest assured that if I want to tell you something, I'll say it. I don't use dead rodents to speak for me."

"Whatever," Johanna said. "I need your receipts."

Olivia held open the door and stepped aside. "Why don't you come in for a few minutes. We can sit down and talk."

Johanna held out her clipboard. "All I want from you is your receipts and your signature."

Olivia tried to read Johanna; she couldn't tell if the woman was just prickly or dangerous or both. She decided to give Johanna something to react to. Olivia would take it from there. "My feelings about my father are very complicated," Olivia said. "We didn't have much of a relationship, and that was his choice from the time I was born. Same with my sisters."

"So why did he leave you this place?" Johanna asked, gesturing at the house. "Why didn't he leave it to me?" Tears came to her eyes.

And we have contact, Olivia thought. At least she knew how to reach Johanna.

"Please come in, Johanna," Olivia said. "Let's talk."

"Just give me your receipts and sign here," the woman said angrily, wiping at her tears. "I'm not interested in talking to you."

Olivia sighed and handed over the receipts for the coffee and the postcards—which she'd almost forgotten she'd bought—and signed the log on Johanna's clipboard. Then Johanna turned and left.

So did you trash the entryway? Olivia mentally called after her. She had no idea what to think. Johanna didn't like her, clearly, and she was angry—or hurt—that she herself hadn't inherited the cottage.

If her father had loved Johanna, if they had been engaged, why hadn't he left her the house? And why would he subject her to being caretaker? Checking up on the house, checking up on the daughter who would receive the house. If Olivia handed over her receipts every day and signed the log, the house would be hers in a month. Why would William ask Johanna to be watchdog?

Because William is a hateful monster, she thought, heading back inside. *Sorry,* she said heavenward, closing the door against the chilly winter air.

She went into the kitchen to call a locksmith. She was in luck. Someone could come out to fix the lock in the next ten minutes

The doorbell rang. *The locksmith can't be* that *fast,* she thought, then wondered if Johanna had come back. She opened the door to find a smiling middle-aged woman carrying a pamphlet.

"Hello, dear," she said. "My name is Pearl Putnam and I'm Blueberry township's manager of recreation. Which is a fancy way of saying I work in the town manager's office and organize town activities, such as Little League and the Fourth of July fireworks display. Well, you get the picture. Anyway, there's a rumor going around Blueberry that an editor from *Glitz* magazine is staying at the Sedgwick house."

Olivia smiled and held out her hand. "I'm Olivia Sedgwick. One of William Sedgwick's daughters. And a *former* editor of *Glitz* magazine."

Pearl squeezed Olivia's hand with both of her own and said, "I'm so sorry for your loss. I didn't know your father well, but he was a longtime home owner and taxpayer in our dear town." Then she added, "And a former editor is just as good! If you have a few minutes, I'd like to talk to you about a community event."

"Sure," Olivia said. "Come on in. I just made a fresh pot of coffee."

Pearl beamed. "That would be wonderful," she said as she came in and glanced around. She took off her wool coat and hat, and Olivia hung them in the hall closet. "What a beautiful home. I've never been here before. Your father wasn't one for socializing."

"Well, I guess when he was up here in Maine he wanted to spend time with his fiancée," Olivia said, gesturing for Pearl to take a seat.

Pearl almost choked on air. "His *fiancée?* He was quite a ladies' man. I'm surprised to hear he could have had a fiancée. He dated a different woman every time he came up here. Not that he came up very often. A few times a year, maybe, especially in the last seven or eight years."

Well, well, Olivia thought. Interesting. Not surprising, but given what Johanna had said, interesting.

"I was under the impression that he was engaged to Johanna, the woman who owns the sweater shop."

Pearl harrumphed. Clearly she didn't approve of Johanna. "In her dreams, maybe."

"I'll be right back with coffee," Olivia said. Pearl

was clearly chock-full of information and gossip. She'd be a good source.

Olivia headed to the kitchen and returned with two mugs of coffee. Pearl was walking around the living room, peering as if to see inside other rooms.

"I'd be happy to take you on a tour," Olivia said.

"Oh, that would be wonderful," Pearl said. "But I'd better ask you about the Inner-Beauty Pageant before I forget why I came in the first place. The pageant is an annual event here in Blueberry. It used to be held in the summer, but the year-round residents began to resent that so many summer visitors were winning that we voted to hold the pageant in the dead of winter."

Olivia smiled. "I can understand that. I myself won the pageant when I was fifteen."

Pearl sucked in her breath. "Really! Oh, my goodness, well now you simply have to say yes!"

"To what?"

"To coordinating," Pearl explained.

"Coordinating the pageant?" Olivia asked. "I don't—"

"Oh, please say you'll at least consider it," Pearl said. "The pageant hasn't changed in thirty years. It's still our town's way of valuing our girls age thirteen to seventeen, who know that beauty is only skin-deep. The prize is still twenty-five hundred dollars and a monthly column for the whole year on the subject of inner beauty in the *Maine Daily News*."

Olivia smiled. That was why she'd wanted so badly to enter the pageant and win; the columns helped her secure her internship at *Glitz* after college.

"I don't know the first thing about coordinating a pageant, though," Olivia said. "I—"

"The former coordinator's materials are all in order," Pearl interrupted. "She had a folder full of everything you'd need to know. You just have to follow her schedule. The pageant will be held in two weeks, the day after Valentine's."

"Why did the coordinator quit when the pageant is in two weeks?" Olivia asked.

Pearl harrumphed again. "I have half a mind to locate her and tell her just what I think of her leaving us in the lurch that way. She just up and left yesterday, leaving me a note saying she's sick of Maine in the winter and is going to Florida to be with a man she's been corresponding with on-line. Do you believe her nerve? As if that relationship will last, anyway."

"Pearl, I—"

"Your presence will be such a boost not only to the girls, but to the entire pageant itself. Not only a winner of the pageant, but one who grew up to become a distinguished editor of a major New York fashion magazine. Oh, please, Olivia."

Olivia sipped her coffee. Even if she wanted to say yes, she couldn't very well do so without finding out what Zach thought. Kayla was entering the pageant. And she'd promised to keep her distance.

"I'd try to take over the pageant myself," Pearl said, "but my hands are so full right now. Give me one more thing, and I'm afraid all the balls I've got up in the air will come tumbling down." She sighed. "As recreation manager, I'm responsible for the pageant, but Shelby—that's the runaway coordinator, Shelby Maxwell—loved the role so much and managed it so well that I took it off my to-do list years ago. It would take me two weeks just to get up to snuff on how the pageant operates." Pearl sighed again for effect.

"Let me think about it," Olivia said.

Pearl clapped her hands. "That's not a no! Oh, do think fast, dear. The girls really need direction."

"I'll let you know tomorrow," Olivia promised.

"Wonderful," Pearl said.

And then after a brief tour of the house, Pearl finally left. The locksmith arrived and set to work, leaving Olivia time to think. The Inner-Beauty Pageant. Olivia would actually love to be involved in coordinating. That pageant had meant so much to her. She thought about the summer she suggested that her sister Ivy enter the pageant. Ivy was so interesting, so passionate about forensic science, but Ivy had taken it the wrong way: *"You think I should enter because I'm ugly! Because I don't look like you! Well, I know why you're not entering. Because you don't have inner beauty! You're ugly inside!"*

Later that night, she and Ivy had made up.

"You're not ugly inside," Ivy had said, tears in her eyes. "You're one of the nicest people I know, actually."

Olivia had been thrilled at the compliment. "And you're not ugly outside," she'd said. "In fact, you're very pretty."

"Pretty schmitty," Ivy had said. "I'd rather be smart."

"You are that," Olivia had said.

Ivy had inner beauty in spades. So did Amanda. And when Olivia won the pageant, she'd finally been assured that she did too.

"I have a daughter," she said to the air. "I have a daughter! I am someone's mother!"

She tried to remember as much as she could of the girl she'd seen at the gazebo, but Kayla had been too far away for Olivia to get a good look at her face. She'd seen the hair, the same hair as her own, light blond and long.

"I am a mother," she said again, twirling around for no reason other than the pure joy that filled every bit of her heart.

Her mood much improved, Olivia grabbed her coat and mittens and headed out. She had no idea when Zach would be returning her car, so she might as well walk into town. She had her two items to buy, one of which was a good set of blinds for the bathroom. And if she ran into Zach and Kayla while shopping, all the better.

Chapter 8

Zach was just getting into Olivia's car in order to drive it back to the cottage when Marnie drove up in her little red car. He closed the door and walked toward her, lest she shove him in Olivia's car and pull a repeat of last night. Though he doubted even Marnie would dare that in the light of morning.

It was incredible sex, and crazy as his life was at the moment, Marnie had managed to clear his mind of all but what she was doing to him. He'd gone inside last night, paid the sitter, checked on Kayla, and then fallen fast asleep. Exactly what he needed. Without that lovely little interlude last night, he would have lain awake, thinking, wondering.

As he strode toward Marnie, beautiful, sexy Marnie, what he was thinking, wondering, was why he couldn't feel for her what he'd felt for Olivia. He hadn't felt that for any woman since. He liked. He lusted. But that crazy I-would-die-for-you feeling had never stirred inside him again. Until he saw Olivia in Blueberry the other day. At first he'd been shocked, then, yes, scared, for what it meant in terms of his daughter, but the overriding feeling was that same lift of his heart, a surge he could only compare to how he felt for his daughter.

"Thought I'd bring you some coffee and fresh muffins," Marnie said, then kissed him full on the lips.

"Appreciate it," he said. "And I appreciated last night, too," he added.

"Look, Zach," she said, eyeing Olivia's car, "I really need to talk to you. Or do you have company?"

"No. Olivia left her car here last night when she drove over after coming home to the break-in. I drove her home and told her I'd drive her car over this morning."

Her expression darkened. "Don't be silly, Zach. You go to work. I'd be happy to drive her car over. Then she can drop me in town."

He didn't think Olivia would appreciate that at all. "There's something I wanted to talk to her about, so . . ."

"Because there's something going on between the two of you?" she asked, her eyes narrowed. "If you're cheating on me, Zach Archer, I'll—" She stopped, and then her expression changed again. Sweeter. Softer.

"You'll what?" he asked.

"I'll be devastated," she said. "That's what. So can we go talk somewhere?"

He glanced at her, then led her into the heated barn, where he'd set up Kayla's gymnastics equipment. Upstairs was a heated loft that contained a sofa, a desk and chair, and a table and chairs. They sat down on the sofa, their coffees and muffins on a small coffee table in front of them. He could tell

Marnie had a lot on her mind, and he had no doubt her questions would concern Olivia.

We were catching up at Barker's. . . .

"I just need to know that things are okay between us," Marnie said. "All of a sudden, this woman turns up and you're acting differently."

"Things are fine between us, Marnie," he said, covering her hand.

She searched his eyes. "So is Olivia an old girlfriend?"

He nodded and bit into his muffin to avoid having to elaborate.

Her eyes widened. "She's Kayla's mother, isn't she. They have the same hair."

"Marnie, I'm sorry to be so evasive, but I'm just not ready to answer any questions about Olivia. She and I do have a history, but I'd like to leave it at that for now. Okay?"

"Okay," she said, but she looked anything but satisfied. She placed his hand on his belt buckle. "How about a little morning delight?" she asked, rubbing against his fly. Before he could blink her tongue was in his ear and she was straddling him. "Lookie," she said, taking his hand and putting it up under her skirt, "no underwear."

Oh, Marnie, he thought. *You don't have to do this. You don't have to try to keep me yours with sex.*

She started unzipping his pants. In seconds he could be inside her, neither of them having to even undress. But it was eight o'clock in the morning, and though Kayla was fast asleep and probably wouldn't awaken until nine, he'd never allow himself to be caught in a compromising position by his daughter.

"Kayla might come looking for me," he told Marnie, as her hand stroked him. He put his hand on hers to stop her, and she flinched. "Why don't we continue this tomorrow night," he said.

She smiled. "How about tonight instead? I can't wait."

"You're hard to resist, Marnie, but Kayla's a little all over the place with the pageant and I think I'd better stick close to home tonight."

That was true, actually. The fact that he couldn't get Olivia out of his mind was also true.

She pouted, but his expression must have seemed unyielding because she smiled and said, "Tomorrow night, it is."

Marnie was his girlfriend. He was doing nothing he hadn't been doing for a month. So why did he feel so guilty?

Because Olivia was in his heart and always had been. Thirteen years and all the terrible circumstances hadn't changed that.

Zach drove Olivia's car to the cottage, the faint smell of her trademark perfume assailing him. He used to love just sitting beside her, breathing in that beautiful clean scent. One of his assistants was trailing him in the pickup so that he wouldn't have to walk the two miles into town. Good thing, too, because today was a cold one. And a waiting assistant meant he'd have to keep this meeting short.

Truth was, he was glad for an excuse to see her again this morning. Despite how easily he'd fallen asleep last night—thanks to Marnie—he'd woken up several times and tossed and turned for thinking of her alone in the house, a nasty message scrawled on the mirror, some stupid figurines smashed.

It was a warning. A warning of what, he had no idea. Who gave two figs if Olivia Sedgwick was in town? She hadn't been in town to get on anyone's bad side in ten years. Olivia was right: it made no sense.

He was pulling into her driveway when she came out of the house. He got out of her car, hating his response to the sight of her. It wasn't just her beauty that always stopped him dead in his tracks. It was her aura, if he could use a word like that, her confidence, the intelligence in her eyes, the old-soul quality in her eyes. There were those who'd written Olivia off as a spoiled Sedgwick girl, but Zach had always known the real Olivia.

Even bundled up in a down coat, she was sexy as hell.

"Perfect timing," he said. "Were you planning to walk into town?"

She nodded. "It's colder than I realized today." She glanced over at Zach's truck. "Is someone waiting to give you a ride back home? I was hoping to talk to you about something important."

He glanced at her. "That's one of my assistants. I'll tell him to drive on ahead to the office. You can drop me off there. We'll talk on the way."

"Okay," she said and watched as he walked over to his truck and spoke to the driver, who then drove off.

"Did you call a locksmith?" Zach asked as he got into the passenger side of her car.

Olivia buckled her seat belt. "He's come and gone. I feel a lot better now. Well, as good as I can feel about the situation." She paused. "Zach, there's something I need to talk over with you. It has to do with the Inner-Beauty Pageant."

He glanced at her. "What about it?"

Olivia backed out of the driveway and headed toward town. "Someone from the town manager's office asked me if I'd be interested in coordinating the pageant since the previous coordinator up and left on them. I told her I'd let her know. My answer is dependent on yours."

"Do you want to coordinate?" he asked. "Sounds like a big job."

"Well, I do know the ins and outs of the pageant, and Pearl, from the town manager's office, thinks that my having been an editor at *Glitz* magazine will add cachet and even greater sponsorship from local businesses. But the main reason I'd want to do it is to get to know Kayla."

He nodded. "We'd have to tell her that you're her mother immediately, though. No lies. Just the truth. I wouldn't want her to get to know you as the coordinator and then have it sprung on her that you're her long-lost mother."

Olivia's entire face lit up. "I agree."

"We'll tell her tonight," he said. "I think we should do it on her turf. Can you come for dinner? Seven?"

"That would be great," she said.

He had no idea how Kayla was going to react. He was only grateful that something had forced his hand.

Olivia felt eyes on her in the Eat-In Diner. She glanced around, and indeed people were staring.

Blueberry was a small town and didn't attract outsiders in the dead of winter. She didn't recognize many of the diners; she'd only spent two weeks a year in Blueberry and she and her sisters had rarely come to town. They'd spent most of their time at home or at the private beach behind the cottage.

She stood at the counter and ordered a cup of coffee and a cheese Danish to go.

"New here?" asked the waitress, an attractive young woman.

"Just visiting," Olivia said.

"Visiting whom?" the waitress asked.

"Nosy!" snapped another waitress, an older woman who shooed the younger one away. She turned to Olivia. "Sorry about that, hon," she added, handing Olivia her coffee and Danish.

Olivia smiled. "No problem."

As she left, she saw Marnie getting out of her bright red car. The woman didn't look happy. When she noticed Olivia, her expression changed in a snap.

"Olivia," Marnie said in what sounded like the fakest I'm-so-happy-to-see-you voice. "How did you sleep last night? I stopped by your house just a few minutes ago to see if you'd made it through the night all right, but you weren't home. Now I know why! Join me for breakfast?"

Olivia shifted her bag of food from the Eat-In Diner. "I'd love to, but I just got takeout, and I have an appointment. Another time."

This time Marnie wasn't as quick with her smile. "Of course. Another time. I'm disappointed, of course. I would loooove to compare notes about Zach."

"Compare notes?" Olivia repeated.

Marnie grinned. "The former girlfriend and the current girlfriend. Although, you were only teenagers when you dated and it was only for what—a couple of weeks? I know your little summer fling with Zach can hardly be compared to our serious relationship, but I still thought it would be fun to talk shop."

Summer fling. . . Was that how Zach had described their relationship? And was Marnie and Zach's relationship serious? Or was Marnie just baiting her?

Oh, for God's sake, Olivia thought. It's not like she herself had any claim on the man. And if she were in Marnie's position, she'd be threatened too. The old girlfriend comes to town—and Marnie didn't know the half of it—and of course the new girlfriend would be worried.

"Well," Marnie continued, "if you're free for dinner tonight, we could have a girls' night out." Her expression turned teasing, and she leaned close. "I can tell you all about last night. After leaving your house, I stopped by Zach's to return a T-shirt he'd left at my house the night before, and, oh, my God, we didn't even make it out of his truck. Okay, I know this is TMI, but I can still feel the impression of the steering wheel against my back." She laughed and rubbed her back.

Way too much information, Marnie.

Olivia wondered if it was true. "I wish I could join you for dinner, but I just made other plans."

The smile disappeared again, then returned. "Another time, then."

"How long have you and Zach been dating?" Olivia asked before she could stop herself.

She *should* have stopped herself. First of all, she

didn't want to know. Second of all, she was talking about Zach behind his back, which felt wrong. And third, she was playing right into Marnie's hands.

But she couldn't help herself.

Marnie grinned. "Hmm, let's see. We've been a couple since just before Christmas. So, a month. The holidays were so wonderful this past year. A real family affair. Zach and Kayla came over for Christmas Eve dinner, and then we spent Christmas and New Year's together. I wouldn't be surprised if he surprised me with a ring for Valentine's Day."

Olivia's back went up. Were they that serious?

"Have you and Zach talked about getting engaged?" Olivia asked. Perhaps Zach and Marnie had talked about blending their families. Perhaps Marnie had been a mother figure to Kayla this past month.

Perhaps, perhaps, perhaps. Speculating was stupid. She should just ask Zach what was going on. The problem was, she barely felt entitled. Yes, Kayla was her daughter. And Olivia had missed out on Kayla's entire life through no intention of her own. But Olivia couldn't just waltz into Kayla's life after thirteen years and demand to be mom. It didn't work that way.

Marnie glanced at her watch. "Ooh, I'd better run, actually. Let's make plans to get together soon."

Olivia smiled, and Marnie headed inside the diner.

Evasive. Interesting. Olivia doubted there was talk of engagement or Marnie would have told her all about it. *I think I can still feel the impression of the steering wheel against my back. . . .*

Which meant that *that* little we-didn't-make-it-out-of-his-truck episode was very likely true, Olivia thought, her stomach flip-flopping.

Olivia crossed the boulevard, glancing back at the diner. Through the plate-glass window she could see Marnie watching her.

Creepy. Maybe Marnie *was* responsible for last night's welcome to Blueberry surprise. Or perhaps Johanna was, she thought, as she passed the sweater shop. She glanced in to find Johanna folding sweaters. The woman did not look happy.

Pearl's words came back to her. *His* fiancée? *He dated a different woman every time he came up here. . . .*

Olivia wouldn't have thought that possible—for one woman to believe she was a man's one and only when he was clearly playing the field. Johanna was either deluded, believed what she wanted to believe, or William was just that good of a liar. Olivia knew that last one was dead-on.

The wind picked up, and Olivia zipped up her coat. She passed a pickup truck—not Zach's—and immediately envisioned Marnie straddled on Zach's lap in the driver's seat.

She squeezed her eyes shut to shake the image.

Focus, Olivia, she told herself. *You need blinds for the bathroom. You need something to bring for tonight's dinner. Dessert?* She glanced across the street. There was a hardware store just a few shops up from a bakery and the General Store.

At least she'd easily fulfill her receipts quota. She headed into the hardware store and estimated the measurements; she'd had so much on her mind this morning that she'd forgotten to look for a tape measure. After dropping off the heavy carton in her car, she continued on down the boulevard on foot, thinking about what she'd contribute to tonight's dinner with Zach and Kayla. A dessert, definitely. And she'd bake it herself, from scratch.

I wish I knew what Kayla's favorite flavor is. I don't even know what my own child is allergic to.

Chocolate cream pie and apple pie were her favorites and seemed safe, so she entered the General Store and filled a shopping basket with everything she'd need.

As she debated about ice cream, she felt eyes on her and turned around. A woman she'd never seen before was staring at her, her expression . . . angry? No, that wasn't quite right. Olivia couldn't quite place it. She was in her midthirties, attractive, but dressed like a teenager in a tiny pink jacket and tight jeans with rhinestones and embroidery that read "HOT!" dotting the pockets and hem. She had shoulder-length blond hair and bangs, a rhinestone clip holding back one swath of hair above her ear.

"Hi," Olivia said, trying to summon a smile.

The woman didn't respond. She simply turned and walked away. Olivia stepped back to see where she went; the woman had left the store and was walking fast down the street.

Creepy, Olivia thought. Perhaps she's one of the women her father dated and, like Johanna, thought Olivia a heartless opportunist.

Yup, Daddy dearest, all my dreams are coming true, all right, she thought as she brought her basket to the checkout counter.

She froze. *All your dreams will come true. . . .*

She only ever had one dream, albeit for just a short while, that she and Zach would run away together and raise their baby.

Her father knew that Zach and Kayla were living in Blueberry. He'd been sending Kayla birthday cards and Christmas cards in Olivia's name for years. William Sedgwick had known exactly where they were all these years.

Why had he chosen now to let Olivia learn the truth? Why after he was gone? Had he not wanted to deal with the fallout of what he'd done? Olivia couldn't imagine he'd care one way or another who was angry at him. Perhaps he worried about legalities.

Olivia, again full of questions with no answers— and no way to get answers—lugged her heavy basket atop the checkout counter.

She would definitely pay a visit to the home for pregnant teenagers where she'd spent seven long months. Have a little chat with a certain doctor and nurse. Thirteen years wasn't too long ago. There was a good chance both were still there.

How much had their lies been worth? Olivia wondered as the clerk rang up her purchases. A lot, she imagined.

Receipts safely tucked in her purse, she headed back to her car with her bag of groceries.

She stopped dead in her tracks.

"Rich bitch" was written in marker on the passenger-side window of her car. And two of the tires were slashed—on the passenger side. Whoever had done it had been blocked from view by the hedges that lined that edge of the lot.

The "HOT!" blonde in the general store immediately flashed into her mind. So did Marnie. And Johanna.

Which one of you is doing this? Or is it someone who has yet to let me know what he or she thinks of me? More furious than scared, as she'd been last night, she pulled out her cell phone to call the police. She asked to speak with the officer who'd been at the cottage last night.

"Someone sure doesn't like you," the officer said. "What did you do to anger someone to that degree, anyway?"

Jerk. "I didn't *do* anything," she said.

"Well, you've pissed off someone."

"I thought I was the victim here," Olivia snapped.

"Someone will be out in a few minutes," the officer said and hung up.

She wouldn't be surprised to find out the ever-so-concerned officer was Marnie's cousin.

Chapter 9

Zach was pleased to see Kayla doing her homework when he arrived back at the house after work. He'd collected her assignments from the principal and warned Kayla that if she didn't do her schoolwork, there would be no Inner-Beauty Pageant.

"Yay, pizza!" she said, eyeing the two big boxes he'd set down on the kitchen counter. "Wow, you must be hungry."

"Actually, we're having company for dinner," he said, walking toward her.

"Not Marnie and Bri-asshole again," she said, glaring.

Zach stopped dead in his tracks. "Kayla!"

"Sorry," she said. Without meaning it. He'd add another day of being grounded to her already packed month, but given the bombshell that was going to change her life tonight, he couldn't bear to.

"And no, it's not Marnie and Brianna. It's the woman you saw yesterday morning in town, the one with the blond hair—"

"The beautiful one," Kayla said, perking up. "So

you're dating her now? Did you dump Marnie for her?"

I am so out of my element, Zach thought. Out of his element with Kayla and her constant questions and certainly out of his element with the emotions and questions tonight would bring. Which was why he'd opted to pick up pizza instead of cook something fancy. He had no doubt there would be more talking done tonight than eating.

"We're not dating," he said. "Come help set the table, please."

She surprised him by jumping up and heading into the kitchen for the silverware and plates. "Why is she coming, then?"

Zach stiffened. He needed to tell Kayla the truth now. Before Olivia arrived. His daughter deserved to hear the truth of her history from him; to have Olivia there as she learned the story would be overwhelming. And Kayla would need some time to digest what she heard. "Sweetheart, I have to make a quick phone call. Can you finish setting the table?"

She nodded and got to work and Zach headed outside with his cell phone. He pressed in the phone number for the Sedgwick house, a number he'd never forgotten. He'd only dialed it once before, when he was seventeen and in love. King Sedgwick had asked his name.

"Archer? It's not ringing a bell," William had said.

"My father is a mechanic at Joe's Auto Repair."

There had been silence. And then, "Don't call here again. Olivia is not permitted to date while she's visiting." And then he had hung up.

That was his first conversation with William

Sedgwick. There had been one other, when he'd learned about his daughter. When William's lackey had placed her in Zach's arms.

Zach paced the front yard, hoping Olivia hadn't already left.

"Hello?"

"Olivia," he said. "I'm glad I caught you. Look, I think it's best if I tell Kayla about you myself. It's been just the two of us her entire life, and to spring the truth on her with you there strikes me as incredibly overwhelming. I hadn't thought of that before."

"That's true," she said. "I think you're right."

"Give us an hour," he said. "I think after hearing what I have to say, she'll want to see you, even if it's just for a few minutes. She'll need to see that you're real."

"I couldn't agree more," Olivia said. "It says quite a lot about you as a father."

He was silent for a moment. "See you later, then." He put the phone back in his pocket, took one hell of a deep breath, and then headed back inside. It had been a long time since he had felt this nervous.

Oh, boy, Zach thought as he walked into the dining room and saw what Kayla had done. Lit candles on the table. A lace tablecloth. Dim lighting.

She was wearing a dress. And her hair, which was usually in her face, was pulled back by a pretty clip.

"Kayla, I want to ask you something," he said, taking her hand and leading her to the living room. They sat down on the sofa.

"What, Dad?"

"It's more than clear by the romantic table and

your good-girl appearance that you're hoping this dinner will mean Marnie's out and that a new woman is in."

"Am I that obvious?" she asked, smiling.

He gently yanked her hair. "Yes. But. And there's a big but. Let's say I do fall for someone other than Marnie. Let's say we—whoever it is—start seeing each other. Will you have a problem with that relationship too? Or is it just Marnie you have problems with?"

She glanced down at her feet. "I don't know," she said, and her eyes welled with tears. "You're all I have. I don't want to share you."

There was no better segue. He pulled her close and hugged her, stroking her fine hair. "Sweetheart, I understand that. I really do. I know it must be hard. Listen, I need to tell you something. Something very important."

She wiped away her tears. "What?"

"It's about your mother."

Kayla stared at him. "What about my mother?"

Here goes. He looked at his daughter, his precious girl, and knew that he was about to change her entire world. For the better, he knew, but for a thirteen-year-old, this was going to be mind-blowing.

"Kayla, the woman you saw me talking to yesterday, the one who's coming over tonight . . . she's your mother."

Her mouth dropped open. "She's my mother?"

He nodded. "Olivia Sedgwick."

Kayla jumped up and stared at him. "She came back for me?"

He took her hand. "Sweetheart, it turns out that she didn't even know you were alive all these years—"

"What?" Kayla interrupted. "She gave birth to me!"

"I'm going to tell you a story, a true story, most of which I heard for the first time yesterday. I know you're going to have a lot of questions, and I want you to ask anything. Anything at all."

She took a deep breath, then stared at him as he recounted his relationship with Olivia when they were teenagers and then what William Sedgwick had done.

"She was told I was dead?" Kayla whispered. "Oh my God."

"And I was told that your mother didn't want anything to do with us," he said. "Which wasn't true. Olivia loved me then. And she loved you."

Kayla covered her face with her hands and cried. He held her. "I'm glad whatshisname is dead!" she screamed. "He deserves to be dead."

"Sweetheart, Oliv—your mother—is due here in about a half hour. Are you up for it? Or should I have her come tomorrow?"

"Is she nice?" she asked.

"Yesterday was the first time I've seen her in thirteen years, Kayla. But she was nice when I knew her. I was madly in love with her then."

"Oh my God. Oh my God. Oh my God," Kayla said, pacing the room. She broke into a smile, then burst into tears. Then started laughing. Then another nervous round of "Oh my God."

"Kay? Are you all right?"

"I have a mother," she said, her expression happier than he'd ever seen. "I have a mother!"

She flew into his arms and he held her close as she continued to cry and laugh and utter, "I have a mother. I have a mother like everyone else."

Oh, Kayla, he thought, his heart twisting.

The doorbell rang, and Kayla turned white. "I'm not ready! Tell her to come back in a half hour. I'm not ready! No, wait. I'm ready. Do I look okay?"

"You look beautiful, Kayla," he said.

She smiled and took a deep breath and accompanied him to the door. But standing on the doorstep wasn't Olivia.

It was Marnie.

"Kayla! How pretty you look!" Marnie exclaimed. And then her eyes zoomed right to the dining room table, where Kayla had set the stage for romance. "Expecting someone?" she asked, her eyes narrowed.

"Olivia Sedgwick is coming for dinner," Zach said.

Marnie's expression turned from hurt to anger to just peachy in seconds. "Just peachy" was a favorite expression of hers. "Well, I don't want to intrude," she said, hesitating.

But an invitation to join them would not be forthcoming.

"I'll call you later, Marnie," Zach said.

She leaned close, pressing her breasts against him. "Please do," she whispered in his ear, adding a twirl of her tongue, another of her favorite moves. Sometimes the hot breath shot straight to his groin. Now it did absolutely nothing. He hated playing games, and he felt like he was playing one right now, but he couldn't exactly pull Marnie aside, tell her the truth, and let her know things would go on as they had been between the two of them. He had no idea if they would. He had no idea of anything right now.

Marnie was already back in her car and driving away when a car he didn't recognize passed hers on the road. Olivia was behind the wheel. He hoped there hadn't been another incident.

"Here she comes," Zach said. "You ready?"

Kayla nodded.

The conversation had exhausted Kayla. By ten, she'd fallen asleep on the couch. Olivia had told Kayla everything: finding out she was pregnant, her father's reaction, the home for unwed mothers, believing that Zach had abandoned her, and being told that her baby had been stillborn.

First Kayla had been angry, then moments later, the anger had been replaced by tears. "How could your own father have done this? Don't you hate him?"

Good question, Olivia had thought. "I need to sort out my feelings for my father and what he did."

"Well, I need to sort through my feelings about my *mother,*" Kayla had said. "So I guess I can understand that."

It had been a breakthrough.

"Aren't you really, really mad at your father?" Kayla had asked. "I mean, how could you not be?"

"You know what, Kayla?" Olivia had said. "One feeling overrides any other: joy at knowing that you're alive."

Kayla had smiled. And she'd clearly had enough for one night. Before Olivia had returned from the kitchen with the two pies, Kayla had been snoring on the couch.

Zach had carried Kayla upstairs, and Olivia had followed, her heart beating wildly in her chest.

"Can I tuck her in?" Olivia had asked. "For the first time?"

He had smiled. "Go right ahead."

She had sat down on the edge of the bed and pulled the pink comforter up, then just watched Kayla breathe for a minute, her chest rising and falling.

You're my daughter, she had thought, marveling at Kayla's face, at her features, a combination of Zach and herself. She had Zach's eyes and Olivia's nose. Zach's smile, and Olivia's hair.

From somewhere deep inside her, a feeling of love so strong had burst up, and tears had come to her eyes. "I'm so sorry I missed out on your childhood," she had whispered. "I'm so sorry I wasn't there. And that you thought I didn't want you."

She had felt a strong hand on her shoulder and turned; Zach had stood there.

"You're here now. That's what matters. Today and the future."

She had nodded, unable to speak for a moment. "Thank you, Zach. I know how hard this must be for you, too. Suddenly sharing your daughter after thirteen years."

"It's what I've always wanted, Olivia," he had said. "For Kayla to have her mother too. How could I not want that for her?"

She had smiled and glanced back at Kayla, who had snaked an arm around her Winnie the Pooh. "I know tomorrow may bring a lot of questions, and I'm prepared for that."

"Your talk with her went very well," Zach had

said. "It was a great start. She reacted so much better than I thought she might."

It still felt surreal to Olivia. She'd been talking to her own daughter. *Her* daughter. They would both need time to get to know each other, become familiar to each other. When Olivia had first come to the door tonight, she and Kayla had just stared at each other for a full minute, taking in each other's faces, bodies, expressions, mannerisms. There was so much to see, let alone know.

Olivia reluctantly stood, and she and Zach stepped out of the room. As they headed downstairs, she said, "Zach, there was another incident today."

"I had a bad feeling when I saw you pull up in a different car," he said. "I meant to ask you about it, but with all that was going on with Kayla, it went out of my head. What happened?"

"Someone slashed my tires and defaced my car window with another nasty note. This time it said, 'Rich Bitch.'"

Zach shook his head. "This is ridiculous. Who's pulling these kinds of immature stunts?"

"Maybe it's Johanna. She told me she and my father were engaged, but according to Pearl, who seems quite the gossip, my father dated a different woman every time he came to Blueberry."

"Well, that wasn't often," Zach said. "I certainly never saw him around town. And I had to pass the house a few times. There were never signs of life."

"So is Johanna living in a fantasy world?" Olivia asked.

Zach shrugged. "I don't know her at all."

"There's another person I've been wondering

about," Olivia said, hesitant about saying something at all. "Look, Zach, I feel really uncomfortable about even bringing this up, but Marnie does seem to have a problem with me."

Zach nodded. "Yes, I'd say she does. I don't know if she's capable of trashing your entryway and car, though. Doesn't sound like her. I've seen her angry and frustrated and she's never resorted to back-handed retaliation or subterfuge."

She's probably never felt her relationship with you threatened before, Olivia wanted to say, but Zach headed into the kitchen to make coffee, and the subject of Marnie was most likely better left alone.

In a few minutes, Zach returned with two mugs of coffee. He set them on the coffee table, then sat down next to her on the sofa. He was so close that their thighs could almost touch if she leaned over just a little. Which she wouldn't, of course.

But she wanted to.

He glanced at her for a moment, and Olivia almost thought he might just reach over and kiss her, but he didn't. He picked up his mug and sipped his coffee.

I do want him to kiss me. More than anything, she realized. This was the first guy she'd ever loved. And what had torn them apart hadn't been either of their faults.

They were silent for a moment. She wondered if he was thinking the same thing.

"I really want to get to the bottom of who's leaving you these nasty notes," he said. So much for him thinking the same thing. But she was touched that he cared. "I'll stop by the police station and see what I can find out."

"Thanks, Zach," she said. "I also had a strange run-in at the General Store today. A woman I've never seen before stared at me with total disdain, then just turned and left when I said hello. Ten minutes later, my car was trashed." Olivia described the woman as best as she could remember.

"Sounds like Jacqueline McCord," Zach said. "We grew up next door to each other. Her family barely had it together better than mine. I remember being eleven, twelve, and watching guys crawling in and out of her bedroom window. She got pregnant at sixteen and dropped out of high school, and I never saw another guy around her house after that. When I was sixteen, she showed up in my bedroom when no one was home and told me I could do anything I wanted to her. She's four years older, so I have no idea why she'd be interested in a high school kid. I lied and told her I had a girlfriend, and she got enraged." He shook his head.

"What happened?"

"She said a high school girl could never satisfy me the way she could, a woman. She lifted up her sweater and showed me her breasts, as though I wouldn't be able to resist. So I told her I would never cheat on my girlfriend, and she told me I was a loser and left. She replayed that scenario at least ten times until I left Blueberry. And then when I came back five years later with Kayla, she tried everything to get closer to me—volunteering to baby-sit, be Kayla's nanny, always bringing over dinners in Tupperware. Once she even came over in nothing but a raincoat and said, "This is all I have left to entice you," and held open her raincoat. She was buck naked."

Olivia recalled how attractive Jacqueline was, even with a murderous expression. "What did you do?"

"I pulled her coat closed and told her that I thought she was a beautiful woman, but that I couldn't possibly get involved, what with having a five-year-old and starting up my career, and that I thought too highly of her to take advantage of her."

"That sounds nice," Olivia said.

"I thought so, but she told me that she wanted me to take advantage of her. That's when things turned ugly. She started screaming that I thought I was better than she was since I'd left Blueberry and come back with a college degree. It took a while for me to calm her down."

"Have you spoken since?" Olivia asked.

"I'm always polite to her when I see her in town, but she glares at me and huffs away."

Olivia took a sip of her coffee. "Well, if she gave me the evil eye because she's seen us together, she must really stare down Marnie."

Zach smiled. "She does. But there's little Marnie's afraid of. She marched up to Jacqueline the first time Jacqueline stared her up and down and told her off."

"So Marnie does have a hot temper?"

Zach leaned back against the couch. "It's hard for me to say. I guess I don't really know. Marnie and I are dating, Olivia. So we see each other at night for dinner or movies; there's little to rile her up." He paused for a moment. "Look, Olivia, I think I'd better tell you that Marnie and I are a couple. We've never had any talks about exclusivity, but we see each other a few times a week. We saw each other last night, as a matter of fact, after I left your house."

"I know," Olivia said, offering a hint of a smile. "In fact, Marnie can still—and I quote—'feel the impression of the steering wheel against my back.'"

Zach looked shocked. "She told you that?"

"I ran into her this morning."

Zach shook his head. "How does our sex life possibly work its way into conversation with someone she just met the evening before?"

"I think she's just trying to tell me that you're hers."

He let out a deep breath. "I don't know if I'm hers. I don't know anything right now."

"I can understand that," she said. "I gave you quite a shock."

He glanced at her. "You did at that, Olivia."

For a moment they were silent.

"Zach, if it's all right with you, I'd like to spend some time with Kayla tomorrow. Maybe I can take her out to breakfast and tell her I'll be coordinating the pageant." She froze. "Oh, no. The pageant. I'll need to tell Pearl that I'm Kayla's mother. I don't know if she'll allow me to coordinate under that circumstance."

"Well, let's see what she says. It's not as though you're *judging* the pageant. And taking Kayla out to breakfast sounds great. You don't even have to be too early. She's suspended from school for a few days."

"You mentioned that at Barker's," she said. "What did she do?"

"She was caught smoking—for the second time."

"Smoking!" Olivia couldn't believe it. Smoking at thirteen?

Zach sighed. "We had a long talk. She's grounded—her third or fourth grounding this month alone. "The Inner-Beauty Pageant couldn't have come up at a better time. I think it'll do a lot of my work for me."

Olivia nodded and sipped her coffee. "I can only imagine how tough it must be to raise an adolescent girl. I agree that the pageant will do so much good for Kayla. It asks girls to really focus on who they are inside. And for young girls just forming their identities, like Kayla, you're right that it couldn't have come into her life at a better time."

They each ruminated on that for a moment, and then Zach got up to refill their mugs. She couldn't possibly ask for a third cup, but she'd take any excuse not to leave. Being in this room, in this house, with Zach, with her daughter—*her daughter!*—sleeping upstairs—it was like a dream from which she never wanted to awaken.

"You're welcome to the spare bedroom if you don't want to go home," Zach said, reading her mind. "Two incidents at the cottage in as many days—I'm not too comfortable with you there overnight alone."

She was so surprised that he *did* care about her that she almost dropped her cup. In a moment, he was beside her on the couch, steadying her hand.

His hand felt so good on hers. She closed her eyes to savor it, and then she felt his lips on hers. She opened her eyes, amazed to discover she wasn't imagining it. Or dreaming. He held her gaze, giving her the opportunity to say no.

"I must be crazy," he said. "Because things are crazy enough right now. But I've been wanting to do that for two hours."

"Me too," she whispered.

"I remember our first kiss," he said. "On the beach, at night. The warm July wind blowing your hair all around. I thought you were the most beautiful person I'd ever seen."

She smiled, the image of Zach at seventeen filling her mind. "I thought the same about you."

"I couldn't believe you were really interested in me. But it wasn't like I had anything but myself to offer you, so I figured you must actually like me for me."

She laughed. "I did."

And then she kissed him, tentatively, questioningly. Giving him the out, time to change his mind, tell her it *was* crazy to do this with everything else that was going on.

But he slid his arms around her, pulling her closer, his chest crushing against hers. He kissed her the way he used to, with all the passion inside him, kisses that always led to their making love.

He pulled away and looked at her, and for a moment, she was looking at the Zach she'd loved so much. He took her hand and led her to the room off the living room. It was a spare bedroom, with French doors, which he closed behind them, then locked.

He pressed her against the doors in another kiss, his hands unbuttoning her blouse and then making quick work of her bra. He groaned at the sight of her breasts and cupped them, teasing her nipples until her legs almost buckled. He undid the snap of her pants and slid them down her hips and thighs, then used a finger to ease off her panties.

She stood naked before him and he stepped back to take her in, groaning again. In moments his clothes had joined hers on the floor and he pressed her down with his body onto the fluffy white rug by the bed, his hands and mouth roaming every inch of her until she almost screamed.

"Now, Zach," she breathed, unable to wait a moment more.

He reached for his pants and removed a condom from his wallet. She didn't care that last night he might very well have been making love to Marnie on this very rug. She only wanted him inside her.

And then he was. Her nails dug into his back as he entered her, and he groaned against her hair. He then lifted her hips and shifted them to a sitting position against the bed so that she was on top of him. He lifted her up and down against the hard length of him until the waves overcame her and she exploded in pleasure. And then he laid her down on the rug again and rode her hard and fast until he too was spent.

They lay there, catching their breath, until Zach suddenly bolted up.

"What is it?" she asked.

"I thought I heard noises outside the window," he said, glancing up at the window in front of the bed. The curtains were drawn, but there was a slight gap between them. And the low lamp from the bedside table could have illuminated them enough for someone to have seen them. "It was like the sound of a foot breaking a branch."

"Maybe it was a raccoon," Olivia said. *Or Marnie,* she thought.

"Maybe," he said.

He looked at her, then down the length of her naked body. "You're exquisite, Olivia."

She felt herself blush. "You are too."

"I'd like you to stay the night."

"I wish I could," Olivia said, "but rules of my father's will stipulate that I spend every night of a month at the cottage."

He rolled his eyes. "Your father's rules never made any sense."

She smiled. "I know."

"Keep a phone beside you at all times," he said. "And I want you to call me when you get home."

Pleased, she reached over to kiss him, but he'd already moved away. She suddenly felt very naked. Exposed. And like a fool for moving so fast. What had she been thinking? She *hadn't* been thinking. The man had just told her himself that he'd been with another woman last night. No, not just another woman. His girlfriend. And yet she let herself get caught up and carried away, let him make love to her.

No again. Let him have *sex* with her. Sex, that was what it had been. Hot, fast, lusty, unemotional sex. Always good during the doing. Not so good during the aftermath, when you lie there feeling . . . alone.

I'd like you to stay the night. . . .

There was that. Men didn't say that unless they meant it. A few years ago, she'd dated a man who'd pressured her for weeks to sleep with him, and then when she did, he handed her a ten-dollar bill for a cab because "he had to get up early to hit the gym." Another lover had said the first morning they'd woken up together, "Do you know what I wish? I wish you were a Swiss cheese omelet and side of home fries. And a large cup of coffee."

Olivia had had her share of bad dates and worse relationships. She knew what it felt like to be lonely in a man's company, in a man's bed, in his arms.

She didn't feel quite that way now. She felt . . . unsure. Unsure even what she was unsure of.

She was thinking too hard. "I'd like you to stay the night" was about safety. She'd been targeted twice. And it was late. And then there was Kayla; it seemed perfectly fine and natural, given the circumstances, for Olivia to sleep over in the guest room, to be there in the morning for her daughter, who'd surely be full of questions, want to make sure the whole thing hadn't been a dream.

"You'll call the minute you get home?" Zach asked as he stood, now fully dressed.

"The very minute," she said, wondering herself if what had occurred between them not five minutes ago hadn't been a dream.

Chapter 10

When Olivia woke up in the morning she could still feel the imprint of his lips on hers. She closed her eyes and let the memories surround her. Zach. Zach. Zach.

Last night, when she'd arrived home, she'd almost been surprised to find the house standing. Nothing seemed out of place. She'd called Zach and they'd spoken for just a minute, less really, and she'd felt bereft when they'd hung up.

It was early now, not quite six, but Olivia couldn't fall back asleep. Not with Zach to think about. Or Kayla. Or whoever it was who was trying to run her out of town. Olivia was eager to get up and out to meet with Pearl at the town hall to find out if she could still coordinate the pageant if her daughter was a contestant, but then she remembered she had to wait for Johanna. And the town hall probably didn't open until nine, anyway.

She showered, loathe to wash away the scent of sex, of Zach, from her body. As the hot water poured down, she thought of him making love to her and instantly wanted him again. She had no idea if there would be a next time, though, or what it would mean. She'd never knowingly been with a man who was involved in a relationship. That was against every code she'd lived by since the first grade, when she developed a wild crush on the very boy her best friend had a crush on. The boy had chosen Olivia, and Olivia had chosen her friend.

You didn't fool around with other women's men. Unknowingly was one thing. But Olivia knew. Zach had done the right thing—at least by Olivia, anyway—by telling her about Marnie before things had gotten out of hand between them last night. Olivia would have been wise to walk away. At least until either of them knew what they wanted.

Maybe she was rationalizing, but it seemed that last night was less about romance and more about history. What was between them was overwhelming; what they'd gone through last night with Kayla amazing. In any case, there wouldn't be a next time. Not while Zach was in a relationship with another woman.

That settled in her mind, she dressed and made coffee, then sipped in dread as the minutes ticked toward eight o'clock. But eight came and went without the ringing of the doorbell. At eight-twenty, Olivia was about to head out, figuring she'd drop off the receipts at Johanna's shop, when the doorbell rang. Johanna held out her hand without comment. Olivia gave her the receipts, then signed the log and the woman was down the path before Olivia could even say good morning.

Or ask if Johanna, had, say, slashed her tires yesterday. Or been involved romantically with her father at all. If William had rarely come up to

Blueberry, how serious could their relationship have been?

Johanna taken care of—as far as the terms of the will were concerned—Olivia headed to the town hall. As she passed the auditorium, she couldn't resist going in and walking across the stage, where so many years ago, she'd stood at the podium and read the essay she'd written on the most influential person in her life, her half sisters. A young girl in the audience, a candidate's younger sister, probably, had stood up and said, "She's disqualified, 'cause that's two people!" But the main judge had stood and said that two half sisters made a whole and therefore beautifully fulfilled the topic, and the girl had sat down with a huff.

It was true: Amanda and Ivy had been the most influential people in her life when she was fifteen, even though she saw them around three times a year: once for the two-week vacation in Maine, and then two or three more times for a dinner here or there to celebrate a holiday—if they were invited to their father's. They often weren't.

Even though we couldn't possibly be considered close, she'd written, *my half sisters, Amanda and Ivy, are the most influential people in my life because I strive to make them proud. They probably don't know that, couldn't know that, actually, but I want Amanda to see during the brief times we have together that I'm kind and compassionate, like she is. And I want Ivy to see that I'm intelligent and questioning, like she is. I want them to know that I have inner beauty, like they do. . . .*

Olivia smiled at the memory of what she'd written so many years ago. Amanda and Ivy hadn't heard Olivia read the essay; they hadn't come to the pageant. Neither had her father. Olivia had been the only contestant without a reserved section in the audience for family. And the only winner in history, probably, who hadn't been swept up in relatives' cheers and hugs when her name was announced. Her sisters hadn't come because they simply hadn't been close then. *Wary* was a good word to describe their relationship, fostered by their mothers. Though not so much Amanda's mother, who didn't seem to have a spiteful bone in her body. Amanda had been raised by her mother in a borough of New York City in a tiny apartment, and Olivia always got the sense that Amanda had felt she was looked down upon by Olivia, especially, but by Ivy too. That hadn't been the case at all. And since birth probably, Ivy's mother had been filling Ivy's head with diatribes about how Ivy was the only legitimate Sedgwick child and therefore should be treated differently than the other two "bastard children" and given the biggest room and the most expensive gifts. Olivia had heard a few of Dana Sedgwick's famous rants with her own ears.

So, no, the girls hadn't been close growing up. And they weren't close now. But they were getting there. At the reading of their father's will, the three Sedgwick sisters had somehow bonded, despite Olivia's and Ivy's bickering mothers demanding their daughters get the lion's share. Once work was less hectic for Ivy and Amanda was back from her honeymoon, Olivia would try to arrange a get-together.

If I'm in one piece, she thought as the door to the auditorium slammed shut.

Olivia hurried up to the double doors and pushed. Nothing. Someone had locked her in.

Oh, good Lord, she thought, banging on the door. "Hello!" she called out.

She'd been banging and calling out for fifteen minutes before Pearl herself opened the door.

"How did you manage to lock yourself in?" Pearl asked. "Oh, never mind that. I'm always dallying and dallying with silly questions. I hope you're here to tell me you've agreed to coordinate the pageant!"

"I would love to accept," Olivia said as they headed to Pearl's office down the hall. "But I need to inform you of a serious conflict of interest."

Pearl's eyes widened. "A conflict of interest? What could that possibly be? It's not as if you're related to any of the entrants, are you? Someone's aunt? Second cousin?"

"Actually," Olivia said. "I'm one of the candidates' mother."

Pearl stopped in her tracks. "Mother," she repeated. "Whose?"

"Kayla Archer's."

"Ah," Pearl said, resuming walking. "That does make sense, as she's the only girl in town without a mother." She hesitated, then bit her lip. "Were you . . . abroad or something?"

Olivia shook her head. "To be very honest, Pearl," she began, figuring the terrible truth was the best possible explanation, "I gave birth to Kayla when I was sixteen. My father had sent me to a home for pregnant teenagers up the coast and arranged for a private adoption. Only he didn't. And I was told that my baby was stillborn. Only she wasn't."

Pearl's mouth dropped open. "I don't understand."

"My father manipulated things," Olivia explained. "Why, I don't know."

Because if Kayla had been adopted by a loving couple, you would have been out of Olivia's reach until she was an adult, or possibly forever.

Olivia froze, her mind reeling. The thought came to her so suddenly and from out of nowhere, but it was the only explanation that made sense. If that had been her father's master plan, it gave him an iota of decency. She preferred the iota to believing that her father was a monster.

"So you see, Pearl," Olivia continued, "now that there's a serious conflict of interest, I'm not sure you'll still want me to coordinate the pageant. The other entrants and their mothers may feel it gives Kayla an unfair advantage."

"Oh, I'm sure they will feel that way," Pearl said. "Oh, dear, how to handle, how to handle. I certainly don't want to lose you as a coordinator, what with your experience as both a former *Glitz* editor and a former winner of the pageant. Let me call a meeting of all entrants and their guardians and let's discuss the situation. Perhaps they'll be open to a neutral assistant coordinator being on scene to make sure that everything is on the up-and-up, that you're not giving Kayla information you're not giving the other girls, that sort of thing."

"Do you think that would make everyone feel comfortable?" Olivia asked, surprised.

"Well, the Inner-Beauty Pageant isn't exactly Miss Teen Maine," Pearl whispered. "The girls who enter the Inner-Beauty Pageant tend to be more self-motivated than entrants of beauty pageants, where, let's just say, there can be a certain type of stage mother. . . ."

Olivia smiled. "I understand."

"Well, I'd better skedaddle to my phone calls," Pearl said. "I'll call you after I've set up the meeting. I'm thinking six o'clock tomorrow night in the auditorium."

"Sounds good," Olivia said. She didn't think it would sound too good to Marnie, though.

When Olivia arrived at Zach's house to take Kayla out to breakfast, Marnie's car was in the driveway. She stopped short; perhaps she should return later.

Too late. Kayla was peering out the window and spotted her. The girl smiled and waved and Olivia waved back.

Good, Olivia thought. They were off to a fine start this morning.

She rang the bell, and Marnie answered.

"Olivia!" Marnie said. "What brings you here *again?*" Olivia caught the emphasis on the *again*. The woman had fight in her eyes, and Olivia couldn't exactly blame her. "Zach's just finishing getting dressed," she added quickly. She then giggled and buttoned the cleavage button of her blouse. "Oops."

Did I just interrupt them from making love? Olivia wondered, *or is Marnie simply trying very hard to protect what is hers?*

"Omigod, Mom, guess what?" said a girl who came running down the stairs.

She has mud on the heels of her boots, Olivia noticed as Marnie whirled around. *Had she been prowling around outside Zach's last night?*

"This is my daughter Brianna," Marnie said, her arms around the pretty dark-haired girl.

Olivia smiled at the girl. "Very nice to meet you, Brianna."

"You have the exact same hair as Kayla," Brianna said. "Doesn't she, Mom?" she added to Marnie.

Marnie looked like she wanted to spit. And then she regained her composure. "You know what, Bri, you're right. They do have the same pretty hair."

Brianna's eyes popped. "Oh. My. God. You must be Kayla's mom!" She turned to her mother. "Mom, that's the major secret that Kayla just told me! I can't believe it!"

"It's true," Olivia said. "I'm Kayla's mother."

Marnie did not look pleased. Clearly, Zach had not told Marnie yet. And Marnie didn't seem to appreciate her daughter's knowing something so important about Zach Archer before she herself did. "Brianna, why don't you go on up to Kayla's room for a few minutes so Olivia and I can get better acquainted."

"Okay," Brianna said and headed back upstairs.

Marnie turned to Olivia, her anger barely veiled. "Actually, before we chat, will you excuse me for a moment? I'd like to talk to Zach for a moment. Privately."

"Of course," Olivia said. *This would be a good time for me to get my earrings off the bedside table in the guest room. Just in case Marnie goes in there for any reason. Like if Zach has a date with her tonight,* she thought, her heart squeezing.

She hurried into the room, the sight of the white rug instantly bringing to mind Zach's naked body, his lips on hers, his hands all over her. She blinked to bring herself back to the present. Her earrings weren't on the table.

She glanced on the rug; had they fallen down?

No. Something caught her eye on the bed. It was a picture from a magazine like *National Geographic*. Her earrings lay atop the picture.

She screamed.

The photograph was of a castrated man. Scrawled in the white space above the man's head was: "This is a warning. Don't see that bitch again. Or you'll be next."

Zach and Marnie rushed into the room. "Olivia?" Zach said. "I didn't realize you were here yet. What's wrong?"

The blood drained from her face. She showed him the picture.

Zach crumpled the piece of paper. "That's it. I've had it. I'm getting to the bottom of this."

"What's that?" Marnie said, taking the picture from Zach. She uncrumpled it and smoothed it out; then her gaze went to the gold hoop earrings on the bed, gleaming against the dark coverlet. "I'm assuming the bitch in question is you," she practically spat out at Olivia, her eyes on the earrings. "I assume you left these here last night. And I can only think of one reason why a woman would take off her earrings in a man's home." She glanced back at the picture in her hand. "Zach, did you cheat on me with her?" Marnie demanded.

"Marnie, I didn't mean—" Zach began.

"Yeah. You didn't mean for things to get out of hand between you and the bitch who abandoned you with a newborn. She waltzes back into town and seduces you all over again and you fall right for it? You're a sucker."

"Marnie, can we just sit down and talk this through?" Zach asked. "There's a lot I need to tell you."

"Such as the fact that Olivia is Kayla's mother?" Marnie spat. "I heard that choice piece of news from my daughter, who heard it before I did. The two of you make me sick. When she blows you off again, Zach, don't come crawling back to me. I'll have found someone decent by then."

Zach placed his hand on Marnie's arm. "Marnie, please let me—"

Marnie yanked her arm away. "I guess someone doesn't like cheaters," she said to Zach, then rushed out of the room. "Brianna, we're leaving!"

The girl came rushing down looking full of secrets.

"We need to leave right now," Marnie said to her daughter. She hurried the girl out the door.

"Marnie, wait," Zach said. "I—uh—"

"There's nothing to say," Marnie snapped and pulled the door closed behind her.

Zach let out a deep breath. "What a mess."

"Why don't you go after her," Olivia said. "She deserves that. I'll take Kayla out to breakfast. And I'll try to put that picture out of my head."

He nodded. "She came over here this morning to ask what's going on with us. With you and me. With me and her. And I wasn't honest with her. I should have been, but I wasn't ready to tell her about what happened last night between you and me. I blew it. She deserved the truth."

Olivia squeezed his hand. His handsome features were so troubled. She didn't know what to say, what to think.

"Look, Olivia, I don't even know what last night was. I don't know what it meant. What it means. It just happened."

"You don't have to explain or understand it, Zach," she said. "Let's just let it be."

"Daddy, Olivia," Kayla called from upstairs, "I'm almost ready! I'm deciding between outfits! Brianna has no taste at all. She said my sweater was all wrong for my body type."

Olivia smiled. "At least she didn't hear the scream. Zach, this is my department. I'll go up. You go after Marnie."

"Okay," he said. "Let's meet back here around noon."

A few precious hours to spend with her daughter. Olivia forced herself to put the picture, the warnings, Marnie, and even Zach out of her head.

"So should I call you Olivia or Mom?" Kayla asked as they arrived at the Eat-In Diner.

Olivia was so touched she couldn't contain it. She squeezed Kayla's hands. "I would love it if you called me Mom."

"I'm not sure yet," Kayla said, spinning a lock of her light blond hair around her finger. "I might just not call you anything for a while, okay?"

Olivia smiled. "Perfectly okay."

The waitress came over and took their orders, then returned in seconds with coffee for Olivia and a glass of orange juice for Kayla.

"Ick," Kayla said. "Don't look now, but a girl I totally hate just came in."

Olivia glanced at the door. A beautiful blond girl and her equally lovely mother were led to a table by the window.

"Why do you hate her?" Olivia whispered.

"She thinks she's so perfect. Perfect grades, perfect face, perfect body, perfect hair. Perfect life. She's a total fake. Her name is Cecily and I hate her guts."

"Did you two have an argument or something like that?"

Kayla shook her head and sipped her orange juice. "She goes to the high school, but tutors in math and science at my school. I got stuck with her like ten times for help with tests. She thinks she's too good to even speak to lowly me. I asked her if I could borrow a pen in math class a couple of weeks ago, and do you know what she said?"

"What?"

"She said, 'We don't use pens in math class. Pencils only.' In this total tone. So I asked if I could borrow a pencil, and she acted like I was asking to borrow her head or something."

"Did she give you a pencil?" Olivia asked.

"Yes, but with attitude."

Olivia tried to remember being thirteen. Every slight felt like the end of the world.

"And she entered the Inner-Beauty Pageant, too," Kayla continued, shooting sulking glances at the blond girl. "So of course she'll win. She wins everything."

"You have a lot of inner beauty, Kayla," Olivia said. "And that's all you need."

"You really think so?" Kayla said, brightening. "You think I can win like you did?"

Olivia nodded. "Absolutely."

"It's so cool that you'll be coordinating the pageant," Kayla said. Olivia had explained about Pearl's request on the ride into town. "You'll be able to help me win."

Olivia sipped her coffee. "Actually, that's the reason we'll need to get the permission of the other contestants and their moms before I can officially be named coordinator. The other girls and their moms might not think it's so fair that your mom is coordinating."

"But you've only been my mom for a day," Kayla pointed out as the waitress returned with their breakfast. "Not even a day. A night!"

Olivia laughed. "I'm just glad that we'll get to spend a lot of time together over the next couple of weeks." She squeezed Kayla's hand. "We have so much time to make up for."

Kayla smiled, then gobbled up her pancakes.

Olivia's cell phone rang. It was Pearl, informing Olivia that she spoke with the other five contestants' mothers and the meeting was set for tomorrow evening at six at the town hall to discuss the open coordinator's position.

If Pearl had managed to get hold of Marnie, she must have *just* spoken to Marnie. Very bad timing.

"There's an Inner-Beauty Pageant meeting tomorrow night to discuss the coordinator issue," Olivia told Kayla. "We'll see then what everyone thinks."

She had no doubt what Marnie would think.

Chapter 11

"Just tell me the truth," Marnie said, her hands on her hips in the doorway of her house. "Did you sleep with her?"

Zach glanced away from her intense stare. Although he was still standing in the doorway, her expression and body language said she might take the vase of flowers on the coffee table and crack him over the head with it. "Yes," he finally said.

Her expression changed from fury to sadness and back to fury within seconds. "Then turn around and go." She pointed behind him. "We have nothing left to talk about. If it was only some kissing, I could live with that."

"Marnie, I—"

"What could you possibly have to say?" she asked. "You cheated on me. You let me look like a fool. You're total scum."

He had cheated on her. But he hadn't meant for anything to happen between him and Olivia. Not last night, anyway.

Interesting, he thought. So he *had* expected

something to happen. Wanted something to happen. He'd been so focused on his daughter's feelings that he'd forgotten to check in with his own. Last night there had been no time to think about repercussions. He'd *felt,* and he'd acted on that. And Olivia had responded.

He certainly hadn't meant for Marnie to get hurt. She was a good woman, a good mother, and their relationship had seen him through some rough patches with Kayla this past month. The last thing he wanted was to hurt Marnie.

He reached for her hand, but she backed away. "I hate how you found out—about last night, about Olivia being Kayla's mother. I wish I could take that back. I should have told you myself about both, and I did plan to this morning, but then you saw the photograph. I'm very sorry."

"Sorry doesn't cut it," she said. "No one cheats on this," she added, waving her hand down the length of her body. "No one. Do you know how many men wish they could be with me?"

She certainly had a high opinion of herself. "I have no doubt of that, Marnie," he said. "You're a beautiful, sexy woman. And I've been very lucky this past month. And I'm not saying this in defense, but we never said this was an exclusive relationship. You yourself told me that you didn't want labels, didn't want rules."

She crossed her arms over her chest. "Why would you want to be with someone who abandoned you with a newborn? That's who you're choosing over me?"

"You don't know the whole story," he said. "It's a huge mess and was completely out of Olivia's control.

What we both learned in the past couple of days was so overwhelming that—"

"That you needed to screw each other to make things less overwhelming. Right. Just answer this," she said. "Was it a one time thing, a roll in the hay for old time's sake, or are you two dating?"

"I honestly don't know what we're doing," he said as gently as he could.

"Just get the hell out of here," she screamed, shoving him backward. "You make me sick."

"Marnie, I am sorry."

"Oh, trust me. You have no idea how sorry you'll be," she said before slamming the door in his face.

He rang the bell again, needing to say again that he was truly sorry he hurt her, but Marnie didn't answer.

He hated this. Hated hurting someone, making her feel the way Marnie felt right now. He did wish she could cut him a little slack, though. He was going through something crazy, something totally unexpected. The mother of his child was back. And something had happened between them last night. Marnie didn't have to take that into account, of course; cheating was cheating. But sometimes there truly were mitigating circumstances. Marnie didn't seem to think so, though. It wasn't as though he'd made love with just *anyone*.

Maybe he was rationalizing. Maybe Marnie could have been a little more understanding. Who the hell knew?

Actually, he did know. He'd been having these kinds of scenes with women since he was seventeen. They wanted more. He couldn't give it. Either they were hurt or they were hurt *and* angry.

That first year in Boston, when he had an infant and no clue how to care for her in any sense of the word, he'd started seeing a woman named Jen, a college student who lived in his apartment building. He'd thought his life circumstances would be explanation enough of what kind of commitment he could make to a relationship, but Jen had been devastated when he had responded to her inquiry about status with: "I just don't know." Those words had come out of his mouth so many times over the past twelve, thirteen years.

But he had known; he'd always known. Not one of the women he'd dated, even down the line, when he was older and more settled in his life as a single father, could he possibly imagine as the mother of his daughter. Because he didn't love them? Because he'd loved Olivia, however short and ultimately heartbreaking their relationship had been, in a way that could never be measured up to? That was crazy. People fell in love again all the time. He did believe it was possible to feel the way he'd felt for Olivia again. He'd just never felt it. Not with Jen all those years ago and not with Marnie. Nor with anyone in between, and he'd known some wonderful women.

He sat in his truck for a few minutes, just staring out at the forest surrounding Marnie's property. A vase came careening out a second-floor window and landed on the hood of the truck. It missed the windshield by a sliver.

Get off her land, already, he told himself. *Before she hurls a desk at you.*

He planned to drive over to the police station for a status report on the break-in at Olivia's and the tire slashing, but he found himself stopping at the turnoff for Blueberry Point, the stretch of beach where he and Olivia had met. He pulled over and walked down the narrow, icy path to the ocean. It was beautiful even in winter on a gray day like this one. And it was just the same. Primitive and age-old and natural, as their feelings for each other had been.

Zach picked up a rock and threw it in the water, hard and fast. It felt good to release . . . what? He wasn't even sure what was pent up in him. Just the suddenness of it all—Olivia, back in his life. But he'd always expected it. Countless times he'd come down here to the beach, this particular strip, where it had all started, and he'd stare out at the water, brilliant blue or a cold gray, as it was now, and he knew with absolute certainty that the day would come, that Olivia would come back. He'd never had any idea when. He used to find himself looking out the window on Kayla's birthdays, even when they still lived in Boston. And when he moved back to Blueberry five years after he'd been handed a bus ticket and a newborn, his college degree and new job as an architect, albeit low on the totem pole, had meant something to the snobby neighbors who'd once deemed him as worthless as his parents. The important thing he'd come back home with was confidence in himself, something he'd never had growing up, something Olivia had had in him.

Zach picked up another rock and flung it as far as he could, angry at himself for not believing in her back then. He had believed what he'd been told: that rather than ruin her life with a no-good punk like him, she wanted nothing to do with him or the baby and was going to college, where she planned to forget she ever knew him. He hadn't believed it at first, of course. Scrounging for change to call all the way to New York, he'd rushed to every phone he could find, and then taken the train down to try to find her. But when she remained so unfindable, so unreachable, he began to believe what he'd been told.

But then Kayla, an unnamed baby girl who looked just like him, had been placed into his arms, and scared as he'd been, his life suddenly had a purpose. If he couldn't be the guy Olivia wanted, he'd damn well become the father Kayla needed. And he had.

And now here Olivia was, all of a sudden. No matter what happened, Olivia was good for Kayla. He believed that even though he hardly knew Olivia.

He stared out at the ocean. A little self-control would have done a lot of good too last night. It was crazy to bring sex into the mix. Or maybe bringing sex in would clear things up.

At least he could clear his conscience about one thing: he hadn't lied to Marnie about the status of his relationship with Olivia. He really didn't know a damned thing about how he felt.

The police station was across from Zach's office. He stopped in and asked to speak with the detective handling the Olivia Sedgwick case, but apparently, there was no case.

"Hijinks," the officer said, stamping paperwork.

"Or she got on someone's nerves and they paid her back. There are no leads."

"Someone *did* break into her house," Zach reminded him. "Isn't breaking and entering a crime in Blueberry?"

For that Zach got a steely stare. "We'll let Miss Sedgwick know if there are any developments." He then continued stamping.

Yeah, well, I wasn't planning to report the latest incident anyway, jerk, he thought as he left. Blueberry was a small town, and the last thing he wanted was Kayla affected by what was going on in his life. With Olivia coming into her life and with the pageant, his daughter had enough for one thirteen-year-old.

At noon, Olivia and Kayla were in the kitchen of Zach's house, making hot chocolate. Zach came in, his expression letting Olivia know that things hadn't gone well with Marnie or the police.

As Kayla chattered on about how she liked her hot cocoa super chocolatey, Olivia realized that this was all she cared about. Being with Kayla, getting to know her daughter, sharing tiny moments about hot chocolate on a cold winter day. They were together. And not only did Kayla not hate her for being absent from the first thirteen years of her life, but she seemed thrilled by Olivia. Kayla would be staring at her one moment, then peppering her with questions the next. When did Olivia get her period? Had she also been thirteen? When did Olivia go to second base with a boy? Startled, Olivia had asked Kayla if *she'd* been to second base with a boy, and Olivia had been happy to hear she hadn't even French-kissed yet.

Zach had to go into the office for a few hours, and Olivia had been delighted to stay with Kayla all day. They gave each other facials and pedicures, talking and laughing and having a blast—until the doorbell rang.

Standing on the welcome mat were two girls who looked to be Kayla's age.

"So she's not a total liar?" one of the girls said. "You're really her mother?"

"If you're talking about Kayla, yes, I am her mother," Olivia said, startled by how rude the girl was.

"You're not so great," the other girl said, blowing a bubble, which she popped with her finger. The girl looked Olivia up and down.

"Olivia? Who's at the door?" Kayla asked, cotton balls between her toes to protect her freshly polished lavender toenails. At the sight of the girls, Kayla's smile was triumphant. "Told you," she said to them.

"If she's really your mother, why do you call her by her first name?" the red-haired girl asked.

"If she was really her mother, they'd look alike," the other said. "And they totally don't. Except for the hair. But you could have dyed yours," she told Olivia. "There's no proof she's your mother, Kayla. Nice try."

"She is my mother, you stupid freak!" Kayla shouted.

"Don't call me a freak, loser!" the redhead shouted back. "You're the freak. Only a freakizoid loser would pretend her dad's new girlfriend is her mother. You're only doing it to win the ugly girl pageant."

"Okay, that's more than enough," Olivia said. She'd read that thirteen-year-old girls could be very cruel to each other, but this was a little too much proof of that. "For your information, girls, I am Kayla's mother. Excuse us, please." Olivia waited for the girls to turn and go, but they didn't.

"I have a new name for you," the redhead said to Kayla. "Kayliar."

The other girl snickered. "Later, Kayliar."

"I hate you both!" Kayla yelled at them. "Go to hell!"

Olivia took Kayla's hand and stepped back from the door, then said, "Good day, girls," and closed the door in their faces.

"What was that all about?" Olivia asked Kayla.

"They were my friends until they turned losers," Kayla said. "We were all smoking in the bathroom the day I was caught, but they threw their cigarettes in the toilet before that bitch gym teacher could see their lit butts. Only I got caught. That's so unfair."

"Kayla, please don't refer to someone as a bitch," Olivia said.

"Oh, so now you're telling me what to do?" Kayla yelled and ran upstairs.

Olivia stood in the center of the hallway, wondering what the heck had just happened to her perfect day. *You've got yourself a new teenager, that's what,* she told herself, remembering all the drama of her life at thirteen. *You can't just have the daughter without the reality,* she reminded herself.

She had to hand it to Zach. Raising a daughter by himself all these years, no family, no relatives, had to be so difficult. Yet his relationship with

Kayla was wonderful, a testament to him as a person and as a father.

She had a bad feeling about those girls. Add that to her bad feelings about Johanna and Marnie and whatshername from the general store who'd stared her down.

Chapter 12

As Olivia got into bed that night, she picked up the framed picture of Kayla that she'd placed on her bedside table earlier that evening. After her breakfast with Kayla, Olivia had bought a disposable camera and had taken shot after shot of Kayla, then someone had asked if she wanted a picture of the two of them, and thanks to the one-hour photo lab at the drugstore, Olivia had a photograph of herself and her daughter. She'd bought a beautiful pewter frame for it.

She held the photograph close, marveling at what was. Days ago, there was only Olivia. Now there was a daughter. A daughter with her hair, her nose. Her laugh, even. And definitely some of her stubbornness.

Olivia had knocked her knuckles raw on Kayla's door before the girl had unlocked it. Kayla had then thrown herself on her bed and sobbed, but she'd allowed Olivia to hold her, and when Olivia told her that mothers were supposed to say things like "No calling someone a bitch," Kayla sniffled and then laughed and said she guessed so.

Later, when Zach had come home, Olivia filled him in during a brief walk around the property. He'd shaken his head at what had occurred; all the girls had once been so sweet, and now they threw around words like *bitch* and *loser*. He'd assured himself that once she got busy with the pageant, she'd stop reverting back to some of her old ways. At least he hoped so.

Zach had looked exhausted. And so she'd gone home, wishing she were there with the two of them.

Now, she drifted off to sleep, thoughts of Kayla and Zach floating through her mind, but then half awake, she realized she was dreaming of the dream girl, just the girl this time. And she looked exactly like Kayla.

But the dream girl was angry. Very angry. She was shouting, or at least her mouth was moving frantically, her fists flying in the air, but no words came out.

Something was scratching her neck. Her eyes opened wide. The dream had gone. In its place was darkness. She sat up and something dropped to her lap. Before she could see what it was, she heard a movement, then saw a shadow.

Someone was in her bedroom. Running away.

She reached out for the glass pitcher of water on her bedside table and threw it at what appeared to be the intruder's head just as he or she turned. She heard a grunt—a female's grunt, she was sure—and then the person continued running. Olivia turned on her bedside table lamp and saw what had fallen from her neck.

A noose. A note attached said: "Next time I'll tighten it."

She flung the noose to the floor, her heart beating a mile a minute, then raced into the bathroom with her cell phone and locked the door.

Her knees trembled and she slid down to a sitting position on the cold marble floor. Her hands shook so wildly that she dropped the phone. She snatched it back like the lifeline it was and pressed in Zach's telephone number. It was just past midnight. In some fuzzy corner of her mind, she hoped that Kayla was in such a deep sleep that the phone wouldn't wake her.

Zach answered on the first ring.

"Zach," Olivia said and then couldn't speak.

"Olivia, what's wrong?" he asked, the alarm in his voice matching her own. "Olivia?"

"Someone . . ." The reality of what she was about to say was too much and Olivia broke down, the phone dropping onto the marble floor. She could hear Zach's voice, calling her name. She reached for the phone. "Zach, someone was in my bedroom," she said, her heart beating too fast, her breath rushing in and out in gasps. "Someone tried to . . . there was a noose lying across my neck and chest." She took a breath, and then told him about the note.

He sucked in a breath. "Did you call the police?"

"No. I ran into the bathroom and locked the door and called you. Oh, God, Zach, I'm so scared."

"Don't move, okay? You don't know if they're still in the house. It'll take me two minutes to get to you. Stay on the line with me."

"Okay," she said, her voice shaking. "Hurry, please, Zach."

"I'm just going to leave a quick note for Kayla in case she wakes up that I went over to your house for a bit." After a moment he said, "I'm out the door now. In the car."

He talked to her through the drive and when he said he was at the front door, she bolted up and raced downstairs.

She flung herself into his arms, and he held her.

"Let's get inside and close the door," he said. "You must be freezing in that nightgown."

She vaguely realized she was wearing nothing but a short ivory slip. She'd been so tired when she'd gotten home that she'd taken off her clothes, but hadn't put on real pajamas.

"I'm so cold," she said, her body shaking. "And so scared."

Zach bolted the door, then scooped her up and carried her to the sofa, where he sat her up against the cushions. He grabbed the chenille throw from the armchair and draped it around her shoulders. "I'm going to call the police."

She nodded. She then opened her mouth to speak but just shook her head.

"It's okay, Olivia," he said. "Just catch your breath. You don't have to speak right now."

She took a deep breath. "They have to catch this psycho. Stupid pranks are one thing, but tonight, someone was in my room. They could have gotten that thing around my neck before I woke up."

He came close and sat down beside her. "Let me see your neck."

She arched her neck up and he tenderly ran his fingers over her neck.

"I'm just grateful they didn't get the chance," he said. He let out a breath, then an expletive. He held her hand as he called the police and tersely explained the situation. He placed the cell phone in his back pocket. "The police will be right over."

"Who could possibly want to kill me?" she asked, her shoulders trembling. "And why? What did I ever do to anyone in Blueberry? I don't get it. Yeah, I was ready to point the finger at Johanna or even Marnie over the nasty notes or slashed tires, but attempted murder? Would my father have dated someone nuts enough to kill someone? Would *you?*"

"Olivia, I hate to say this, but you just never know about people. What makes them snap. What's lurking, festering inside them. What your father did to both of us was unforgivable. Would you ever have thought your own father capable of such a thing?"

"Even with the way he treated me and my sisters— no," she said. "So I guess you're right, that you never know. But that's damned scary, Zach."

The doorbell rang, and the police did their work, dusting for prints, asking questions, checking the entrances, hunting for clues.

"This time we have a footprint," one of the officer's said as he came in through the living room from the back door. "Appears to be a woman's size eight."

"The grunt I heard—it did sound like a woman's voice," Olivia said. "Size eight—that's a very common size. *I* wear a size eight."

The officer nodded. "And it doesn't necessarily

mean anything, either. The footprint could have been left by anyone, not necessarily the assailant."

"Is there anything else you can tell us?" the officer asked. "Did you smell anything? Perfume? Soap? A strange smell?"

Olivia shook her head. "I'd been barely able to breathe."

"What about the rope?" Zach asked the officer. "Special kind?"

"Well, I'll have it sent through the lab," the officer said. "But it looks like standard-issue rope you can buy at any hardware store. Oh, and we found the point of entry. There's an unlocked window in the basement. The assailant probably just lifted it and entered. Outside the window is where we found the footprint. Anyway, I locked it for you."

"I appreciate that," Olivia said. "I'll double-check all the windows."

"I would do that if I were you," the officer said, and then after a few more questions, the police left.

"You can't stay here tonight," Zach said. "Come stay at my house."

"I'll forfeit the cottage and the inheritance," Olivia said. "My mother is depending on me to clean up the mess she made of her finances."

"The will says you have to spend every night here?" Zach asked.

Olivia tried to think. "Let me get the letter." She rooted through her tote bag and found the envelope from her father's lawyer. "You must live in Blueberry for at least one month etcetera." She breathed a huge sigh of relief. "It only says I have to stay in Blueberry for thirty days—not necessarily this house. So I can stay at your place. As long as I'm back here to give Johanna my receipts at eight tomorrow morning."

"You'll be back. So will I. And then we're going to see what your father's supposed fiancée does with her time."

"What about Marnie?" Olivia asked. "How did things go when you went after her this morning?"

"Terribly," he said. "She was more than angry."

"Angry enough to threaten to kill me?"

"I don't know," he said. "I don't think so—I don't want to think so, but I can't say for sure. She said some stupid things, like that I'd be sorry. And she hurled a vase out the window at my truck. She was aiming for the windshield."

Olivia shook her head. "Then perhaps we've got two women to pay very close attention to."

He nodded. "I'm an architect, not a detective, but hopefully we'll find something that'll point us to the right person."

"Thank you for being here, Zach," she said.

He nodded. "I want to make sure every door and window is locked tight. And then we're out of here. I can't stand the thought of you being here alone tomorrow morning—and opening the door to a psychopath."

Because maybe, just maybe, there's a chance you could care about me again, Olivia thought.

"I'll be fine here," Olivia said as Zach pulled the comforter over her in the guest room of his house.

He sat down on the edge of the bed. "I hate

leaving you alone," he said. "After what you've been through. I hate leaving you, period."

He could have kicked himself. Why had he gone and said that?

She glanced up at him, clearly surprised too, and took his hand. "I feel the same way."

He stood, gently pulling his hand away. "I'll sleep on the sofa in the living room. If you get scared, I'll be right there."

"I'd rather have you right here," she said. "At least until I fall asleep."

More than anything he wanted to get out of his clothes and tear off hers. She still wore that incredibly sexy little ivory slip. She'd pulled on clothes over it for the police, then they'd driven back to his house, and now she lay in bed in that scrap of lace. He could rip it off her with one hand.

But he wouldn't.

"Olivia, I need to be honest. After what happened today with Marnie, I don't want more omissions of the truth."

"Be honest," she said. "That's what I want."

He glanced away, then back at her. "I don't know how I feel about any of this. You. You coming back to Blueberry. It's more than clear that our old chemistry is still there. But thirteen years is a long time. I want you like crazy, Olivia. But beyond sex, I can't say."

"That was honest," she said. "Zach, it's okay. I don't know how I feel about anything either. We were taken from each other thirteen years ago, and there's so much water under the bridge. So I understand."

He nodded and turned to go, but she stopped him by reaching for his hand.

"Don't leave, Zach."

He'd been planning on sitting guard on the sofa right outside the guest room door. "Are you sure you want me to stay?"

She nodded and placed her hand on the empty side of the bed next to her.

He held her gaze. "You're so vulnerable right now, Olivia. I won't take advantage of that."

"For God's sake, Zach, I'm only asking you to keep me company. I'm a little afraid of the boogeyman right now. I wouldn't mind someone bigger and stronger next to me while I'm sleeping. If I can sleep at all."

"You've got it," he said, sitting down next to her. He stretched out, his hands behind his head.

"Remember how we used to do this on the beach?" she asked. "Just stare up at the night sky, our hands behind our heads?"

"I remember."

They both turned on their sides to face each other. "Do you ever wonder what would have happened if my father hadn't intervened?" Olivia asked. "If we had run away together?"

"I'm sure we'd be right here, right now. Except for the part about the rope earlier."

"So you think we'd still be together?" she asked.

"I'm not much of a what-iffer," he said. "But I know how I felt back then."

"Me too," she said.

He reached to touch her neck. "Does your neck or chest hurt?"

She covered his hand with her own. "No."

He held her gaze and then kissed her. She was so close, so right there, in her beautiful ivory nightgown, that he couldn't resist. She kissed him back.

"Maybe we should stare up at the ceiling some more," he said. "To keep things straight."

"I'd rather stare up at you," she whispered.

That was all he needed. He moved on top of her, one hand in her silky blond hair, the other moving down the soft length of her.

"Are you sure, Olivia?" he breathed against her ear. "If you're not, I can try very hard to stop."

"Make me forget what happened tonight," she whispered.

He rolled off of her so that he could slip off her nightgown. God, she was beautiful. So, so beautiful. He could barely take his eyes off the swells of her breasts, her nipples just visible through the thin material of her nightgown. He felt his erection strain against his jeans and he took them off, then his shirt. She watched him, her eyes following his hands, and her appreciation of his body made him want her all the more.

He lay next to her on the bed, and already she was breathing hard, her eyes asking him, begging him, to make love to her. But he waited. He lifted up her nightgown to see what she wore underneath. Tiny white cotton panties. He groaned at the sight of them and then yanked them down hard, explored inside her with his fingers, then his tongue. She moaned and writhed, her hands clawing at his back, grabbing at his hair.

He kissed his way up her stomach so that he was

lying on top of her. He wasn't willing to take off the nightie. It was too sexy on. He pushed aside the silky material from one breast and suckled her nipple, hard, gently biting, licking, while using his hand to ravage her other breast. And then Olivia moved on top of him, unwilling to wait.

Neither could he. He grabbed her hips and lifted her until he could thrust up inside her, then slid his hand up to her breasts and massaged their weight against his palms.

Olivia teased by sliding up off him and then down again, then stretching his arms over his head and lying down on top of him, all the while grinding against him, her breathy moans against his neck, his ear, his hair. He turned her over onto her back and thrust into her, his mouth on her breasts, her nipples, her mouth, her neck, back to her nipples.

"Oh, Zach," she murmured, her eyes fluttering open and closed.

He thrust harder, harder, harder, and she opened her eyes. Too hard, he realized. Too rough. But he needed it this way. Hard. Unromantic. Sex.

He turned her over and lifted her hips until she was on her hands and knees, then thrust into her from behind, fisting her hair. He jammed into her, hard, harder, his own breath ragged.

"Zach, I don't like—" she whispered, inching up a bit, trying to move away.

But he edged her down onto her stomach and slid his hands underneath her breasts and ravaged them with his fingers, while grinding into her so hard he thought the bed might collapse.

"Zach, stop," she said.

But he couldn't stop. Couldn't stop ramming into her. He snaked his hand around her thigh and teased her clitoris, thrusting, thrusting, thrusting. She tried to move, but she was pinned beneath him.

"Zach, please stop," she said, her voice breaking.

The pain in her voice got through. He stopped, and she scurried up on the bed, sat up, and wrapped her arms around her legs as if to conceal her nakedness. She was crying.

"Olivia, I—" But what? *Olivia, I wanted to hurt you? Olivia, I wanted to just screw you? Treat you like a whore so that I don't have to feel anything?* "Olivia, I'm sorry," he finally said. And he meant it. He closed his eyes for a moment and let out a breath. "I should have stopped when you first said you didn't like it that way. I shouldn't have done it in the first place. I am sorry, Olivia. If I have some aggressions to work out I should do it at the gym or basketball court. I shouldn't have—"

"Lie down with me, Zach," she said, getting under the blanket.

He did as she asked, their shoulders touching.

"You did what you wanted to me," she said. "Now I want to do what I want to you."

He glanced at her, surprised. "What do you want to do?"

She straddled him, her expression unreadable. She wasn't smiling. She didn't seem angry or hurt anymore. She lifted her hips and slid onto him again, arching her back, then leaned over him, bracing her arms on either side of him. Her silky hair brushed his chest. She rocked against him, and for a moment he wanted to grab her hips and grind against her, flip her over and take her hard like he did before. But he lay back and closed his eyes, letting himself be drawn into her rhythm, the sweet, insistent rocking, the pliant wetness of her sliding all around him.

She kissed him, lightly, gently, her breasts brushing against his chest. He leaned his head down to tease her nipples with his tongue, and she moaned, rocking against him a little faster, a little harder. He lifted her off him and gently laid her down next to him, then moved down the length of her until he could slip his tongue against her clitoris. He licked and teased and gently bit. Olivia grabbed at his hair and arched her back and moaned and he slipped two fingers inside her, his palm rubbing against her, his tongue darting over her swollen clitoris until she grabbed a piece of the blanket and clenched it between her teeth to drown her screams.

And then her body relaxed, her chest rising up and down so fast as she caught her breath.

"You really are so, so beautiful," he said, lying down beside her, propping on his side with his elbow. "And I am so sorry about before."

She caressed his cheek, then flipped over onto her stomach, slightly spreading her legs.

"Is that an invitation?" he asked.

"Yes," she whispered. "Do what you need to do, Zach. We have a lot to work out between us. We're both going to cross lines. But I want it honest. You were way too rough before, and you ignored me when I told you to stop. That was wrong, but it was also honest. It's how you felt."

"I don't want to hurt you, Liv. That's not how I feel."

She turned over onto her back and reached for his rock-hard erection. The moment her hand made contact, he wanted, needed, to be inside her. He lay over her and entered her, not too hard, not too gently, sweeping his lips against her neck. She wrapped her arms around his neck and met his thrusts, her breath in his ear, and he knew that he loved her all over again.

Chapter 13

Bright morning sunshine streamed through the windows. Olivia stretched like a cat in the queen-sized bed, her thoughts going only as far as the middle of the night, when her every question about how she should feel about a man had been answered. And not just sexually.

This, this incredible satisfaction, the wonder, the excitement so deep inside her, was how she'd always wanted to feel with the men she'd dated. The depth of emotion between her and Zach, the beautiful and the ugly—and parts of last night had been very ugly—demanded their honesty, demanded they talk things through. How they felt. What they wanted. Needed. But the only time she'd felt the way she did right then was thirteen years ago. Either there was something very special about Zachary Archer, or there was something very special between them. Perhaps both.

He was gone when she'd opened her eyes. *Understandable. His daughter is sleeping upstairs,* she'd thought. Our *daughter,* she'd corrected herself and wondered if the *my*, the *our* would ever roll off her tongue.

Regardless, the last thing they needed was for Kayla to find them in a "compromising position" and send a whole new set of questions loose in her head.

Olivia heard a shower running and pop music playing upstairs. She was dying to go up and see Kayla, but she'd wait until Zach explained her presence.

Yeah. Someone is trying to scare your mother out of Blueberry. Trying very hard. But not succeeding. Olivia bolted up in bed.

The shower stopped. Olivia quickly dressed and slipped into the bathroom that opened from the guest room. She washed up and made herself look as presentable as she could. Just in time, too. There was a knock on the guest room door.

Zach. Looking gorgeous. He wore jeans and a dark green sweater that brought out the green of his intense hazel eyes.

"Kayla's back to school today," he said. "So I figured we'd drop her off, then wait for Johanna at the cottage and trail her for a while, see what she does."

All business, she thought. Granted, she was pleased that he was more concerned than the police seemed to be, but there was nothing in his face or expression that said: "You didn't dream last night." If someone else were there in the room with them, he or she would have no clue that the two of them had made love just hours ago, had been through an emotional wringer together.

"What if all she does is go to her shop?" Olivia asked. "We can't exactly trail her there."

"The shop doesn't open until ten," he said. "So that's two hours."

Olivia nodded. "And when it opens, one of us can pretend we're looking for a cashmere sweater and snoop around."

"I don't want you alone with her in there. Just until we can rule her out."

"*If* we can rule her out," she said.

"Dad, where are you?" came Kayla's voice.

"We're down here," he called back.

"*We're?*" Kayla said as she came into the guest room.

Kayla's eyes widened. She glanced at the bed, which Olivia hadn't had a chance to make yet. "You slept over here last night?"

Olivia nodded. "I heard noises in my house last night and was afraid to stay there alone, so I slept here."

Kayla smiled. "Are you two getting back together?"

Zach turned red. He opened his mouth to speak, but absolutely nothing came out.

Olivia took Kayla's hand and squeezed it. "I've only been back in your lives for a few days."

Kayla nodded. "Will you feel like my mother soon?"

Olivia's heart squeezed. "I hope so."

"Do I feel like your daughter to you?" Kayla asked.

Olivia nodded. "Yes."

"Good," Kayla said, and with that she flitted out of the room.

"I'm making eggs this morning if you're interested," Zach said, turning to go.

Almost like one big happy family, she thought. It was a start.

She glanced around the living room, surprised at how homey the place was. Zach had chosen big, functional pieces that could withstand a toddler's sticky hands and a kid's somersaults and a teenager's after-school naps. The sofa was huge and slip-covered in durable red cotton, throw pillows everywhere. A large kilim rug added color and warmth to the wide-planked wood floors. One wall was devoted to Kayla's artwork over the years, from preschool finger paints to a self-portrait dated last year. And there were photographs everywhere. Of Kayla. Of Zach and Kayla.

Her favorite was in an antique frame on the piano, Zach and Kayla, around five or six, climbing a mountain. Kayla had on her little hiking boots and held a canteen, and her smile was as big as the land. Zach looked happy and healthy. Olivia wondered who'd taken the picture. A girlfriend maybe. Or a passerby.

But the thing she noticed most of all was that of all the pictures of father and daughter, there was no mother. She could imagine Kayla going through these rooms over the years glancing at her family photographs and noticing the same thing. There was no mother.

I'm here now, she said silently to the room. *I just hope I'm not too late.*

"No smoking, right?" Zach said to Kayla as they pulled up in front of Blueberry Middle School.

"I'm totally over smoking," Kayla said. "Bye, Olivia!

See you at the Inner-Beauty meeting!" she added, then disappeared among the students.

Zach was about to head to the cottage, but Olivia touched his arm.

"Can you wait just a minute?" she asked, glancing around at the hustle and bustle of a school morning. "I'd like to watch."

"Watch kids walking into school?"

She nodded. "This is Kayla's world. I want to know all about it."

He smiled. "On Kayla's first day of preschool, after the teachers assured me she was fine and I could go, I sat in the car in the parking lot for the entire two and a half hours, staring at the front door of the school."

Olivia laughed. "How about the second day?"

"One hour. By the third week, I was able to actually drive away."

"I guess I'm feeling a little like that," she said. "I don't want to let her go now that I have her."

He was about to say, "There's all the time in the world," but everything felt so up in the air. And once again he'd put sex in the mix. Until he knew how he felt about any of this, he needed to keep his hands to himself. Not easy. Olivia was so beautiful, and their strange history—just a couple of weeks of a teenaged love affair so long ago, and thirteen years of estrangement—was too strong a force. There was a daughter between them.

"We'd better get to the cottage before Johanna calls your father's lawyer and gets you kicked out," Zach said.

Olivia nodded. "I wouldn't put it past her."

"And I want to make sure we get there before she

does so that she doesn't see me," he said, pulling away from the curb.

"Do you know Johanna?" Olivia asked, glancing at him. "From around town?"

He shook his head. "I've seen her before, but we've never spoken. Every time I see her in town she's walking fast or has her head down. Odd for someone who owns a shop. You'd think she'd be friendly, cultivating customers."

"Has she always been that way?" Olivia asked. "Or just in the past month, since William died?"

"Don't know," he said, turning in to the cottage's driveway. "I can't say I've really noticed her much at all."

Olivia was staring up at the cottage. She was nervous, he realized. She wasn't easy to read, never had been, but he could tell that she was scared.

"I'll be with you," he said, squeezing her hand.

She glanced at him and held his gaze. "I just don't know what's coming next or from whom."

"I'll be with you," he repeated.

She took a deep breath. "I can't stay with you every night, Zach."

"There's no reason why you can't move into the guest room," he said. "You'll be closer to Kayla, more available to her. It makes sense. We can drive here in the mornings for Johanna. It's a short drive."

And I want you closer to me anyway, he added to himself.

Her heart surged. "I appreciate it, Zach. The idea of sleeping in this house, knowing that someone out there wants me dead . . ." She took a deep breath. "I can't stay here anymore."

"It's settled, then." He glanced at his watch. "It's five to eight. We'd better get inside."

No broken windows. No nasty messages scrawled across the front door. And inside, nothing seemed out of place. They checked all the rooms. Nothing was disturbed.

When the doorbell rang, Zach headed into the kitchen, which was within earshot of the front door, but out of view.

"Receipts and sign here," he heard Johanna say, her voice clipped. She was angry, that was for sure.

"Is that a bruise on your forehead?" Olivia said, her voice cracking a bit.

A bruise. Olivia had mentioned that she'd thrown a glass pitcher of water at the assailant and that she'd gotten a grunt of pain in response. Suddenly Johanna had a bruise on her forehead? A bruise that wasn't there yesterday?

"I bumped into a door in the middle of the night," Johanna said. "Your concern is touching," she added, her tone dripping with sarcasm. "Now give me your receipts and sign this sheet or I'm calling the lawyer to tell him you didn't keep up your pathetic enough end of the bargain."

"Johanna, do you want to keep up these barbs back and forth for three more weeks, or do you want to sit down and really talk and hear the truth? I'm hoping you'll want to talk."

"The truth? What truth? Yours? I already got the truth from William. He was my fiancé. I think I'll believe him over you, thank you very much."

"And there are two sides to every story," Olivia said. "I'd like to tell you mine. Come in, and let's have some coffee and talk about William Sedgwick."

"What's the point?" was Johanna's response. "He's dead."

"But you loved him."

"You didn't," Johanna snapped.

"Actually, that's not true," Olivia said. "As a child I loved him even though I saw him for just two weeks a year. I had all these daydreams and fantasies of him magically deciding that he did want me in his life. But it never happened."

Zach knew how true that was. He and Olivia had talked a lot about that during those two weeks they'd shared. And then over the years, he and Kayla had had similar conversations about Olivia.

"Whatever," Johanna said. "I'll need your receipts for yesterday's items. And sign here."

Interesting, Zach thought. Johanna wasn't willing to give Olivia an inch.

"I just want to know one thing, Johanna," Olivia said. "Given that I didn't have a relationship with my father—and that was his choice—why do you resent me so much?"

Good job, Olivia. Get information. Get her to open up, Zach silently encouraged.

"Just show me your receipts," Johanna said coldly. "You're wasting my time."

A minute later, the door closed. Olivia came into the kitchen, shaking her head. "She grabbed my receipts, shoved the clipboard in my face so I could sign it, and left."

"Well, let's see if we can find out what's bugging her," Zach said.

Johanna was in a hurry. She practically ran down the road and got into a beat-up car parked at the opening to the main road.

"Why doesn't she park in front of the cottage every morning?" Olivia asked as she and Zach got into Zach's truck and headed at a snail's pace down the road. "I mean, why walk a half a mile and back every morning in the cold?"

"Add that to our five pages of questions for Johanna," Zach said, turning onto Blueberry Boulevard. Johanna passed the center of town and then turned left onto Mayfair.

"What's out this way?" Olivia asked.

He glanced at her, surprise mixed with suspicion in his eyes. "Marnie."

"Johanna and Marnie are friends?"

"I don't know," he said. "I've never met any of Marnie's friends. And I never see Johanna out and about."

"I'd love to be a fly on the wall in Marnie's house right now."

"Maybe I could be," Zach said. "Let me drop you off at a safe place, the Eat-In Diner. I'll go over to Marnie's to apologize again and try to get invited in."

"Be careful," Olivia said.

Zach stood on Marnie's porch and rang the doorbell, but there was no answer. He heard a door close behind him and he turned around; Marnie and Johanna were coming out of the barn, which was really just a garage.

They stopped dead in their tracks when they spotted him.

"What are you doing here?" Marnie said.

"Can I talk to you for a few minutes?"

"No."

He headed toward them, his arm outstretched toward Johanna. "I'm Zach Archer. I don't think we've met."

She glanced at Marnie and kept her hands in her pockets. "No foe of Marnie is a friend of mine," she said.

"Well, I can understand friends sticking by friends," he said. He turned to Marnie. "I really wish you'd talk to me, Marnie. Let me explain myself as best I can."

"There's nothing to say, Zach. You made your bed. Now you're going to have to lie in it."

He raised an eyebrow. "Meaning?"

"Meaning cheaters get what they deserve."

Oh, brother. "Well, I hope we can talk things through one day," he said. "You know where to find me."

"At that greedy little bitch's house?"

Her anger now seemed over the edge. They'd dated for a month, never talked about an exclusive relationship. Yes, he hadn't been honest with her when she'd asked about Olivia, but Marnie's bitterness struck him as excessive.

Cheaters get what they deserve. . . .

You'll be sorry. . . .

Olivia was the one being targeted, though. Not him. Was Marnie trying to get to him through Olivia? Hurt him by hurting her?

He thought of her in the diner, sitting there alone, vulnerable. Not that anything could happen to her at the Eat-In Diner. Still, he had this need to be with her, to make sure she was safe.

Because, as he knew without a doubt last night, he did love her. And not with the innocence of a seventeen-year-old boy, unfettered. He loved her the way he'd been waiting to love someone again. He simply had no idea that person would be Olivia herself. He shook his head at the irony of it. The magic of it.

He glanced at Marnie, her eyes shooting sparks. "All I can do is apologize, Marnie." With that he got back into his truck and drove to the diner to pick up Olivia.

He saw her through the plate-glass window; she was poking at a salad and looking nervous. Worried. He went in and sat across from her and filled her in.

"So Johanna must have told Marnie what she knows about me. What she *thinks* she knows, anyway," Olivia said.

He leaned close. "All I know is, Johanna has something against you. Marnie has something against both of us. And suddenly the two of them are fast friends. I'm glad you're going to be staying at my house from now on. There's no way I'd leave you alone, especially at night. Stay in town until it's time for your meeting. And keep your cell phone on you at all times. Okay?"

She nodded. "The tension in the town hall auditorium should be pretty scary tonight. Hopefully, Marnie will focus on her daughter and not on me. I don't doubt she'll want Brianna to win at all costs."

Which was what worried Zach.

Chapter 14

All the contestants and their mothers were early. At a quarter to six, Pearl was able to take the stage to welcome everyone to the meeting for contestants to enter the thirty-first annual Inner-Beauty Pageant. Eleven girls and their mothers were sitting in the first few rows of the auditorium, everyone checking out the competition, including Olivia. She could tell who Kayla was worried about by the expressions the girl made as her gaze stopped on each entrant. Brianna barely got a glance; clearly Kayla thought the girl had no inner beauty. Marnie hadn't looked Olivia's way once since arriving.

The pretty blond girl whom Kayla had complained about in the diner got Kayla's poutiest pout.

If Olivia thought the dirtiest looks sent her way would come from Marnie, she was wrong. Jacqueline McCord took that honor. She sat with a tall girl who stared at her shoes.

"All rightie!" Pearl said, clapping her hands. "First order of business is to formally enroll our candidates in the pageant. So, we'll need to verify that all entrants meet the age requirements of thirteen through seventeen. You cannot be younger than thirteen or older than seventeen to enter."

"But Jennifer's birthday is next month!" said a woman sitting in the front row. "She'll be thirteen in just a few weeks!"

"Which will make her eligible for next year's pageant," Pearl said, with a smile.

The woman smacked her lips and practically yanked her daughter out of her seat. Olivia knew from experience that girls entered the pageant because their parents had their eyes on the prize money.

"Please line up with a birth certificate or other proof of age," Pearl said.

"Dad put my birth certificate in my packet this morning," Kayla told Olivia. She opened up the pink folder and handed Olivia the document.

Olivia sucked in her breath, her fingers shaking as she took the piece of paper, its raised seal assuring her of its authenticity.

Mother: Olivia Kaye Sedgwick

Father: Zachary Archer

She would never, ever forgive her father for the lie. No matter what he tried to undo thirteen years later.

"Olivia?" Kayla said, tugging on her sleeve. "Everyone's in line except us."

Olivia regained her composure and smiled at Kayla. "I'm just so thrilled to see this," she told Kayla. "It's the first time."

"Oh, yeah," Kayla said. "I didn't think of that. Sometimes I would take it out of my special box and just look at your name to remind myself that I did have a mother out there somewhere."

Olivia squeezed her hand, and they got in line. There seemed to be a bit of a commotion up ahead.

"This is a proper form of ID!" a girl with curly brown hair screeched. "It's my driver's license!"

"Dear," said Pearl, "this is not a valid Maine driver's license. It's a fake ID just like my own daughter used to have before I found it and cut it up. Maine licenses have six numbers, not seven. If you don't have another valid form of ID to prove your age, you will need to leave."

The girl's mother tried arguing, but Pearl held up a hand and said, "Eh, uh-uh!" She then clapped her hands, hard. "Listen up, people. If there is anyone on line who does not have a valid form of ID—and trust me, I know what they look like—you must leave now."

There were grumbles, and five girls and their mothers left the auditorium.

"I see we're down to a very manageable number now," Pearl said as the next girl handed over her birth certificate.

Left were Kayla, Brianna, the blond girl who Kayla sulked about, and three others: Jacqueline McCord's daughter, a tall brunette who seemed to stoop as though she was uncomfortable with her height; and, interestingly enough, one set of twins.

"All rightie!" Pearl said once everyone was seated again. "I am now proud to introduce the six contestants for this year's Inner-Beauty Pageant! When I call your name, please stand up. Cecily Carle."

As the pretty blond stood, her mother clapped excitedly.

"Cecily, please state your age and why you want to enter the Inner-Beauty Pageant."

"I'm fifteen and want to enter because it's what's inside that counts," said Cecily. Her mother clapped again.

Kayla pouted. "That's what I was going to say," she whispered.

"Next is Brianna Sweetser."

Brianna popped up. Olivia saw Marnie doing a silent clap for her daughter. "I'm thirteen and I want to enter because I want to show all of Blueberry that there's a lot more to me than just a pretty face."

Kayla rolled her eyes. "Do you believe her?" she complained and Olivia smiled.

Pearl consulted her roll sheet. "Next is Emily Abernathy."

One of the twins stood and moved out to the aisle. "I'm fourteen, whooo!" she said, breaking into cheerleading moves. "I want to enter because it's what's inside that counts." She added a few twirls and claps.

"I already said that," Cecily pointed out, with something of a restrained smile.

"Well, if you hadn't gone before me, I would have said it first," Emily shot back, slipping into her seat.

"Our next entrant is Eva Abernathy. And I will note for the record that Eva and contestant number three are identical twins."

"Identical except that I have slightly more inner beauty!" Eva said, also moving out to the aisle and breaking into a cheerleading routine as she spoke. "I'm fourteen and I want to enter because it's what's inside that counts."

"She already said that!" Brianna contributed. Marnie grabbed her daughter's arm in admonishment.

"Well, if she hadn't gone before me, I would have said it first," Eva sing-songed.

"No, because Cecily said it first," Kayla threw in.

Olivia had a feeling that coordinating this pageant—if she was allowed to—would lead to a massive headache. She glanced at Jacqueline McCord and her daughter. Both had been silent, not joining in the bickering.

"Before we continue," Pearl said, "I should point out that during the judging round, it would be wise not to repeat an answer that someone has already said."

"Yeah, but what if the answer you were going to give is the same as what someone else gave?" Kayla asked.

"I guess you'll just have to think fast," Pearl responded.

"I don't think fast," Kayla whispered to Olivia.

"Our next contestant is Kayla Archer," said Pearl.

Kayla stood and smiled. "I'm thirteen years old." Silence.

"And the reason why you want to enter the pageant?" Pearl prompted.

Kayla turned red. She looked to Olivia for help, but it wasn't like Olivia could—or would—whisper an appropriate answer. "Um . . . I was going to say the thing about what's inside counting, but there's another reason I want to enter." She glanced at Olivia. "My mother won the Inner-Beauty Pageant when she was fifteen. I want my mom to know that even though we're just getting to know each other, like from scratch, that I'm just like she is."

Olivia felt every set of eyes in the room on her. Even Marnie's.

"Girls, if that's the case, I'd keep your boyfriends under lock and key," Marnie said, with a laugh. But the deadly look she leveled on Olivia was anything but funny.

Pearl cleared her throat. "Our last contestant is Deenie McCord."

The only girl in the room who hadn't yet stood up remained seated. Olivia could see her cheeks tinged with pink.

"Deenie McCord?" Pearl called, lifting her bifocals from around her neck to her face.

Olivia saw Jacqueline nudge the girl's thigh, and Deenie stood, her stoop more pronounced. She said nothing until Pearl prompted her. "I'm seventeen years old. I . . . I want to enter because this is my last year to show everyone that I have inner beauty."

"She certainly doesn't have *outer*," someone whispered. One of the twins. Olivia wasn't sure which.

"Who said that?" Jacqueline demanded, bolting up. "Name callers should be disqualified immediately."

Red faced, Deenie sat down.

"Name-calling is not allowed," Pearl announced. "Are we understood?" The rounds of nods must have satisfied Pearl. She called for a round of applause, and then each girl was handed a sheet of paper listing the rules and regulations, which Pearl went over in agonizing detail. "And now, I have some news about the open coordinator's position. As some of you have heard, our present coordinator, Shelby Maxwell, has left Maine for warmer weather. Therefore, we need a new coordinator. It came to my attention that a former editor of *Glitz* magazine in New York City is residing in Blueberry and she is also a former winner of the Inner-Beauty Pageant. I thought with her credentials she would make an excellent coordinator. However," Pearl continued, "she is also the mother of one of our entrants, Kayla Archer."

All eyes swung to Olivia.

Pearl cleared her throat. "As there is a possible conflict of interest, I thought I would throw out the issue to you all and see how you felt."

"I, for one, would not feel comfortable with one of the contestants' mothers coordinating," Marnie clipped out.

All the other mothers agreed.

"Okay, then," Pearl said. "I did have an assistant coordinator lined up, so she can take over the general role, though she isn't very experienced in such events. In fact, I'll even suggest that all of you moms become co-coordinators this year."

Everyone liked that idea. And with that settled, the very long meeting was called to an end.

"Co-coordinators?" Zach asked as he and Olivia entered the cottage to pick up some of Olivia's belongings. "Will that work?"

"It has to," she said. "But, to say there are some big personalities involved would be a serious understatement."

Zach had been beyond confused when Olivia had filled him in on what had gone on at the meeting. The girls and the mothers sniping at each other.

Marnie's nasty dig at Olivia, but at Kayla's expense. "How exactly is Kayla going to turn into an angel with all that muck going on?"

Olivia smiled. "Sometimes, when you're in the right place at the right time, trying circumstances can do wonders for building character."

He glanced at her. "I know what you mean."

"I know you do."

"I want to see the home you were sent to," Zach said. He had no idea where that had come from. He hadn't even been thinking of it at the moment.

"Really?" she asked. "Why? It's not an example of the right place, right time during trying circumstances." She glanced down at her feet and took a deep breath. "I don't even like to remember that place."

"What was it like?" he asked, imagining her alone and scared.

"The place itself was fine. The care was good. I even had some friends, well, acquaintances really. But there was somewhere else I wanted to be, somewhere else that felt right to me. But I couldn't be there."

He glanced at her. "With me, you mean."

She nodded.

"I want to see it," he said again. "I want to see firsthand where you spent those lonely months of your pregnancy. I want to know where you were."

"I suppose we can just drive up and surprise them with a visit," Olivia said. "It's about three hours north." She froze. "I wonder if the doctor who attended the birth is still there."

"I hope the hell not," Zach said. "Who knows what other lives he interfered in."

"I'd like to go tomorrow, so I'm not anticipating the trip for too long," Olivia said.

"Tomorrow it is."

Olivia glanced around the cottage. "I guess I'll just bring some basics, clothes and toiletries. I'll need to be back here every morning at eight, anyway."

Zach dropped down on the easy chair in the living room while Olivia went into the bedroom.

"Zach!" she screamed. "Zach!"

He rushed in. Olivia stood by her bed, her hand over her mouth, her face pale.

Her bed had been slashed to ribbons, some sticky red substance oozing all over.

"What is . . . that?" she asked, her voice shaking.

"I'm sure it's paint or something like that," he said. He banged the wall with his fist, and pulled his cell phone from his pocket.

"Zach, look at this," Olivia said, pointing at something on the bed.

He leaned over. A note, typewritten on a plain piece of paper, was pushpinned to one of the pillows. It said: "You're next."

As Zach dealt with the police, Olivia sipped the tea that was supposed to calm her down. But the more the officers said they had no leads, the more agitated Olivia became.

Could it be Marnie? Johanna? Both? One of the contestants' mothers? No, that was stretching. Granted, the four other mothers—besides Marnie— were hardly friendly, but this nasty business had begun before Olivia had had anything to do with the pageant.

The police left, and Zach joined Olivia in the kitchen.

"I packed a bag for you," he said. "Let's get the hell out of here."

"You packed for me?" she asked, surprised. And then she remembered that any man who's single-handedly raised a teenager knows something about packing for a girl. She smiled. "You always manage to make me feel better."

He placed his hand over hers. "We're going to get this creep. Whoever it is will slip up, Olivia."

"I'm surprised he or she is reverting to stupid notes on pillows," she said, twisting her hair into a knot on her head. "To go from trying to strangle me to a threatening note and some food coloring or whatever it was is pretty weird."

"That's a good point," Zach said. "Although slashing your bed with a butcher knife is more than aggressive."

Olivia shivered. "I thought I left mean and back-stabbing at *Glitz* magazine. I never expected to encounter this here." She wrapped her arms around herself. "Maybe my ex-boss sent a henchman up here to pay me back for quitting on her."

"All I know is that you're not spending another minute alone unless you're in the center of town," Zach said. "If the police won't protect you, I will."

She stood up and went to him, then traced a finger down his chiseled cheek. "I feel safe when I'm with you. I feel safe just knowing you're there."

He pulled her close and kissed her, and that was when a stone came careening through the kitchen window, narrowly missing both of them.

They raced to the front door and looked in every

direction, but all Olivia saw was the movement of the trees and brush from the wind.

They made it out to Zach's truck unscathed. Once back at Zach's house, Olivia saw him release a breath after they checked in on Kayla and found her sleeping peacefully. Zach paid Mrs. McGill and sent her home and then joined Olivia in the guest room.

She opened the suitcase Zach had packed for her. There were jeans and sweaters, a bunch of underwear, her fluffy bathrobe, and the slinky slip. She smiled at him and took his hand, and then they both lay down on the bed, fully dressed. She curled against him so that they were spooned, and she closed her eyes as the rhythmic beating of his heart lulled her into relaxation. Tomorrow they would drive to the Pixford Home and possibly confront the staff. In any case, Olivia would be transported back in time to when she was truly scared. She realized that nothing could ever top how fearful she'd been then. Of the unknown. Of giving up her baby. Of how she'd feel afterward. Of course, she'd never for a moment thought she might lose the baby.

Nothing would ever scare her as much as her time in Pixford had. Not a rock through the window, nor someone trying—and not very well—to strangle her in her sleep.

"Penny for your thoughts," Zach said, rubbing her shoulders.

"Just thinking about tomorrow. About going to the home I stayed at."

"You okay with it?" he asked, his warm, strong hands under her sweater, massaging her back, her shoulder blades. "If you're not, we don't have to go."

"I need to go. I need the closure. And I want

answers. I want to know how the administration allowed my father to pay off their staff."

He kissed the back of her head and continued rubbing her back, and then his hands moved around her side and found her breasts. She closed her eyes as he explored, his warm lips on her neck. And then she turned around and kissed him.

"Make me forget everything, Zach," she whispered, snaking her arms around his neck.

And he did.

Chapter 15

In the morning, Olivia and Zach went back to the cottage to wait for Johanna. Zach listened in from the kitchen, but there was nothing much to listen to. Johanna asked for the receipts with her usual dripping venom, Olivia handed them over, signed the clipboard, and all but shut the door in the woman's face.

Olivia wanted to bait her, to tell her what she'd learned without naming names (Pearl's) of her father's active love life. That seemed to be the only way to get Johanna talking. But today wasn't the day for that. Not with the trip to Pixford looming.

Johanna seemed surprised at how easily Olivia capitulated. The woman eyed her, clearly curious that Olivia was suddenly not interested in making nice.

That settled, Olivia wanted to get out of the cottage as quickly as possible, so they got back into Zach's truck and headed into town to pick up breakfast to eat along the way. She had no idea how long they'd be in Pixford or if she'd have time to buy her two items later, so she figured she might as well buy coffee and egg sandwiches from the Eat-In Diner and a couple of bottles of orange juice from the town store. In the diner she ran into Cecily Carle's mother. Cecily was the girl who most worried Kayla, but of all the mothers, Rorie Carle was the nicest. She offered a warm and friendly hello when she saw Olivia at the counter, asked after Kayla, and chatted briefly about the pageant and how wonderful she thought it was for developing self-esteem in their girls.

The positive interaction actually perked her up a bit. She was so used to sidelong glances or out-and-out hostility that Rorie Carle's smile and warmth was like a soothing balm.

And then Olivia and Zach headed north on I-95. She stared out the window for most of the three-hour drive, the passing scenery not bringing back a single memory. It was just trees and the occasional rest stop, like on any highway she'd ever been. Only when they turned off the highway in Pixford did a knot begin to form in Olivia's stomach. The town center was as she remembered. Not very interesting or the slightest bit quaint. Just some shops and a church. The pregnant girls hadn't been welcome in town, so they'd rarely gone.

"Turn here," she told Zach as they approached the dirt road leading to the home. There was a blue sign reading "Pixford Home, Private Property." Pixford was in a rural area of Maine and the home was located a mile down the curving, bumpy road. She remembered how her mother's tiny sports car had bumped on the holes and rocks on the road thirteen years ago, Olivia's morning sickness at an all-time high. Back then she'd thought it a very bad sign that the powers that be at the home didn't ensure a smooth ride for pregnant girls.

It was early fall when Olivia had been driven down this road for the first time, and the grounds were beautiful. Huge, leafy trees on both sides of the road covered the sky above so that there was almost an element of cocooning, an assurance that she would be protected, safe. At the end of the road, a circular driveway looped in front of the stately brick house.

Her mother had driven her, and they'd barely spoken during the ten-hour drive. Olivia had been a nervous wreck, staring out the window at the passing trees, at other cars. She'd been numb. In the dimmest recesses of her mind, she had heard a voice telling her to throw open the car door and run, right in the middle of the highway, or at least when they'd stopped for bathroom breaks. There had been many of those. So often Olivia had gone into a bathroom at a rest stop and come out with the vague idea of simply disappearing. She'd spot her mother smoking a cigarette by the picnic tables or waiting on line for a cinnamon bun or coffee, and it would have been so easy to simply walk away. Of course, there were few places to go on a highway, but the freedom that had been hers during those breaks had been so tempting.

But then what? Go where? Take care of her baby how? She was sixteen. Two months pregnant. Her mother was her only family. Her father hated her. She had a few friends from school, but no one she could confide in.

The only person she could go to, wanted to go to, had abandoned her. Or so she'd thought. She should have trusted her instincts, which had told her Zachary Archer wouldn't run from the pregnancy. She'd thought it so out of character. But she'd been too naïve to even consider what her father had done behind the scenes, behind her back.

"It's the right thing to do," her mother had said at least ten times during the trip.

Olivia had said nothing to that. Her baby had deserved better than what Olivia, at sixteen, could offer. She'd comforted herself with that knowledge. And with the knowledge that her father had arranged a private adoption with a wonderful couple who'd love her child.

"Ready?" Zach asked, startling her out of her memories. "If you just want to sit here for a while and get your bearings, that's fine. We don't have to go in at all."

Olivia took a deep breath. "I would like to just sit here for a little while. Thanks, Zach."

He reached over and squeezed her hand.

In the dead of winter, the grounds weren't quite as welcoming. There was no cocoon factor. Just bare trees and snow cover. Olivia could see a figure moving past an upstairs window, the silhouette of a heavily pregnant girl.

I hope you're okay, she said silently to the teenager. *I hope you're all okay in there.*

Olivia glanced at Zach. He seemed shaken, and she had no doubt he was imagining her here alone thinking she'd been abandoned.

"I can't believe what you had to go through all these months," he said, his voice breaking. "God, it kills me."

"It's okay, Zach. I was treated well enough. And our baby was born healthy—that's apparent now."

He stared up at the building. "I can't even begin to imagine sending my child here. If Kayla, God forbid, got pregnant at sixteen, I wouldn't send her away."

"Good," she said, placing her hand on his.

In her mind's eye she could see her old room as if she were standing in it right then. Pixford had ten bedrooms, three girls to a room. There were five bathrooms—and always a line. Three square meals a day. Prenatal vitamins and checkups. Lamaze-type classes with no coach. Olivia spent most of her time in the library, reading or staring into space. The library had a fireplace and several rocking chairs, and she'd often rocked herself while staring out the window at nothing. Wondering where Zach was. Wondering who their baby would be. She never thought she'd get the opportunity to find out.

"Let's go in," she said. "I'm ready, if you are," she added.

"Ready."

The moment they walked through the door, Olivia could see that absolutely nothing had changed, including the staff. Mrs. Mimbly, the effusive receptionist, sat chatting on the phone to someone who was clearly a prospective "client." Olivia always figured Mrs. Mimbly had been hired to give girls and their families the illusion that Pixford was a warm and welcoming environment, that the pregnant teenagers would be treated with TLC. None of the other staffers were like Mrs. Mimbly. The nurses and social workers and directors and aides were all disapproving. Olivia had heard from a few of the girls that they'd heard of other homes where the girls were treated with respect and kid gloves. Olivia sure hoped so. It wasn't the case at Pixford.

Mrs. Mimbly hung up the phone and turned her attention to Olivia and Zach. "May I—" She paused, staring at Olivia. "Wait a minute. You're one of our girls!"

Olivia smiled. "Olivia Sedgwick."

"Of course! I remember you. Prettiest girl we ever had. Your baby must be—" She stopped again, her smile gone in an instant. "I'm sorry. I just remembered that your baby was stillborn."

Was she lying? Or had the doctor and nurse conned everyone on the staff?

"We don't have many stillborns," Mrs. Mimbly continued. "I remember being so sad when I heard the news."

"Thank you," Olivia said. "I appreciate that. I'm wondering . . . is the doctor or nurse who handled the birth still working here?" She held her breath.

Mrs. Mimbly shook her head. "Goodness, no. In fact, both that OB and the nurse—Lindy was her name—left Pixford in the days after your delivery."

Olivia and Zach glanced at each other. "Really," Olivia said. "That's interesting. Do you happen to know where they're working now?"

"Well, Dr. Franklin retired," Mrs. Mimbly said. "Somewhere in France, if I recall. He always used to talk about retiring to the French countryside. And Lindy left no forwarding information. She just up and quit and seemingly disappeared."

With a wallet full of cash, no doubt.

"Thanks very much," Olivia told the woman as

the phone rang. She turned to Zach. "Let's just get out of here."

Once they were back in Zach's truck, Olivia let out the breath she didn't even know she'd been holding.

"William must have paid them well," Zach said, shaking his head. "I have a birth certificate for Kayla. It was sent to me out of the blue a year after she was born. I assumed by your father. We're named as parents. And Kayla's full name is on it."

"I saw it," she said. "At the pageant meeting. I almost cried at the sight of it." She shook her head. "My father really thought he was God," Olivia added.

"God with a huge bank account."

That afternoon, with Zach at work and Kayla still at school for an extracurricular activity, Olivia stopped in at the Eat-In Diner for a solo lunch. Ever since she'd returned from Pixford, her heart and stomach had been in knots. She couldn't quite catch her breath. But she couldn't seem to cry either, and she had a feeling a good long cry would help. Then again, she'd have to burst into tears in public, since she couldn't go to the cottage alone. Not with someone out there who liked to slash beds and leave nooses around people's necks. She'd have some lunch, treat herself to something gooey and good for the soul, like cheesecake or a chocolate milkshake.

As she pulled open the door to the Eat-In Diner, she did a double take.

"Camilla?"

None other than Camilla Capshaw turned

around, her dazzling white teeth gleaming. "Olivia! I was just asking for directions to your house. And here you are!"

Olivia hugged her friend, thrilled to see her. "What in the world are you doing here?"

"Bitch Face is ripping off *Allure*'s feature of best beauty treatments around the country. Portland, Maine, has two incredible spas, so she sent me up here to write them up. Isn't my face amazingly smooth? Seaweed facial. Anyway, I knew you were just an hour north, so I figured I'd surprise you."

"I'm so glad you did. It is so good to see you, Cammie."

Camilla linked an arm through Olivia's. "Do they have rabbit food here, or is it total greasy spoon?"

Olivia smiled. "Don't worry. There's a whole section on the menu for people on low-carb diets."

"Perfect. Let's sit and have an early dinner. I have to be back on the road by fiveish or I'll fall asleep somewhere on I-95 in Massachusetts."

As Olivia sat down across from Camilla in the booth, she realized that she hadn't given much thought to her old life. She didn't miss her job or Manhattan at all.

"So tell me everything," Camilla said after their Diet Cokes were served. "Has it been hard to be back?"

Olivia filled in Camilla on everything that was going on.

It took a lot to shock Camilla, but her eyes widened. "Are you sure you're safe here?"

"I'm staying at Zach's, so I think so," Olivia said.

"With your daughter," Camilla said. "I still can't believe it. Do you have a picture?"

Olivia pulled out the pictures of her and Kayla that they had taken the other day and handed them to Camilla.

Camilla sucked in her breath. "She has your hair!"

"Otherwise she looks exactly like her dad."

"Well, her dad must be very handsome," Camilla said, "because Kayla is gorgeous. She's at that awkward becoming-a-teenager phase, but I can see it. She's going to be a knockout."

Olivia stared at the photo of Kayla, her heart surging in her chest. "I'm in love with them both," she said, her eyes suddenly filling with tears.

"Hey, sweetie," Camilla said, covering Olivia's hand with her own, "what's the matter? Everything sounds great between all of you. And now you're even living with them."

"I guess I'm a little overwhelmed," Olivia said. "I don't want to do anything wrong by Kayla. But I hardly know how to be a mom. Here I am stepping in thirteen years later. What do I know about motherhood?"

"I think I know what this is about," Camilla said. "I think it's about that awful place you visited today. You left without her the last time you were there."

"I signed my rights to her away," Olivia said. "How could I have done that?"

"Olivia, first of all, you were sixteen. Second of all, it doesn't matter how old you were. When you're not in a position to take care of a baby, the right thing to do is to sign your rights away so that someone else who can do right by the baby will take good care of her. You were not in a position to take care of a baby then. Not emotionally, financially, or otherwise."

"Zach was only seventeen," Olivia said. "Not much older than I was."

The waitress delivered their salads and paninis. Camilla waited until the woman was gone before she leaned in. "I'll repeat what I just said. It's not so much the age as the person at the time. Yeah, maybe you could have risen to the occasion when you were sixteen, Olivia, but maybe not. From what you told me, Zach had years of experience relying only on himself, taking care of himself. He knew how to take care of that baby or how to find help, as he did for himself. Maybe your dad knew that."

"Are you saying my dad thought that I was too immature to care for my baby but that Zach, whom he thought was a total loser, would make a fine father? Camilla, that makes no sense."

"I'm saying your father didn't want his daughter to have a baby at sixteen and he made that baby go away. Poof. Gone. Gone to the baby's father, a streetwise kid who'd had to raise himself for seventeen years and clearly had something special about him if his own golden child daughter saw something in him."

Olivia gasped. "You think my dad gave Zach the baby because I supplied Zach with some stamp of approval?"

"By default," Camilla said. "It happens in fashion and beauty all the time. You know that. Olivia, you won the Inner-Beauty Pageant at fifteen. That told your father, along with all your other achievements, that your voice, your heart, who you are meant something. And the boy you chose to fall madly in love with, to lose your virginity to, to risk getting pregnant by was Zach Archer. That had to tell your dad something about him."

Olivia sat across from Camilla stunned. She'd never looked at it that way before, never dared consider that her father actually respected her, albeit in a very bizarre, backhanded manner.

"Camilla, how in the world does the assistant beauty editor of *Glitz* magazine get to be such a genius in the field of psychology?"

"I read a lot of self-help," Camilla said, pulling out a hardcover titled *Thirty Days to Self-Esteem.*

Olivia laughed. "How long have you been reading that?"

"Four months," Camilla said, cracking up. "But I'm still on chapter three, "Three Days to Demystifying the Authority Figure in Your Boss."

Olivia grabbed Camilla's hand and squeezed it. "I am so, so happy you came to see me today, Mill. You have no idea how much the sight of you has done for me."

"Me too, Livvy. So is there anywhere to shop in this town?"

Olivia had a brainstorm. As she filled in Camilla, her friend's eyes got wide and excited. "Oooh, I love being a spy girl!"

As Camilla and Olivia entered Johanna's Cashmere Emporium, a bell above the door jangled. Johanna was ringing up a sale at the counter; she glanced at Olivia and frowned.

As the other customer left, Olivia said, "Johanna, this is my friend Camilla. She's visiting from New York City. She's an editor at *Glitz* magazine, and she's looking to buy a gift for the fashion editor. I suggested a gorgeous cashmere sweater from a local Maine shop."

Johanna was flustered. "*Glitz?* Wow. Do you think you might be able to get a mention of my store in the magazine?"

Camilla smiled. "I can certainly try. I'm like this"—she twisted her fingers together—"with the fashion editor."

Johanna rushed around the counter, falling all over herself to help Camilla choose among styles and colors. "Let me show you what just came in. To die for. So soft! The most gorgeous dark purple."

In one minute, Johanna had said more to Camilla than she'd said every morning at eight to Olivia.

"Oooh, I think Larissa would love this!" Camilla said. "Don't you think, Olivia? You were such good friends with her."

Johanna stared at Olivia. Waiting. Hoping.

Olivia eyed the sweater. She let a few moments pass. "I can't decide between the purple and the black, though. Larissa loves both colors so much. Maybe get both?"

Johanna's eyes widened.

"Ooh, they're pricey. But worth it!" Camilla said. "Okay, I'll take both." Camilla made a show of glancing down at Johanna's shoes. "Oooh! I just love your shoes, Johanna. Are those Choos? Manolos?"

Johanna beamed. "Payless, actually."

"You're kidding! They're gorgeous! I wish I could try them on, but we're probably not the same size. I'm a ten. Huge feet."

Good job, Camilla! Olivia thought. Johanna was

about to walk into their trap and admit she was a size eight. Just like the shoe print left outside the basement window of the cottage.

"Sorry," Johanna said. "I'm an eight. But I'm sure Payless will have them in your size."

Camilla smiled. "I'll stop in. Thanks so much!"

Johanna beamed and rushed back around the counter to the cash register. Once the sale was rung up, Olivia said, "See you in the morning, Johanna."

Johanna smiled. Not a light-up-her-face smile, but a smile nonetheless.

Olivia had a feeling Johanna would be a little more talkative tomorrow.

Chapter 16

Olivia was right. Not only did Johanna offer her a smile the next morning, but she actually agreed to come in for coffee. Zach waited in the kitchen. No matter where she was, Olivia could smell his combination of Ivory soap and delicious maleness; she worried that Johanna could too, would spring up and find Zach listening in.

The moment Johanna sat on the sofa, she burst into tears.

"Johanna?" Olivia said gently. She ran to get a box of tissues from the kitchen. Zach squeezed her hand on the way back.

Johanna accepted a tissue and dabbed under her eyes. Her mascara was running down her cheeks. "At first I was doing it for the money," Johanna said cryptically. "But then I really started to like the old guy."

"Doing what for the money?" Olivia asked, her tone as gentle as possible.

"William liked to pay for sex," Johanna said. "He wasn't interested in calling an escort service and having a strange woman, however hot, for the night. He liked to pick someone he was attracted to. So one night when I was working at Hotsie's, a strip club a few towns over, he came in and started paying more attention to me than to the dancers. I was a waitress and also helped out in the girls' changing room, mending a costume or finding someone's mascara, that kind of thing."

Olivia's face must have registered some kind of shock because Johanna stood up. "Look, she said, if you're gonna sit there all high and mighty and judge me . . ."

"I'm not judging you, Johanna. I'm more picturing or trying not to picture my father in a strip club."

That calmed down Johanna. She sat and took a deep breath. "Is the coffee ready? And if you have some Danish or something . . ."

Olivia smiled and headed into the kitchen. Zach shot her a thumbs-up. She poured two mugs of coffee, added milk and sugar to a tray and the box of cinnamon rolls she'd bought yesterday.

"Mmmm, do I smell cinnamon rolls?" Johanna asked, eyeing the tray. "I just love those."

Half a cinnamon roll later, Johanna said, "Now where was I?"

Olivia sipped her coffee. "How you met my father."

"Oh, yeah," she said, then took another bite of the cinnamon roll. "Your dad kept watching me. I saw how free he was with his money, and I couldn't believe he was more interested in a forty-three-year-old waitress than a twenty-two-year-old dancer, but he was. One night, he waited for me to come out after my shift and he asked me on a date."

"Were you interested?" Olivia asked. "I only ask because of the big age difference."

"Interested in a handsome, older, wealthy man?" Johanna asked. "Of course I was."

"He asked me over to this house for dinner. I arrived and he had the whole thing set up in the dining room. A four-course meal, complete with waiter. I've never been treated like that in my entire life."

"So it was a 'date' date," Olivia said. "How did money factor in?"

"Well, after dinner we . . . ended up in the bedroom. Afterward, he gave me five one-hundred-dollar bills. He said he thought it was hot to pay for sex, to role-play that I was a high-priced call girl and he was a strapping young guy. So I thought I was supposed to give him back the money when I left, but he always tucked it in my purse."

Olivia's face must have registered some surprise because Johanna added, "It wasn't like *that*."

"Like what?"

"It wasn't like I was really a *prostitute*," Johanna said.

"How long was your relationship?" Olivia asked.

"Just a few months," Johanna said. "But it wasn't all sex. We talked a lot. About my dreams, his. I told him how it was my dream to own a real cashmere sweater, and the next day, three were delivered to my apartment. When I told him it was my dream to open my own clothing store, he suggested I have a cashmere sweater shop and made all the arrangements. Put everything in my name, too."

"That was very generous of him," Olivia said. "And then he asked you to marry him?"

Her cheeks pinkened. "Well, he didn't 'ask me' ask me. I mean, we talked about it. We were more like preengaged. We were going to live in this house together. And then he died. And left the place to you."

"So I guess he must have talked about our estrangement. That's why you were always so hostile to me."

She nodded and sipped her tea. "He said you ran around behind his back when you were a teenager and got yourself knocked up by a local boy. He said you were an embarrassment to the Sedgwick name."

"Well, that shows how he estranged himself from me," Olivia said. "But why did you think I was the one who spit it in his face?"

"He said he was worried sick that one day you would come back and take everything that was coming to you. He said it just like that."

"And you took that to mean this house?"

She nodded. "The house and Zach. Your father dropped dead and there you were, all moved in. You even moved in on my cousin's boyfriend. She was worried about that before you even turned up, of course."

Cousin! So Marnie was Johanna's cousin. Very interesting. "Worried about me before I arrived?" Olivia asked, leaning closer. There was something crucial in all this and Olivia didn't want to miss a word. She adopted a nonchalant look and jumped up to water the plants by the window. Anything to show Johanna there was nothing out of the ordinary about what she said.

"Well, when your father's health started going, and I mean going bad—he'd already had a heart attack—he began talking a lot about you. He told me all about how you had a daughter at sixteen by someone who lived in town and that you gave custody of the baby to the guy. I was trying to figure out who, and Marnie, who has a thirteen-year-old daughter, was able to pinpoint Kayla Archer in two seconds. She and Brianna are in some classes together at the middle school. There aren't too many thirteen-year-old girls without mothers in Blueberry."

Olivia wondered what was going on in Zach's mind right now as he took all this in. That Marnie knew about Olivia before Olivia had even come to town. Had Marnie started dating Zach because she knew William Sedgwick was dying—and that Kayla might come into a huge inheritance soon? The timing added up. They'd started dating in December.

"Johanna, what you said about my making moves on your cousin's boyfriend. It wasn't like that. When I came to Blueberry I didn't even know that my child was alive."

At Johanna's confused expression, Olivia filled her in on the entire story.

"So it was more like unfinished business between you and Zach," Johanna said. "I can understand that."

Olivia took a deep breath, drained from talking about her father's manipulations. Drained from the entire day. "I hope we can be friends, Johanna. We see each other at the crack of dawn every morning. We might as well be friends, right?"

"I don't know about friends," Johanna said. "I

mean, Marnie's my cousin, and you're like the enemy, you know?"

"The enemy?" Olivia repeated. "Does she really hate me that much?"

"Oh, yeah," Johanna responded. "She does."

"So, my car, the figurines, the noose, the size-eight footprint found outside my basement window the night someone slashed my bed—was that all you guys?"

Johanna stood up, suddenly nervous. She made a show of looking at her watch. "I really have to go. I have to be somewhere."

As Johanna practically ran to the door, Olivia said, "Johanna, if it was the two of you, will it stop now?"

Johanna glanced at Olivia. "I don't know what you're talking about." She bit her lower lip. "I'll see you tomorrow. I probably won't be able to chat or anything, though, because I'm opening up the shop earlier from now on."

With a last nervous smile, Johanna fled down the stairs, walk-running down the road on her high heels until she disappeared from view.

"All that because your friend bought a couple of sweaters?" Zach said when Olivia closed the front door.

"It's almost as though Johanna was looking for an excuse to talk. She's so high-strung and nervous. I get the feeling that Marnie is pulling the strings, and Johanna's freaking out. One more sweater and she might break down and confess."

"I wouldn't trust her, though," Zach said. "It's hard to tell what's real and what she's deluded herself into thinking is real."

"Well, a little kindness seems the way to get

through to her," Olivia said, "so perhaps the incidents will stop now. She might see me as more allied with my father now, whereas before I was the enemy."

"Yeah, but as she said, you're even more of the enemy because of me."

Olivia let out a breath and flopped down on the sofa in the living room.

"So Marnie came on to me because she thought I might get very rich soon?" Zach said, shaking his head as he sat down next to Olivia. "That makes me so sick."

"Well, if it's any consolation, she fell in love."

"That's not a consolation. She came on to me because she thought my daughter—and therefore I—was going to inherit a fortune. That's revolting."

"Zach, did you ever see William when he was in town? Did he ever meet Kayla?"

He shook his head. "Well, he saw her at least one time that I know of. From a distance. I didn't speak to him. He looked from me to Kayla and then turned away."

"Why do you think he sent the birthday and Christmas cards?" Olivia asked. "I keep thinking about that; it would mean he cared about Kayla's feelings. He wanted her to know her mother was thinking of her at least on those two big days."

"Olivia, we'd go out of our minds trying to figure out the inner workings of your father."

"Ever since my friend Camilla left, I've been thinking of something she said yesterday."

"What's that?" Zach asked, glancing at her.

"Well, Camilla thinks my father gave you Kayla because of my stamp of approval. He didn't want his sixteen-year-old daughter to raise a baby, but he didn't want the baby to be raised by strangers, all ties to me gone forever. So he gave the baby to you, knowing she'd be fine in your care."

"But your father thought I was pond scum."

"Clearly not. Or he wouldn't have given you Kayla."

Zach seemed to be taking that in. "I hadn't thought of it that way. But I also don't give a rat's butt what your father thought of me."

She smiled. "I know. And I'm glad. I just thought it was interesting. It hurts less not to hate him, Zach. And these little tidbits keep adding up to me being unable to hate him. I don't like him, but I don't hate him the way I did that first day I arrived in Blueberry."

He took her hand and held it. "Good. Hatred doesn't do anyone any good."

"Do you think Johanna will tell Marnie about our little chitchat?" Olivia asked as Zach caressed the tender skin of her inner arm.

"I don't think so. I have a feeling Johanna wants to be written up in *Glitz* magazine too much for that. I think Johanna thinks she's found a more important, useful ally than Marnie. Cousin or no cousin."

"We have another pageant meeting tonight," Olivia said. "I have a feeling it's going to take hours to make a single decision."

"I'll be waiting outside in the truck just to make sure the hours aren't because you've been locked in a basement."

"Don't even joke," Olivia said. But she knew he wasn't joking.

Chapter 17

"No, I think Cecily should go first. She's the prettiest," Cecily's mother announced.

"*Hello!*" Kayla yelled. "It's an *inner-beauty* pageant. So looks don't matter."

"Then *you* go first," another girl snapped.

Kayla's face fell for a moment, but then she recovered. "Jerk-face."

The six contestants and their mothers stood on the stage in the auditorium, bickering back and forth, as they'd been doing for the past fifteen minutes. All that was required of them this evening was to agree on the order in which the girls would present themselves to the panel of judges and the audience in two weeks.

Olivia waited for Colleen, the assistant coordinator, to intervene, but the shy woman bit her lip and then buried her nose in the pageant manual. She was clearly intimidated by the mothers *and* the girls.

Olivia might not be the sole coordinator, but she was taking charge *now*.

"Rule number one of Blueberry's Inner-Beauty

Pageant is that contestants must demonstrate inner beauty all the time, not just during the actual pageant. So let's all put that into practice, okay?"

"I agree with Olivia," trilled Cecily Carle's mother.

There were eye rolls from everyone else.

"Well, I think either Eva or I should go first," Emily said. "Because we're twins."

"So you should both go last," Kayla said. "You already call too much attention to yourselves."

As the arguing reached headache-inducing levels, Olivia called out, "The pageant guidebook suggests we go in alphabetical order. That way, the judges know the order is random."

"And your daughter's name just happens to start with *A*," Marnie said coldly.

"But Emily's last name is Abernathy, so she's first!" said Emily's mother. "Then Eva."

"Colleen," Olivia said to the assistant coordinator, "why don't you take over now that we've got that settled."

The woman practically jumped. "Okay, so the order is Emily Abernathy, Eva Abnernathy, Kayla Archer, Cecily Carle, Deenie McCord, and Brianna Sweetser.

"Best for last, baby," Olivia heard Marnie say to her daughter.

"Attention, please," Colleen called out in such a low voice that no one heard her. "Attention!" she suddenly bellowed.

All heads swung to her.

"We will have one placement rehearsal one day prior to the pageant next Saturday," Colleen said, reading from the clipboard in her hands. "Each

contestant must by pageant day be formally sponsored by a town establishment. I'll hand out forms
that must be signed by the proprietor at the end of
the meeting."

"Can it be any type of business?" Brianna asked.

"Any type as long it's located within Blueberry,"
Colleen said. "And no, you can't be sponsored by
your kid sister's lemonade stand or something like
that."

"I don't have a kid sister," Brianna snapped.

"I'm speaking to the *group*," Colleen responded.
She seemed to be relishing this new position of
power. "If I may continue. At the pageant, each
contestant will read an essay of between seven hundred fifty and one thousand words on what inner
beauty means to her. Each contestant will give an
oral presentation on the most influential person in
her life. Finally, each contestant will answer three
questions chosen at random by the judges. After a
short break, the judges will then review their scores
and announce a runner-up and the winner of the
pageant."

"Who are the judges?" Cecily Carle's mother
asked.

Colleen flipped a page on her clipboard. "The esteemed judges are Donald Hicks, town manager
of Blueberry; Laura Maywood, Blueberry Memor-
ial Library's reference librarian; and Valerie Erp,
president of The Blueberry Historical Society."

"Are we done?" Marnie asked, glancing at her
watch. "I have an important engagement. And Brianna would like to work on her oral presentation."

"She'll need all the practice she can get," Eva or
Emily whispered.

"Shut up, you stupid cows," Brianna snapped.

"Inner beauty!" Colleen singsonged. "At all times, please!"

Well, at least Colleen had found her voice.

As Zach watched Olivia and Kayla walk out of the town hall, laughing, chatting, smiling, he was so overcome with emotion that he had to take a deep breath. This was exactly what he'd always dreamed of for Kayla. A mother—if not her biological one, then a woman who could fulfill that role for his daughter. And here was the best of both worlds. Kayla looked so happy. So did Olivia.

Olivia and Kayla stopped and turned around; they were joined by Cecily Carle and her mother, Rorie. He saw Olivia point at Zach's truck, and then they all headed over.

"Hi, Daddy!" Kayla said, leaning up to kiss Zach through the window. "Cecily invited me over to her house to work on our oral presentations. Can I go?"

It amused Zach how Kayla could go from hating someone's guts to adoring them in two seconds flat. Last week, Kayla despised "the perfect Cecily Carle."

"I'd be happy to drop her home around eight," Rorie said. "We don't live very far away."

At Zach's "sounds good," Kayla squealed, and off she went with the Carles.

"Nice girl?" he asked as Olivia got inside the truck.

"The nicest one of the contestants," Olivia said. "I like her mom, too." Her eyes were on Marnie's car, speeding out of the parking lot. "Marnie mentioned she had an 'important engagement' after the meeting. Curious as I am?"

As they trailed Marnie at a reasonable distance, Olivia filled in Zach on the meeting.

"Doesn't exactly sound like the good influence I'd wanted for Kayla," Zach said. "Sounds more like an Inner-Baddie contest."

Olivia smiled. "The good news is Kayla seems so self-motivated to write her essay and work on her oral presentation. She needs to be sponsored by a local business. Have anyone in mind she can ask?"

"Yeah, my architectural firm. We're a one-man shop, but she's got my vote."

Olivia smiled. "I'll check with Colleen to make sure she can be sponsored by a family member's business. I'm sure it's fine, as long you donate a certain amount of money to the kitty of prize money."

Zach began slowing down as Marnie pulled into her driveway. "I have a feeling she'll drop off Brianna and then head out again. Let's wait."

They didn't wait long. In another few minutes, Marnie was back on the road and heading down a rural highway. Twenty minutes later, she exited and pulled into the parking lot of the Boxboro Township Motel.

"I guess her important engagement is sex," Zach said as they watched Marnie dash from her car inside the Boxboro Township Motel. A sign at the main entrance said: *By the hour or week!*"

"Why meet someone here?" Olivia asked. "It's so out of the way—" They glanced at each other. "Maybe her new boyfriend is married?"

Zach glanced around the parking lot, his gaze stopping on a familiar green Subaru Forester.

"Now, granted, the Forester is a popular car in Maine, but I can think of one particular person who has that car."

"Who?" Olivia asked.

"I'll give you a hint. He's definitely married. But more important—or perhaps I should say more *sickeningly*—he's the only male judge of the Inner-Beauty Pageant."

Olivia's mouth dropped open. "The town manager?" she asked. She shook her head. "Do you think they started seeing each other before Brianna entered the contest?"

"If that's the case," Zach said, "she's one hell of a hypocrite."

The next morning, Zach waited in the kitchen as Olivia dealt with Johanna.

"Um, just forget everything I said yesterday," Johanna said. "I was just really emotional about William. I don't even know if what I said was true or not. It's all jumbled."

"Would you like to come—" Olivia began.

"I'm in a hurry," Johanna interrupted, "so could you just give me your receipts and sign the roster?"

"Maybe next time," Olivia said.

"Oh, I almost forgot," Johanna said, "of course, I'm sponsoring Brianna. She is my cousin's daughter."

"Of course."

At the sound of the door closing, Zach met Olivia in the living room. "Let's take a ride to the town hall and check our esteemed town manager's license plate."

Five minutes later, they had a match. One minute after that, Zach was in Donald Hicks's office.

"What can I do for you, Zach?" Don asked.

"Look, Don, we go way back, so I'm just going to come out and say this. I happened to be passing by the Boxboro Township Motel tonight and—"

The man's face reddened. "You're not going to tell Suzette, are you?"

"No, that's your business. My business is the fact there's now a conflict of interest concerning the Inner-Beauty Pageant. I'm talking about one of the contestants in particular. As my own daughter is a contestant, I don't want to see the pageant judged on any merit other than the rules dictate."

Don played dumb for a moment, then slapped his hand to his forehead. "Oh my gosh. Is Marnie's girl a contestant in the pageant?"

Zach tried not to roll his eyes. "Yes, she is."

"I had no idea, Zach," Don said. "But don't give it another thought. I'll tell you what. You keep this between us, and I'll resign as a judge immediately. I'm really too busy as it is. You're doing me a favor."

Zach had a pretty good idea that the understanding between Marnie and Don was unspoken. A tit-for-tat kind of relationship. For example, you give me hot sex in a motel a couple of times a week, and maybe there's something I can do for you, such as waive a town ordinance or, say, vote for your daughter in any pageants for which I'm a judge.

"We have a deal," Zach said and shook the man's hand. Karmic justice would take care of him. "By the way, Don, if you don't mind me asking, how long have you and Marnie been seeing each other?"

He broke out into a smile. "Couple of months.

Nothing serious, of course. I realize we were both seeing Marnie at the same time, but she assured me that you two had an open relationship."

"We certainly did," he said. "Thanks again, Don."

As he left the town hall, he realized that Marnie was a better liar than he'd ever imagined. He had no doubt she was behind all the incidents at the cottage, and she very likely had had Johanna's help. Marnie would probably be difficult to trap, but Johanna would probably fall right into a confession.

He'd see how this interesting little development of her secret boyfriend resigning as a judge affected Marnie. And then he'd plan his next move.

Chapter 18

Zach barely slept the next couple of nights. For two reasons. The first was the beautiful woman, in that nothing of a slip, sleeping downstairs in the guest bed. How simple it would be to creep down the stairs, missing the squeaky sections (he knew where they were, thanks to Kayla's bad habit of sneaking downstairs to go on-line on the computer in the living room), and crawl into bed with Olivia, who'd welcome him in. At least, he thought so. Since she'd officially moved into the guest room, he hadn't allowed himself to linger in there once she turned in for the night. If they were meant to be together, if they were meant to be a family, he didn't want sex to be making the decisions. He wanted to think, to *feel*, with his heart, with a cool head.

Since he couldn't sleep, he often did creep downstairs, missing the squeaky sections of the stairs. He'd do some research on-line, or he'd watch a late night movie using his headphones, and he'd hear Olivia flip-flopping in her bed. Which was how he knew that she'd welcome him in. She couldn't sleep, either.

Then again, who was to say that she wanted him the way she did thirteen years ago? He wasn't that same kid on the beach. And the events that separated him and Olivia had shaped the man he was today. Maybe their old chemistry didn't work with these new variables.

Except it did. Their chemistry felt as powerful and raw and perfect now as it had then. That inexplicable electricity that existed between two people. He and Olivia had very little in common. It wasn't like they both loved boating or dancing or watching kung fu movies. What they had in common was that ridiculous "Snoopy dance" feeling whenever they laid eyes on each other. A happiness in just being near. In being together. A rightness.

The second reason he couldn't sleep had to do with Marnie. Every time he closed his eyes, he saw her jumping through the window like a supervillain wielding a butcher knife. Until he caught her red-handed, he'd get little sleep.

Zach was doing some preliminary sketches for a client's house when the principal of Blueberry Middle School called and asked if he could come right over. He assured her he'd be there in five minutes, then called Olivia on her cell phone.

"Oh no," she said. "I'll leave right now too. What did Kayla do?"

"I don't know yet, but the principal sounded upset."

What could she have done? He was convinced that she'd given up her week as a trial smoker with the two girls who she felt had betrayed her. They were a bit rougher around the edges than Kayla, and she'd gotten into her head that they lacked inner beauty and therefore weren't worthy to be her friends. His daughter had a ton of growing up to do, but she was on the right path, and if she ran into a few huge craters along the way, they'd work on filling those in together.

So what had she done? Cheated on a test? No way. That would disqualify her for the pageant. He couldn't imagine she'd risk doing anything that might interfere.

He and Olivia arrived at the same time from opposite directions. She squeezed his hand in support, and they headed in.

In the office, Kayla sat on a chair outside the principal's office. Through the window on the door, he could see the principal, Marnie, and Brianna. Marnie appeared to be quite agitated. Brianna appeared to be crying.

"Kayla?" Zach said.

She jumped up and flew into his arms. Tears ran down her cheeks. "I didn't do it! I swear I didn't!"

"Do what, honey?"

"I'll let Principal Sykes know you've arrived," the secretary said to Zach, buzzing the intercom. A moment later, she said, "Please go in."

As they walked in, Marnie shouted, "I want her expelled!"

"Mrs. Sweetser, please calm down and sit down," Principal Sykes said.

"Principal Sykes," Zach said, "this is Olivia Sedgwick, Kayla's mother."

The woman shook Olivia's hand, and everyone sat down. "Several of these posters were taped up around the halls and in the bathrooms," the principal said, handing Zach and Olivia the evidence.

Brianna Sweetser is a slut!

Brianna Sweetser thinks she can win the Inner-Beauty Pageant even though she's slept with seven guys.

Brianna Sweetser is a total slut!

"I didn't do it!" Kayla cried.

"Shut up, liar, you did too!" Brianna yelled.

"Principal Sykes," Zach said, "what does Kayla have to do with this?"

"Perhaps absolutely nothing, perhaps everything," she responded. "When Brianna brought the posters to me, she immediately said she thought Kayla was the culprit and explained that Kayla was probably trying to make her look bad because they're both competing in the Inner-Beauty Pageant. When I called in Kayla, she said she didn't do it. Brianna said she wanted her backpack and locker checked for pink and orange markers, and Kayla held out her bag for me to check. This is what I found." She held up pink and orange markers.

"But they're not mine!" Kayla said. "I have no idea how they got in my backpack."

"Oh, please," Marnie said. "Can't you lie better than that?"

"I'm not lying!" Kayla shouted.

"It does seem odd that she'd offer up her backpack if she knew you'd find the markers," Olivia said.

"She probably thought she hid them in a secret compartment," Brianna said. "But she's too stupid for that."

"Shut up!" Kayla yelled.

"Enough!" the principal said, clapping her hands.

"Dad, I didn't make those posters," Kayla said, looking him in the eye. "I didn't."

He believed her in that second. But then he wavered a moment later. Damn! He wanted to believe her. But the posters were something she would do. And the markers were in her bag.

The thing was, Kayla wasn't a big liar. She usually owned up to what she did.

But owning up to this could get her disqualified from the Inner-Beauty Pageant as a display of the opposite of inner beauty.

Where was that damned guidebook?

"Well, is she going to be expelled?" Marnie said.

"Mr. Archer?" the principal prompted. "What's your take on this?"

Zach took a deep breath. "If Kayla says she didn't do it, I believe her. My daughter is not a liar."

"You've got to be kidding," Marnie said. "She's fresh back from a suspension and in trouble right away. She's trouble, period."

"Principal Sykes, I won't sit here and allow my daughter to be spoken about this way. I'm sorry about those posters; they're disgusting. But Kayla wasn't responsible." He stood up, and so did Olivia. "So unless you have proof that Kayla was, I'd like this meeting to come to an end."

Marnie shot up and grabbed her daughter's hand. "Come on, Brianna. I'm not staying in the same room for another minute with these vermin."

As the two huffed out, the principal shook her head. "Thank you for coming in," she said wearily.

On the way out, Kayla said, "You really believe me, Daddy?"

"Yes, I do, Kayla."

She jumped into his arms, tears streaming down her cheeks.

"Do you believe me too, Olivia?"

Olivia smiled and squeezed her hand. "Yes, I do. The girl I've gotten to know wouldn't do something like that."

Kayla let out a relieved breath. "I might as well go to history class, even though there's only a half hour left of school." She leaned close to Olivia. "I like a boy in my class."

Olivia smiled. "See you at home."

Kayla grinned and ran down the hall.

"Why did she have the only two colors of markers used on the posters in her bag?" Zach asked.

Olivia shrugged. "Pink and orange are her favorite colors."

"They are?"

"She told me that three times. She wants to wear her pink sweater dress when she reads her essay, and her orange corduroy miniskirt when she gives her oral presentation."

"So it's just a coincidence that the posters were in pink and orange?" Zach said.

Olivia slung an arm around his shoulder. "I know it's crazy, but yes. I really meant what I said to her. The girl I've come to know wouldn't do that, wouldn't stoop to that. Kayla's not a behind-your-back type. She tells you exactly what she thinks of you to your face."

"That's true," Zach said. "The last thing she is is passive-aggressive. She's aggressive-aggressive."

Olivia laughed. "Go back to work. I'll be home when the bus drops off Kayla."

He kissed her on the lips. He didn't know who was more surprised by that, Olivia or himself.

Chapter 19

The next few days passed without incident. Without bad incident, that was. There were no more calls from the middle school. Johanna didn't revert back to her gruff demeanor. She refused every invitation to come in and talk, but at least she chatted about the weather. And the attacks against Olivia had stopped.

So when Olivia's cell phone rang on Saturday afternoon, Olivia didn't answer with her usual trepidation.

She should have.

"We're holding an emergency meeting for all contestants and their guardians," said Colleen. "If you can't make it this evening, I'm afraid your voice will not be counted in the final decision making."

"Colleen," Olivia said, "what is the meeting about? Did something happen?"

"Something happened, all right," Colleen said. "The meeting is tonight at six at the town hall auditorium. I have several more calls to make, so if you'll excuse me."

Click.

"What was that about?" Zach asked from the kitchen doorway. He was making a gourmet dinner for three tonight, in celebration of Kayla finishing her oral presentation. She wouldn't tell them who she'd chosen as the most influential person in her life, but she was dancing around the house. At the moment, Kayla was in her room, trying to come up with potential questions and answers for the final round of judging.

"I don't know, but it sounds serious, Zach. Colleen has called an emergency meeting of all Inner-Beauty candidates and their guardians for six o'clock."

Zach let out a deep breath. "So much for my homemade chicken enchiladas."

When Olivia, Zach, and Kayla arrived at the town hall, only Deenie and her mother had yet to show. Everyone was seated in the first two rows of the auditorium, Colleen standing in front, looking grim.

"We'll give the McCords a few minutes and then the meeting will begin," Colleen announced.

"We can begin right now because Kayla's here," Eva shouted, jumping up. "And she's the one who sent me the letter!"

Olivia glanced at Kayla; the girl's face registered the same surprise as her own and Zach's.

"What letter?" Kayla asked, staring at Eva.

"Oh, like you don't know!" Emily shouted.

"Will someone tell us what's going on?" Marnie said, arms crossed over her chest. "Though from the sound of it, I can surmise. It sounds like something that happened to Brianna last week," she added, her eyes narrowed on Kayla.

Colleen glanced at her watch, then at the doors of
the auditorium. "Well, it's five past six, and the Mc-
Cords haven't arrived, but I guess we should get
started." She held a letter-sized envelope. Inside was
a piece of paper. "This is what is typed on this letter,"
Colleen said. 'Listen up, Eva. Drop out of the pageant today or I will kill you. Your sister isn't a threat,
but you are.'"

"What's that supposed to mean, anyway?" Emily
Abernathy asked on a sulk. "Why aren't I a threat?"

Zach stood up. "What does this have to do with
Kayla, Colleen?"

"Everyone knows she wears that gross vanilla perfume night and day," Eva said. "And I can smell the
vanilla from that letter from here."

"That is true," Colleen said, sniffing the letter. "It
does smell like vanilla perfume."

"And I happen to know that Kayla has a bottle of
vanilla-scented musk," Marnie stated. "I gave her a
bottle for Christmas."

"And she wears it all the time," Brianna said,
holding her nose.

Kayla jumped up. "So just because the letter smells
like my perfume, that means I sent it? I didn't!"

"Just like you didn't hang vile posters about Brianna at school, even though evidence of your guilt
was found in your backpack?" Marnie said coldly.

Kayla looked wildly from Zach to Olivia, then
burst into tears. "I didn't write that letter! I didn't!"
she shouted, then covered her face with her hands.
"You have to believe me."

"Everyone knows you think Emily is a drip," Brianna added. "So that part about her not being a
threat also points to you."

"Or it all points to someone framing Kayla," Olivia said, standing up. She squeezed Kayla's hand.

"Oh, right," Marnie said. "Someone is trying to make the front-runners drop out and make it look like Kayla's doing it. Right."

"Actually, that makes sense to me," Zach said. "That would knock out Kayla too, wouldn't it?"

All eyes swung to Zach.

"Or so she'd like everyone to think," Marnie said. "But I don't think Kayla is that smart. She's trying to scare the best candidates out of the competition and she left a trail. Twice."

"I did not!" Kayla shouted. "I swear, everyone, I didn't send that letter."

"So why does it smell like your stinky perfume?" Eva asked.

"I'm sure Kayla's not the only person in the world who wears vanilla musk," Cecily said. "I have that perfume too. I know at least three other girls at the high school who have it. It doesn't prove anything."

Kayla stopped sniffling and sat up straighter.

"Attention, everyone," Colleen said, "this letter—and the posters maligning the reputation of another candidate—are unfortunate and unacceptable. If this is the work of one of our candidates and we are able to prove it beyond a shadow of a doubt, you will be turned over to the police. These are serious matters. Please know that we will be watching all of you very carefully. This meeting is now at an end."

The doors to the auditorium opened and Deenie McCord and her mother entered. "Sorry, I'm late," Deenie said, in such a low voice that Olivia barely heard her. "My mom couldn't get off work until now."

Olivia noticed that Jacqueline McCord was staring at Zach. Zach was reading some pageant materials and didn't seem to realize that the woman was boring holes into his profile.

Colleen sighed. "I'll fill you in. Everyone else, I'll see you back here for rehearsals on Friday evening at six P.M."

Cecily and Rorie were waiting when Olivia, Zach, and Kayla left the auditorium.

"Don't let them get to you," Cecily said. "Look, I hate gossip more than anything. But for all Colleen knows, it could be Brianna or even Eva herself who's behind all this."

"Thanks for sticking up for me, Cecily," Kayla said. "That was really cool of you."

After a few minutes of chitchat, Zach's impatience clearly got the better of him. "We'd better get home to those enchiladas," he said, offering as much of a smile as he could muster at the Carles.

As they headed to Zach's truck, Kayla said, "I swear to God I didn't do it, Dad."

"I believe you, Kayla," he said. "I don't know what's going on, but it's getting out of hand. The posters were bad enough, but threatening to kill someone is—" He shook his head. "I'm not even sure you should be continuing with the pageant, Kayla. This is getting too dangerous."

"No!" she screamed. "That's not fair!"

"Kayla, we'll talk about it at home."

"Tell him it's not fair, Mom!"

Olivia gasped. Zach stared at Kayla. Even Kayla seemed shocked.

"Did I just call you 'Mom'?" Kayla asked, tears pooling in her eyes.

Olivia took Kayla's hands in hers. "Yes, you did. And I liked it a lot."

Zach's expression was unreadable.

The family meeting Zach had called wasn't going well.

"Kayla, this is the first year you're eligible for the pageant," Zach said as he stood at the kitchen counter, filling tortillas with chicken and cheese. "With all that's going on—"

"Oh, like it's really fair that I should drop out because someone's trying to ruin it for everyone," Kayla said. "Make us all drop out is exactly what the jerk is trying to make us do!"

Zach looked to Olivia. "What do you think?"

"I think she has a very good point," Olivia said, stirring fragrant Mexican-style rice on the stove. "I think we have to be vigilant, though." She turned to Kayla. "That means being exceptionally careful. It means that at school you can't go into the girls' room alone. You can't go into stairwells alone. You'd have to make sure you're in a group. When you're not in school, either your dad or I or someone we trust would need to be with you at all times."

"So I can stay in the pageant?" she asked, her gaze going from Zach to Olivia.

"If you promise to do what Olivia just said," Zach responded. "The only girl in the pageant who goes to your school is Brianna. Be very careful when you see her, Kayla. And after school, as long as you agree to be in eye view of me, Olivia, or someone we trust, you can continue with the pageant."

"Yay!" she exclaimed. "Okay, I will."

Zach stopped what he was doing and grabbed a chair so that he was at Kayla's eye level. "Kayla, I need to ask. Did you send that letter to Eva?"

"Dad! I can't believe you!"

"Kayla, I'm just asking you so you can answer and I can move on from the question."

"Oh, great, so you move on, and I get to think that my dad thinks I go around telling people they're sluts and I want to kill them."

"Kayla, please answer the question," Zach said.

"Mom, tell him he's being a jerk!"

Olivia sucked in her breath. At being called "Mom" again, and at Kayla's referring to her father as a jerk.

Zach stood. "Kayla Archer, go to your room right now."

"Oh, like that's fair!" she screamed.

"*Now*, Kayla," Zach said through gritted teeth.

Kayla stormed out. Zach turned back to the counter and squashed his fist against the enchilada he'd just rolled.

"I need a few minutes to think," he said, without turning around.

"Okay," Olivia whispered, placing her hand on his back before heading into the living room.

She doubted he was doing much thinking. Cabinet doors were being swung closed a little too hard, and baking sheets were clanging against the counter. He was very likely mangling all the enchiladas in the process.

Kayla was sulking in her room, if her yelling, "This is so unfair!" and slamming the door were anything to go by. And Olivia was sitting in the living room alone, staring at the ceiling, trying to focus on the situation, but unable.

Tell him it's not fair, Mom. . . . Mom, tell him he's being a jerk. . . .

When threatened, when upset, when pitted even against her father, Kayla had, without thought, called Olivia "Mom." What that told Olivia was that her daughter had opened her heart to her.

It was as scary as it was thrilling. She had a lot to learn about being a mother, especially a thirteen-year-old girl's mother. She also had a lot to learn about what her place was in this family. If she was even *considered* part of this family.

No wonder Zach was keeping his hands to himself. Suddenly she realized just how complicated their relationship—to each other and to Kayla—was.

The banging in the kitchen had settled down. Olivia hoped that meant Zach had too.

Olivia's cell phone rang. She braced herself for another call from Colleen.

"Olivia, it's Amanda."

"Amanda! Are you back from your honeymoon?"

"We got back late last night. It's good to be home, but I wouldn't have minded if the honeymoon had lasted forever."

Olivia laughed. "I'm sure it will, Amanda."

"Not with a thirteen-month-old dictating the schedule," Amanda said, chuckling. "Tommy's internal clock is still five hours ahead."

For the next ten minutes, Olivia forgot all her problems as her sister filled her in on everything in her world. Tommy had taken his first step in Paris. Ethan, Amanda's husband, had received the paperwork to adopt Tommy, and Amanda couldn't be happier.

"I'd love to come visit you before you leave the cottage," Amanda said. "Maybe Ivy can come up from New Jersey."

Olivia didn't want to ruin a moment of Amanda's posthoneymoon happiness by filling her in on what was going on in Blueberry, but she wasn't so sure inviting her sisters in the middle of all this danger was such a good idea, either. She did want to see Amanda and Ivy so badly, though.

Then it dawned on her that Ivy was a police officer. If there was any trouble while her sisters visited, Ivy would know how to handle it. She might even be able to get some "professional courtesy" from the Blueberry P.D. and read its reports on the incidents at the cottage.

Another ten minutes later, the Sedgwick sisters' reunion was all set for Wednesday, if Ivy could get the day off.

Zach came out of the kitchen long enough to call Kayla to set the table for dinner. And after a silent first few minutes, Kayla said, "The answer to your question is no. I didn't send that letter. I didn't make those posters, either."

Zach put his hand over Kayla's. "Okay. That's all I wanted. I believe you, Kayla. If you say you didn't do it, I believe you."

"But you think I did it?" she asked, the anger returning.

He shook his head. "No, I don't think so. I think someone is trying to make it look as though you did. You know what else I think?"

"What?" Kayla asked.

"I think it's great that you called Olivia 'Mom.'"

Kayla blushed and looked at Olivia. "Is that okay?"

"It's more than okay," Olivia managed to say. "It makes me very happy."

And with that they settled down to dinner.

Zach couldn't sleep. He glanced at the clock on his bedside table. A minute after midnight. Before he could stop himself he went downstairs and tapped on Olivia's door.

"Come on in," she said.

She was sitting up in bed, the blanket pulled up to her waist. She wore an oversized NYU sweatshirt. How was it possible that she still looked so sexy? Her hair was in a knot on top of her head with a stick through it. He wanted nothing more than to pull it out and run his hands up the sweatshirt, just lose himself under those sheets for a few hours. Days, maybe.

"You okay?" she asked.

He sat down on the edge of the bed. "I feel like I need to tread very carefully with Kayla. On one hand, she's really opened up to you, calling you Mom, looking to you for 'protection' against me. But on the other, she's right in the middle of a major mess. Honestly, Olivia, I don't know if she's telling the truth or not. I hate to admit that."

She let him ramble, scooting closer to him and rubbing his shoulders as he talked and talked and talked.

"Do you think she could be lying?" he asked. "Is she the one everyone needs protection from?"

Olivia shook her head. "I really don't think so, Zach. She's been taking the pageant so seriously. Not the pageant itself, but what it is she's actually competing for—the girl whose inner beauty is shining brightest. She's been internalizing what it means to be a good person, to think before she acts, to concern herself with other people's feelings. I think someone's setting her up."

"Good," he said, releasing a breath. "And I agree with everything you said. Man, it feels good to be able to discuss these kinds of issues with someone who cares as much as I do about Kayla. All these years there's been just me. No doting grandparent, even. It's a huge weight off me, Olivia."

She continued rubbing his shoulders, massaging, pressing, kneading. "It means so much to me that you're giving me a voice, Zach. You could shut me out of what's going on with Kayla. But you're not."

He turned and kissed her then, his hand traveling from her back to underneath her sweatshirt. Her skin was so soft, so warm. He moved his hands from her back to her impossibly small waist, then up her flat stomach to her full breasts. His lips on hers, he massaged each breast, teasing her nipples. She arched toward him, her breathy little moans driving him crazy. He laid her down on the bed and nudged her legs apart, pressing his erection against her. She wore navy sweatpants, which he slid down off her, leaving on her underwear. White. Cotton. Unbelievably hot.

He got rid of the sweatshirt next and leaned up and took in the sight of her, naked save for the scrap of white cotton around her hips. As his erection strained against his jeans, he took her nipple in his mouth, licking, teasing. The more she arched and writhed and let out those breathy little moans, the less he was able to wait. He straddled her and placed her hand on his belt buckle.

As she leaned up to unzip his pants, he suckled her nipples again, then groaned as she slipped her cool hand around his throbbing erection. She urged him down on the bed and he lay flat, naked and waiting, barely able to breathe. He closed his eyes and felt the flutter of her hair brushing across his chest as she licked his nipple and kissed her way down his stomach. She straddled him and rubbed against him for a moment, leaning close to kiss him hot and hard on his mouth, and then she was gone again, the hair fluttering down his chest and stomach until he felt her lips on the throbbing head of his penis. He groaned and fisted her hair as she sucked up and down, licking, her hand moving with her mouth.

He could barely take it. He flipped her over and pulled her arms over her head, pinning her to the bed as he kissed every inch of her, her mouth, her neck, her breasts, her stomach, her inner thighs. He slipped a finger inside her, and she moaned, arching her back. He explored the delicious core of her with his tongue and lips and fingers until her moans exploded into a scream. And then he turned her over onto her stomach and entered her from behind, thrusting so hard that a slick layer of sweat covered his chest. He reached his hands underneath her to cup her breasts, ramming, jamming inside her, again and again until he exploded. He lay there, on top of her, inside her, his breath so ragged. He reached for her hand and squeezed it. She barely seemed to have the energy to squeeze back.

All of a sudden, he leaned up. "I didn't hurt you, did I?" he asked. "I—"

She smiled. "Nope, you didn't hurt me at all. Because you weren't screwing me, Zach. You were making love to me. Passionately."

He caressed her cheek with his finger, trailing it down to her beautiful collarbone. She closed her eyes and breathed in and out. She seemed at peace. For the moment at least, so was he.

They lay like that for a while, and then Olivia slid out from under him and tugged his hand, leading him into the bathroom that connected to the guest room. She turned on the shower and they stepped in under the hot, pulsating spray.

There was no energy to talk, to smile. They dried each other off, and then they padded naked back into bed. Olivia curled herself next to him, her back against his stomach, and in minutes, Zach's eyes had drifted closed.

Chapter 20

The dream boy and girl were running around a brilliant green meadow. The dream boy, a different dream boy, Olivia vaguely realized from the depths of her dream, was holding a piece of paper out to Olivia. She tried to take it, but no matter how close she got to him, she couldn't reach it. The dream girl was pirouetting in a patch of wildflowers. A daisy wrapped around her leg and began dragging her across the meadow, the dream girl's screams silent. Olivia tried to run after the girl, but the boy stood in her way, holding out the paper for Olivia to take.

Gasping for breath, Olivia sat up in bed, the dream already fading. She glanced out the window; dawn was breaking, and the sky was gray.

Zach's side of the bed was empty. Her heart hammering, Olivia pulled on her sweats and told herself she was being silly. Yes, every time she had a dream about the children, something bad happened. But these dream children were different, anyway. Different dream children, different results? Maybe it meant something good would happen.

Still, she raced up the stairs and opened the door to Kayla's room. Kayla's bed was empty. Frantic, Olivia ran into Zach's room to wake him up. But his bed was also empty.

She dashed back downstairs. Silence. Then a faint clinking sound. She followed the sound into the kitchen. And there sat Kayla and Zach, stirring hot chocolate in mugs.

"Sorry," Zach said to Olivia. "We tried to be quiet so we wouldn't wake you."

"We've been talking for like a whole hour," Kayla said, smiling. "Everything's okay again."

Olivia felt her heart move in her chest.

The next morning, Kayla at school and Zach at work, Olivia went shopping in town, looking for something special for Kayla. She wanted to give her something to celebrate the process of competing in the pageant, so that no matter what happened in the end, Kayla had something from her mother that said: You *are* inner beauty.

As she neared a jewelry shop, she decided that a locket necklace would be perfect. A heart to symbolize her love for Kayla. And the space inside the locket to symbolize that what was inside was up to Kayla.

With Valentine's Day just around the corner, Olivia wasn't surprised that the store was so busy. She browsed, settling on just the gold necklace she wanted, when she felt someone staring at her. She glanced up into the cold eyes of Jacqueline McCord, Deenie's mother.

"Hi, Jacqueline," Olivia said.

"How do you know my name?" the woman asked coldly.

That flustered Olivia a bit. "I'm sure I heard your name at one of the pageant meetings."

"No, I'm sure you didn't," Jacqueline said. "Because the mothers weren't introduced. Did Zach tell you about me?"

Olivia glanced around the crowded store. If she were alone with Jacqueline, she'd be very worried. "To be honest, I mentioned that I saw you for the first time at the General Store and described you, and he said it sounded like Jacqueline McCord."

"I'm surprised he'd know what I look like," she said.

Olivia turned her attention to the display case. "I'm interested in buying this locket necklace."

"It figures you're back now," she continued. "Now that Zach is a rich architect and everyone in town thinks he walks on water. Thirteen years ago, you wanted nothing to do with him or his trailer trash kid."

Olivia gasped but quickly controlled herself. "I'll give you one more opportunity to make a sale, Jacqueline. I'm interested in buying the locket necklace."

"You're not even denying it!" she said. "When I was interested in Zach, he had nothing. He barely had parents. He had zilch to offer, and I still fell for him."

This entire conversation was insane. "Jacqueline, I think you're forgetting that I'm the mother of his thirteen-year-old daughter. I fell for him when he was seventeen—although I'd hardly say he had nothing to offer. He had a lot to offer."

"Save it for the Inner-Beauty Pageant judges," she said.

"*I'm* not competing," Olivia said as she turned and left.

She wrapped her scarf tightly around her neck as she stepped back into the cold winter air. There was a jewelry store in the next town. She just prayed no one in there had ever heard of Zach Archer.

Olivia had just finishing clasping the locket necklace around Kayla's neck when the doorbell rang.

The Abernathy twins, Deenie McCord, and Brianna Sweetser.

"We'd like to talk to Kayla," Brianna said.

Olivia didn't like this one bit. "Kayla," she called, "the other contestants are here."

Kayla came running to the door. "Where's Cecily?"

Brianna ignored her question. "We're here as a group to tell you we've voted you out of the pageant. If you really had inner beauty, you'd do the right thing and withdraw."

Kayla glanced at Olivia, then back at Brianna. "Why should I withdraw?"

"Because we all know you're behind everything that's been going on."

"Does Cecily think so?" Kayla asked. "I notice she's not among you."

"We don't brainwash as easily as Cecily," Eva said.

"Girls," Olivia said, "Kayla isn't withdrawing from the pageant. We were about to sit down to dinner, so if you'll excuse us." Olivia closed the door, and Kayla's eyes filled with tears.

"They all hate me," she said.

"Kayla, I'm really sorry this whole experience is being marred by all this trouble," Olivia said. "I know it's hard, but if you could just try to focus on what you're doing, working on your essay and speech, continuing your great job at school, you'll be fine. Try not to think too much about those girls."

"Because they're jealous bitches?"

Olivia was so startled she almost dropped the cup of tea she'd made to calm herself from her encounter with Jacqueline. "Kayla!"

"Well, they are bitches and they are jealous," Kayla said. "I hate them all." She ran upstairs and slammed the door, then blasted her stereo.

Olivia's cell phone rang. *Please be Zach saying he's coming home with takeout and a bottle of wine. . . .*

It was Ivy! She had off Wednesday from work and would fly up in the morning. Olivia was so excited she immediately called Amanda. The three sisters would be meeting at the cottage in just two days.

As always Zach accompanied Olivia to the cottage on Wednesday morning to await Johanna. But Olivia could barely get the door open.

The place was trashed. Everything was upturned. Broken glass and pottery littered the floor. Even the sofa had been slashed. And the painting of William and the three Sedgwick girls had been splattered with what looked like motor oil.

And on her bedroom wall, scrawled in marker

was: "LIKE MOTHER, LIKE DAUGHTER. DIRTY WHORES."

Olivia gasped. Zach let out a string of expletives. "Hello?"

Johanna stood in the doorway, glancing around at the mess. "Looks like someone trashed the place."

"Looks like it," Olivia said. "Any idea who?"

"What's that supposed to mean?" Johanna said, angry yet nervous.

"Here are your receipts," Olivia said, practically throwing the slips at the woman. She took the clipboard out of Johanna's hand, signed it, and handed it back. "From now on, I'll either come to your shop to deal with this or you can come to Zach's house."

"I'll need to check with the lawyer about that," Johanna said. "If he says it's no problem, I'll just come to Zach's every morning at eight."

Zach called the police. In minutes, two officers and half the town were on the doorstep. According to the officers, there didn't seem to be a single clue left behind.

Big surprise when Marnie Sweetser's cousin was on the force.

"Professional courtesy" got Ivy nowhere.

When Olivia called both Ivy and Amanda en route and explained why they should meet at an alternate location—Zach's—instead of the cottage, Ivy said her first stop in town would be the local police.

"You'd think the trashing of a house in that neighborhood would be big news in Blueberry," Ivy said when she arrived at Zach's. "The officer I spoke with acted like it was on a par with jaywalking!"

"I've got a lot to fill you in on," Olivia said, hugging her youngest half sister. "It's so good to see you, Ivy."

"You too, Olivia," Ivy said, her beautiful green eyes concerned. "I'm worried about how personal the attack on the house seemed to be."

And Olivia hadn't even told her about the message scrawled on the bedroom wall.

"I'm okay," Olivia assured her, squeezing her hand.

"Is Amanda here yet?" Ivy asked.

Just then, an unfamiliar white car pulled into the driveway. "Yup," Olivia said, with a smile.

As Amanda got out of her car, her shiny long brown hair gleaming in the bright sunshine, she glanced around at the house and grounds. "Gorgeous property. I don't remember this house, though. And I used to walk down to this part of the beach a lot during my summers."

"Zach built the house around eight years ago," Olivia explained. "He's an architect."

"So tell us everything," Amanda said as they went inside. "How did you meet? Are you having a hot and heavy romance?"

As the sisters settled into the living room, coffee brewing and two full hours before Kayla would be home, Olivia took a deep breath and told Ivy and Amanda everything.

Amanda sucked in her breath. "Oh, Olivia. Just to think of you going through that alone at sixteen. At some home for pregnant teenagers." She shook her head. "I wish I'd known. If only to hug you and tell you everything would be okay."

Ivy was silent for a moment. "I didn't think you

had a care in the world, Olivia. Back then, I thought you were one of the golden people, gorgeous, rich, perfect. Even that next summer, when you came back to Blueberry for the last time, I had no idea you'd been through something like that."

"I guess I learned to hide my emotions," Olivia said. "We all did, huh?"

"The three of us never got to know each other well enough to see past all that," Ivy said.

Amanda sipped her coffee. "Well, hopefully now, that'll change."

Ivy stood up, moved over to the window, and looked out onto the snowy beach. "How could he have let you think your baby died?" She turned toward Olivia. "How could he possibly do that? And then hand an infant over to a seventeen-year-old boy with no family? What the hell was he thinking?"

"Sounds like it worked out just fine," Amanda pointed out. "Zach rose to the challenge and then some."

Olivia nodded. "He was an amazing seventeen-year-old. Of course, our father dismissed him as a worthless townie when he found out I was seeing him and forbade me to date him." She thought about what Camilla had said. "A friend of mine thinks William entrusted Zach with the baby because William wanted me to be able to reunite with both of them one day. What do you think of that?"

"One day seemed to mean William's death, though," Ivy said. "What if he lived another ten, twenty, or thirty years? Would he have kept you from your child forever?"

Huh. Olivia hadn't thought of that.

"As if we could ever begin to understand the workings of that man's mind," Amanda said.

"And William sent birthday and Christmas cards in your name to Kayla," Ivy marveled. "Unbelievable. I can't decide whether that gives him points or not."

Olivia nodded. "I know what you mean. Everything is twisted."

Ivy sat back down. "Well, from what you said, your relationship with Kayla sounds like it's off to a wonderful start."

"It is," Olivia said. "She's so thirteen, though."

Ivy and Amanda laughed.

"Okay, enough about me," Olivia said. "I want to hear about the two of you. Did you bring me pictures of my gorgeous nephew?" she asked Amanda.

Amanda smiled and pulled a manila envelope from her purse. "Of course!"

"Declan wants us to have a baby right away," Ivy said, as the sisters looked at the pictures of adorable Tommy. "I think I want to wait a few years, though."

"He wants to start a family right away even though he's still a student?" Amanda asked. "That's brave."

"Yeah, because he'll be in school all day," Ivy said, smiling. "He has an entire year to go on his M.B.A." She stood up again and moved back to the window and stared up at the sky, her expression troubled.

"Ivy?" Olivia asked. "You okay?"

"I'm a little nervous about what's in my letter," she said. "I'll receive it on March twentieth. And I have to open it on March twentieth. But that's my wedding day. So do I open it before I say 'I do' or after?"

Olivia had learned at the reading of the will that William didn't approve of Declan. The good-looking son of one of Ivy's mother's friends, Declan used to work for William's corporation, then applied to business school.

"Did he work for William?" Amanda asked. "Directly?"

"No," Ivy said. "William was just a figurehead for the last couple of years. So he wasn't even really involved in the day to day. According to Declan, William didn't think a student was worthy of his daughter. I don't know what he could possibly have so against him. All William would ever say about the subject was that he didn't like Declan and that I was making a big mistake by marrying him."

"He wouldn't elaborate?" Amanda asked. "How could he say you were making a big mistake but not say *why?*"

Ivy shrugged. "My mom thinks William is just trying to control me. So does Declan. And I'm so conditioned to not give a flying fig what William thinks. But it bothers me."

"Because you think William knew something about Declan?" Olivia asked.

"I guess so," Ivy said. "But what? If he knew Declan to be a womanizer, say, wouldn't he just tell me? Or if he was an embezzler or whatever. Why not just tell me what his big gripe was? Why keep it secret?"

"Until your wedding day, too," Olivia said. "If he's going to reveal his problem with Declan in the letter you'll receive on March twentieth, wouldn't he specify you had to open it at the crack of dawn? *Before* you married him?"

Ivy ran a hand through her short auburn hair. "That's what I don't get. What I can't figure out. It's as though it doesn't matter to William whether I go through with the wedding or not. My mom thinks he's up to something. But I can't imagine what. I'm sure I'm inheriting the inn he owns in New Jersey. That's the only other property he does own. There'll be a bunch of silly rules for me to follow for a month, just like he put you two through."

"I'm just grateful my letter didn't stipulate that I had to spend the thirty days in the cottage," Olivia said. "I can't imagine ever spending another night there."

"I'm so worried about what's going on here," Ivy said. "Are you sure you and Kayla will be safe?"

"I'm not sure," Olivia said honestly. "And I don't know what's going to happen when the thirty days are up. There are two weeks left to go."

"You mean with Zach?" Amanda asked.

Olivia nodded. "Kayla is my daughter. So I'm going to make my home wherever she is. I just don't know if that will mean in her home. I don't know how Zach feels or what he wants."

"How do *you* feel?" Ivy asked.

"I love him so much," Olivia said. "I want us to be a family more than anything."

"Maybe you should tell him that," Amanda said.

Olivia closed her eyes and thought of him, how he came to her every night now. How they made love with so much passion. It was so hard to tell how Zach felt. He was sexually attracted to her, that she knew. And she was his child's mother. So there was a complex emotional core between them on that level alone.

But did Zach *love* her? That she didn't know.

Chapter 21

When Zach and Olivia arrived at Johanna's shop at eight o'clock the next morning, the door was unlocked, but Johanna was nowhere to be found.

"Johanna?" Olivia called out.

No answer.

Zach tapped Olivia's arm and pointed under the curtain of a fitting room. He'd know those three-inch-high red suede boots anywhere. And that overpowering perfume.

"You two are glued at the hip," came a familiar voice from the fitting room. "Someone ought to separate you with a machete or something."

Ah. All the better that Marnie was here and making vicious comments. He had a small recorder in his pocket. His plan had been to get Johanna talking again on her own turf. But perhaps he'd get the queenpin to incriminate herself.

Olivia shot him an uneasy glance, and he squeezed her hand.

Marnie came out of the fitting room, wearing her usual tight jeans—and a black lace push-up bra.

"Zach, give me a man's opinion, will you? Do you prefer this color on me, or this color?" she asked, holding a white and then a black sweater to her chest.

"I prefer *appropriate* on you," Zach said.

Marnie laughed.

"I heard that Don withdrew from judging the Inner-Beauty Pageant," Zach said. "I don't think you'll be able to seduce Pearl, so the pageant should be fair from here on in."

Marnie's smile faded.

"Johanna, I have my receipts for you," Olivia called out. "Are you here?"

"Johanna's not feeling well," Marnie said. "I promised her I'd handle the collection of your receipts and the signing of the clipboard. We are cousins, after all. It's the least I can do."

Zach stared at her, his gut twisting. "Maybe we'll stop by her house. Keep things on the up-and-up—and bring her some hot soup. Nasty cold?"

Marnie's wheels were spinning. "Nasty bruise, actually. Johanna's a bit of a klutz. Walked right into a door."

"Really," Zach said. "I'd think anyone who could walk on those four-inch heels she favors would be pretty steady on her feet."

"Well, that shows you what you know, Zach," Marnie said. She turned to Olivia. "You can leave your receipts on the counter. The sign-in sheet is there too. Until Johanna's on her feet again, I'll be minding her business," she added pointedly.

"I prefer to deal with Johanna herself," Olivia said. "Let's go, Zach."

"I wouldn't bother her if I were you," Marnie quickly said. "She's got something of a concussion and needs to rest. In fact, she's at the hospital," she added, stepping toward Olivia.

The bell above the door jangled, and a few women came in. Zach saw Olivia's shoulders visibly slump with relief.

"I'll be calling that attorney to inform you that you forfeited," Marnie said. "According to Johanna, you only have a window of fifteen minutes to produce your daily receipts and sign the clipboard. It's now eight-twenty."

"Actually, Marnie," Olivia said, "I read the fine print of the letter from my father's lawyer. It states that if Johanna Cole is unable to conduct her duties as caretaker during the thirty-day period the terms of the conditions are void and the cottage is mine."

A murderous glint shone in Marnie's eyes. "Well, then, enjoy your trashed house." One of the women perusing a display of turtlenecks asked for Marnie's help, and Marnie snapped, "We're closed."

"Let's go, Liv," Zach said, ushering Olivia out. "Is that true about the conditions?" he asked as they headed down Blueberry Boulevard. "No more eight o'clock visits from Johanna? It's yours fair and square."

"Not that I want it," she said. "But yes. I just have to talk to Edwin Harris, William's lawyer. And I suppose Johanna will need to verify that due to illness she was unable to meet her end of the bargain. It might end up being her word against mine."

"Nope," Zach said, pulling out the recorder. "Marnie verified it for you."

Olivia smiled. "Didn't you once say you were an architect, not a detective?"

Zach's cell phone rang. It was Blueberry's finest.

He, Olivia, and Kayla were wanted at the Abernathy residence.

"Now what?" Zach muttered as he opened the passenger door of his truck for Olivia.

Ten minutes later, Zach had his answer. Eva Abernathy woke up that morning to find a dead mole on her pillow—with a note that read: "You're next."

"We found this outside the twins' bedroom window," an officer said to Zach, holding up a pink wool glove with pink sparkly pompoms on the hem.

"And we're pressing charges," Clark Abnernathy said, his arm around his wife. "My daughters are dropping out of the pageant."

"Thanks to Kayla!" Eva screamed from the top of the stairs. "Because of her and her stupid jealousy, we have to drop out. It's so unfair! And now that we're out of the pageant, she gets to go first. It's probably all part of her big plan!"

"Officer, something supposedly connecting my daughter has been found each time there's been an incident," Zach said. "I think she's been set up. If my daughter were going to drop a dead mole on someone's pillow, she wouldn't be stupid enough to drop her very unique glove outside the girl's window. Or leave a perfume trail. Or hand her backpack to the principal when she knows the principal will pull out the evidence that will incriminate her."

"He might be right," the officer said to the Abernathys. "And the glove doesn't prove anything."

"Get out, all of you," Mrs. Abernathy said, her cheeks bright red.

Once they were back in the truck, Zach said, "I've

had it. I don't know what the hell is going on, but I'm getting to the bottom of it. *Now*."

"How?" Olivia asked.

"There are three girls left in the pageant besides Kayla. Marnie's daughter, Jacqueline McCord's daughter, and the Carle girl, Cecily. Two of the mothers have a huge problem with both of us, and one of them may be trying to frame Kayla. Let's go talk to Cecily's mother. Find out if she's gotten any threats."

A few minutes later, they pulled in front of the Carle house, a pretty extended Cape near the center of town. Rorie Carle welcomed them in, and they sat down at the kitchen table to coffee and scones.

"Rorie," Olivia said, "I want to say first that Kayla is not responsible for what's been going on."

"Look," Rorie said, "I'll be honest. I don't know Kayla well. She was over here once and seemed like a sweet, polite girl to me. But so do the Abernathy twins and Brianna Sweetser. I don't know what to make of Deenie McCord. But when one of the girls called Cecily first thing this morning to report what had happened, even Cecily wondered aloud if Kayla was the culprit."

"But Cecily stuck up for Kayla in public," Olivia said. "I'm surprised to hear that she thinks Kayla's the one."

Rorie shook her head. "She doesn't think so. She's just worried that it might be Kayla. If it's not, then it's Deenie. But in the window of time that the posters were taped up, Deenie was taking a makeup midterm exam. And everyone knows that her asthma precludes her from going anywhere near perfume. One sniff and she can't breathe. So . . ."

"So Kayla looks guilty," Zach finished.

"I'm sorry," Rorie said. "I like Kayla. So does Cecily. But we don't know what to think."

"Rorie, has Cecily been targeted in any way?" Zach asked.

Rorie's lips tightened. "I just found out about it this morning. She didn't want to tell me because she was afraid I'd worry, but she did receive a threatening letter just a few days ago. After hearing about the dead mole at the Abernathys', Cecily was so shaken up, she told me about it."

"What did the letter say?" Olivia asked.

Please tell me there is nothing connecting Kayla to this one, Zach thought.

Rorie got up and took her purse from a hall closet. She withdrew an envelope and handed it to Zach.

You're too pretty to win the Inner-Beauty Pageant. Everyone knows it's for ugly girls. So you're no competition. But you'd better keep your mouth shut. Or else.

Zach shook his head. "Unbelievable," he said, handing the letter to Olivia.

"Keep her mouth shut about what?" Olivia asked.

Rorie shrugged. "At first Cecily thought it meant sticking up for Kayla. But now she doesn't know what to think."

The phone rang, and Zach and Olivia quickly thanked Rorie for her time and honesty, then left.

"Now what?" Olivia asked, her expression as glum as he felt.

"Now we go for a walk," he said. "Between Marnie

this morning and this bit of news, I just need
a breather."

He didn't have to think about where to go; he in-
stinctively drove to the beach, and they headed
down the mile-long rocky path to the secluded strip
that was always deserted. Today was no different.

The beach was beautiful. Even gray and cold and
still covered in the last storm's snow, this particular
stretch of beach took Zach's breath away. And it
brought him back to the happiest days of his former
life, which seemed like a million years ago. He could
barely remember being that kid, watching his father
stagger up the road at two in the morning, dead
drunk. Watching his mother get into some stranger's
car at ten or eleven at night. Twenty minutes later
hearing the car door open, then close, then the
front door open and close. Coming downstairs in
the morning before school to find a half-eaten bag
of potato chips on the kitchen table, if he was lucky.
It was worse, of course, when he was younger and
couldn't fend for himself or earn his own money to
feed and clothe himself. But he'd been working
since he was fourteen.

With everything he'd been through, he'd never
once thought about stealing. Or lying. Or doing
anything other than what seemed right to him.
When you had parents whose values were completely opposed to yours, doing right came pretty
easily. If you were unsure of what was right in a
given situation, you imagined what your mother
or father would do and did the opposite.

His parents had died in a car accident not long
after he had left Blueberry with Kayla. He'd been

tracked down in Boston by a Blueberry cop, heard the "I'm so sorry to have to tell you this, son, but . . ."

The ramshackle house was his. Two bedrooms and peeling paint and falling down. At first, he'd been tempted to come back and live in it, enroll in the University of Maine. But he couldn't imagine going back, bringing Kayla back to that nothingness. Boston was new, about new possibilities, about his new life. He wouldn't bring her back to Blueberry until he could make a nice home for her.

"This is where she was conceived," Olivia said, shaking Zach out of his thoughts.

He glanced down at where she was staring, their secret place back under the stand of trees, where they'd made love, hidden from view. In Olivia, he'd thought he'd found the answer to every question he'd ever had in life.

"The last few months have been crazy," Zach said, kicking at the sand. "It was a combination of Kayla starting eighth grade and my starting to date Marnie. Eighth grade is a world's away from seventh," he said. "She slowly changed from this sweet angel girl to this defiant, moody creature who'd lock herself in the bathroom, then come out with so much black make-up on her eyes. She'd take her clothing allowance and buy shirts that said: "I Hate You More." Everything I asked, her answer was: 'Dad, as if!' or, 'You are so provincial.'"

Olivia squeezed his hand. "I'm sorry you had to go through all that alone, Zach."

"I can't tell you how much it means to me that Kayla has your family now," Zach said. "She has two aunts, a baby cousin, a grandmother. She'll have relatives who'll love her."

Olivia smiled. "My sisters fell in love with her the moment they met her. I wish they both could have stayed longer. But we're going to set up another visit in a few weeks. Amanda and Ethan will bring Tommy. And Ivy will bring her fiancé. And then we can all go to the wedding next month."

Olivia had looked so happy yesterday, sitting with her sisters, talking, laughing. When he and Kayla had walked in, Ivy and Amanda had jumped up and enfolded them both in hugs. They had marveled over how pretty Kayla was, complimented her on her shoes, asked her about school and the pageant. He'd always known she needed and would crave that kind of adult female attention, the kind that aunts were especially perfect at. And it took a huge weight off his back to know Kayla would have her Aunt Amanda and Aunt Ivy in her life from there on in.

He picked up a rock and flung it as far as he could into the ocean. Then another, harder, faster.

Olivia put a hand on his arm. "Zach, talk to me."

He chucked his last rock back on the ground. "I guess I'm doubting my judgment, Olivia. I'm the genius who took up with Marnie, thought she and Brianna were good influences on Kayla. I want to go with my gut about Kayla on this pageant business. But I don't know what the hell to think anymore."

"Does your gut tell you she's guilty?" Olivia asked.

"My gut tells me she's capable of everything that's been done. Including that note to Cecily. She's been jealous of Cecily for a long time. Before we even signed up for the pageant, she pointed her out in the school yard and said that Cecily thought she was 'so great.'" He closed his eyes and let the cold air wash over him. "I'm at a loss, Liv."

"Then let me help you out," she said. "I've only known Kayla for a little over two weeks. But as I've said before, in that short time, I've spent a lot of time with her. I've seen her at what I assume is her worst behavior, and I've seen her at her best. She may be capable of doing all those things—the posters, the threats, the dead mole—but I know in my heart she didn't do them."

"How?" he asked. "How are you so sure?"

"I feel it the way I felt it when I met you, Zach. I knew who you were that first day I met you. Those first ten minutes. That's how I feel about Kayla. I know she's *good,* Zach. Just like I knew you were good."

He grabbed her into a fierce hug, holding onto her against the wind. He tried to let go inside, the way he had so effortlessly when he was seventeen. But nothing inside him would budge.

He thought he heard her whisper, "I love you," but he wasn't sure if it was the wind playing tricks on him, or his mind—or if he was just remembering thirteen years ago, when she'd laid under him on this very spot and whispered, "I love you" in his ear.

He glanced at her, then out at the ocean. Whatever the case was, he wasn't ready to deal with it anyway.

After they left the beach, Olivia called all the hospitals in the area. There was no Johanna Cole admitted to any of them. She called Johanna's home several times and got the machine repeatedly.

Olivia drove past Johanna's house, and there were no signs of life. Same with the shop, which had a "Closed for Vacation" sign on the window.

No signs of life.

Do. Not. Go. Near. That. House. Olivia so ordered herself four times but got out of the car. She would just knock, then peer in the windows, just to make sure Johanna wasn't lifeless on the living room floor, having been beaten to a pulp by her dear cousin.

Olivia started up the front steps, her ears perked up for any sounds. But there was only the wind whipping through the trees. She knocked. No answer. She knocked harder. No answer. She peered through the bay window, but the curtains blocked her view.

"Can I help you?"

Olivia jumped. An elderly couple stood on the sidewalk, eyeing her nervously.

"I was looking for Johanna," Olivia said.

"She said she was going out of town for a while," the woman said. "Saw her loading her suitcases into that little car of hers. All that luggage barely fit in the hatchback. Then she peeled out like someone was chasing her."

Interesting. Marnie must have either scared Johanna away or made her leave town. Olivia wondered if Marnie was nervous that Johanna had loose lips.

She headed back to Zach's. No point in buying anything from town.

Time to call Edwin Harris, her father's lawyer.

"Ah, Miss Sedgwick, I'm so glad you checked in," Edwin said. "How are things?"

"Well, the cottage was broken into yesterday, so I

made arrangements with the caretaker, Johanna Cole, to meet at the shop she owns instead, but she wasn't there. This morning, she didn't come by the cottage, and her shop had a closed sign on it. I stopped by her house, and there was no answer. Phone either."

"I see," the attorney said. "Give me a day or two to get in touch with Ms. Cole, and I'll call you back."

Olivia hung up the phone, a chill creeping up her back despite how comfortably warm it was in Zach's house. If the cottage was hers free and clear, not that she wanted it, she didn't have to stay in Blueberry.

Would Zach see it that way? Would he assume she'd pack up and move back to Manhattan? He knew she didn't want to live in the cottage or use it as a summer or weekend residence.

Perhaps that was why he had acted as though he hadn't heard her when she'd told him she loved him. Of course, he might not have heard her; she said it in such a low voice she wasn't sure she said it aloud at all.

Did he think she was planning to leave? Go back to her life in New York? It dawned on her then that they hadn't even discussed it. How Olivia would "fit into" Kayla's life. Was she expected to buy a home of her own nearby so that she and Zach could raise Kayla like a divorced couple? Or like a couple who were sort of dating? If that was what you could call what they were doing.

Her insides twisted, Olivia went into the kitchen to make a pot of coffee. She heard the front door open, and Cecily Carle's voice.

"So your mom sleeps in the guest room," Cecily said. "That's a little weird, don't you think?"

"Totally," Kayla said. Olivia heard their footsteps on the stairs. "I can't tell if anything's going on between her and my dad. Anyway, whatever. I'm just really glad you're coaching me on my oral presentation. No one else will even talk to me."

"It does look pretty bad for you, Kayla," Cecily said. "I hate to say that, but it's the truth."

Olivia could hear Kayla crying. She wanted to rush up, but she needed to let Kayla be, let her and her friend talk the way teenagers talked.

"You want to know something I haven't told anyone?" Kayla said. "No, forget it. I shouldn't even—"

"You can tell me," Cecily said. "I won't tell anyone. If it's a secret."

"Okay. I think my mother might be the one who's been doing all this bad stuff," Kayla said.

Olivia gasped. She moved closer to the doorway of the kitchen to make sure she could hear.

"I mean, she's my real mother, right? And she wasn't around for my entire life, until now. How guilty must she feel? Incredibly guilty. Plus, she won the Inner-Beauty Pageant when she was fifteen. The pageant is probably so important to her. Maybe she'd do anything to see me win. Like make my competition drop out."

"Kayla, I don't know," Cecily said.

"Well, who else could it be?" Kayla said. "Brianna Sweetser wouldn't hang up like ten posters calling herself a slut, even if she is one. So I don't think she's the one doing all this, even though she hates me."

"What about Deenie McCord?" Cecily asked.

"I guess it could be her. I don't know her at all."

"Do you really think your mom could be the one?" Cecily asked.

"I don't know," Kayla said. "I've thought about it. It could be her. I mean, she really loves me. She'd do anything to make me happy. So of course she wants me to win."

"That does make sense," Cecily said. "Anyway, let's go over your speech."

Olivia made as little noise as possible. On one hand, she wanted to make a racket and let Kayla know she'd been in hearing distance. On the other, she wanted her daughter to have this time with her friend to work on her oral presentation.

She poured herself a cup of coffee and sipped it with a heavy heart. She'd talk to Zach about it all later.

That night, Olivia knocked on Zach's door. He sat on his bed, wearing only a pair of faded jeans, a set of blueprints spread out before him.

He was so, so beautiful. The moonlight cast its beams on his silky hair, his strong shoulders. She smiled at the memory of her sisters oohing and ahhing over him yesterday afternoon after he and Kayla had gone out grocery shopping. "He's so good-looking!" Amanda had said. "No—hot, hot, hot," Ivy had put in.

Maybe you should tell him how you feel. . . .

"Are these plans for a house?" she asked instead, her gaze on the blueprints.

He nodded. "This one was just finished. It's so

expensive that it hasn't sold yet. It's on the coast in Marbury, which is about forty minutes north of here."

She sat down on the edge of the bed. "It's beautiful. It looks like it blends right into the rocky coastline. You know what it reminds me of? That house you were sketching when I first met you. Whenever I showed up to meet you, you'd be drawing away, so engrossed you didn't notice I was there yet."

He smiled. "I was always surprised that you did show up. I used to bring my 'life's work' just in case you didn't, so that if one dream got dashed, I'd still have my house." He pointed at the blueprints. "This is that same one."

She saw now that it was. From the wraparound porch to the tree house in the huge oak to the gardens.

"I told myself I'd wait until you came back for Kayla," he said. "I waited until she was ten, and then I guess a part of me believed you probably wouldn't come. That that was a dream I *did* need to let go of. So I started building my dream house in Marbury."

"Do you know how many nights I would stare out the window of my apartment in New York at the glittering lights and wonder if you were out there somewhere, thinking about me, wondering what happened to me and our child? It was actually comforting to me to think that you didn't know. I mean, when I thought she was stillborn."

"Oh, Olivia," he said, taking her hand. "I can't begin to imagine how sad you must have been."

She glanced at him. "If only, if only, if only I'd known. I would have rushed back here."

"I know that now," he said. "But back then, I had nothing to go on but the lies your father told me. I was actually glad the building of the house would take three years. The longer we stayed in Blueberry, the easier it would be for you to find us. I figured you'd come up to visit your father or have some kind of family reunion. But you never did, of course. And then just a couple of months ago, my builder told me the house was ready."

Olivia's stomach sank. His dream house was ready. She'd come back to Blueberry in the nick of time.

And now he could go.

Her heart breaking, Olivia forced herself to focus on why she'd come knocking on his door in the first place.

Because I love Zach. That's why.

"Zach, there's something I need to talk to you about. I overheard Kayla and Cecily talking after school today. And I'm really concerned about some things Kayla said."

Zach gave her his full attention. He rolled up his blueprints and sat back on the bed.

"Kayla told Cecily that she thought I might be behind the posters and dead mole and nasty letters."

"You? Where would she get that idea?"

"She had a few theories. From how much I love her to how much her winning the pageant, as I did, means to me in making up for lost time. I didn't know how to handle it, so I didn't."

"I think you handled it just right," Zach said, running a hand through his hair. He glanced out the window, the moonlight glowing on his profile. "I've learned in the past couple of months that teenagers talk and talk and talk and say everything to each other that pops into their minds. I know she's confused as hell about everything right now."

"Including what's going on between us," Olivia said. "Cecily knew that I sleep in the guest room. So Kayla's definitely talking about her parents' relationship."

"I wish we had something concrete to tell her," Zach said, "but we don't."

Because he didn't know how he felt. Thirteen years was a long time. And he'd raised Kayla alone.

"Did your father's attorney get back to you?" Zach asked. "Is the house yours free and clear?"

"He hasn't called back yet," Olivia said. And when he did, Zach would pack up and move to his dream house on the ocean in Marbury. And Olivia would be in limbo, belonging nowhere in particular.

"Well, after this weekend, after the pageant is over, I'm putting this house on the market. I used to think it would be good for Kayla to grow up here because she was conceived in love here. But now that you're in her life, being here doesn't seem as important. She doesn't need the connection to Blueberry the way she did before."

Olivia was sure she'd hear from the attorney in the next day or so. He'd verify that Johanna was nowhere to be found, and, therefore, the conditions of the will were null and void. The cottage would be hers. Zach wouldn't have to safeguard her anymore; she'd be free to go.

And clearly, he would let her.

Chapter 22

"Dad!"

Zach jumped out of bed and raced downstairs. Kayla stood in the front hallway, pale and shaking in her pajamas, holding a letter. He took it from her just as Olivia ran out of the guest room.

"Kayla, what's the matter?" Olivia asked, her voice frantic. "What happened?"

Kayla pointed at the letter in Zach's hand, her finger trembling. "I . . . I found it sticking out under the front door."

Typed on a plain white paper was: "Kayla, if you don't drop out of the pageant, I will make your life a living hell."

Rage shot up through Zach so fast he almost slammed his fist against the wall. He passed the letter to Olivia, willing himself to calm down.

"What does that mean?" Kayla asked, tears welling in her eyes. "What are they gonna do to me?"

"No one is going to do anything to you," he said, kneeling down so that they were eye level. He wanted to tell her that she didn't have to worry, that they were moving next week, that she'd have a fresh start away from all this madness, but he was afraid she'd ask about Olivia. If she were coming too. And he wouldn't know what to say.

"I won't let anyone hurt you," Zach assured her, tucking the envelope into his pocket. "In fact, you're under parental orders to play hookey from school today."

She pumped her fist in the air. "Yes!"

It was amazing what a free day off from school could do.

I will make your life a living hell. . . .

The rage boiled in his gut again as the threat against his child sank in. *Damn it,* he thought, *what the hell am I missing?*

"Kayla, are you all right?" he asked.

She nodded. "I'm freaked, but I'm okay. I'm sure it's that weirdo Deenie. Or Brianna. I could totally take them. Well, maybe not Deenie. She's, like, a foot taller than me."

"I'm going into my study to think this through," he said, squeezing Kayla's shoulder.

They were definitely missing something, something obvious. But what? he wondered as he stared out the window. A light snow began to fall. With any luck it would accumulate into a blizzard and the damned pageant would be cancelled.

Coffee. They needed coffee and lots of it.

"Kayla, are you hungry?" Olivia asked as Kayla started back up the steps. "I can whip you up some pancakes or eggs."

"No thanks," she said. "I came down and had a cup of juice before I noticed the letter under the front door."

Olivia glanced at the grandfather clock. It was just before six. And still dark outside. Kayla didn't have to be up until seven. "Why are you up so early, anyway?" she asked. "Jitters about tomorrow night?"

"And tonight," Kayla said. "What if I screw up rehearsal? What if I can't figure out which way to exit the stage? What if I lose my place in my oral presentation? Cecily said I should look up a lot while I'm reading so that I'm not just staring at the speech in my hand."

"That's good advice," Olivia said. "You could look up after each paragraph, maybe. And put your finger on where you're up to. That's what I used to do."

"Great idea!" Kayla said. "I'm going to go practice, okay? I'm so glad I have the whole day and now all of tomorrow too." She ran up the stairs, the threat against her forgotten in her excitement.

Zach came out of his study. "She doesn't leave our sight until this pageant is over," he said. "Between the two of us, she should be okay."

Olivia nodded. "I'm going to make a pot of coffee. I'll bring you a mug."

"Thanks," he said, disappearing back inside the study.

Olivia took a filter from the cabinet, then saw that she hadn't emptied the old grounds from yesterday. As she dumped the old filter into the garbage can under the sink, she saw something that made her blood stop.

Scrap paper. With variations of what had been typed on the letter that Kayla found ten minutes ago.

Hey, loser. You'd better drop out of the pageant or I'll make your life hell.

Kayla Archer, drop out of the pageant, or you're dead.

She closed her eyes against the truth of what this meant. Kayla had typed the note herself, slipped it under the door this morning, and then "found" it. And then screamed for her father.

Which would explain why a day off from school had been able to calm her so quickly. There was no threat against her.

"Liv?"

She whirled around. Zach stood there, his expression questioning. She hated what this was going to do to him.

"Are you okay?" he asked. "I called your name three times before you heard me."

She let out a deep breath. "I found these in the garbage can under the sink," she said, as she handed the notes to him.

Confusion, then understanding dawned on his handsome face. He counted to ten, then rushed out of the room, taking the stairs two at a time. Olivia was right behind him.

He knocked, then burst in. Kayla was standing in front of her bureau mirror, a brush up to her mouth as if it were a microphone.

"Your mother found these in the kitchen trash," he said, his temper barely controlled. "Explain yourself."

"What are those?" Kayla asked, taking them from him.

Kayla read them. "Huh? What's this?"

"That's what we'd like to know," Zach said. "They look like practice runs to me. They look like you worked on the letter until you got it the way you wanted it."

"What?" she said, looking from Zach to Olivia as though she had no idea what they were talking about. Her confusion was replaced by anger. "Wait a minute. Are you saying you think I wrote these? And the one I found under the door?"

"That's what it looks like, Kayla," Zach said. "That's what I'm saying."

"I didn't!" she yelled. "I didn't write these!"

"You're looking me in the face and telling me you didn't write these or the one you found this morning?" Zach said.

"Yes," she screamed, tears running down her face.

Zach dropped down on her bed. "I don't know what to think. What to believe. Did someone break in in the middle of the night and leave more evidence to frame Kayla," he directed to Olivia, "and then leave the note under the door?"

"It fits all the other incidents," Olivia said. "Someone got into the Abernathy home to put that dead mole on Eva's pillow."

"And it wasn't me!" Kayla shouted.

"Okay, honey," Zach said. "I saw those notes Olivia found in the trash and *I* freaked out. I thought the worst for a moment and I was wrong."

"The creepy thing is, someone broke into the house," Kayla said. "While we were sleeping, someone was walking around our house. We're lucky we're even breathing right now."

Olivia thought Zach might spontaneously combust. He stood up and hugged Kayla, then apologized again and went back downstairs. "Let me know when you're hungry, sweetie," Olivia said, then followed Zach. Now she knew why he was so conflicted about this entire matter. She'd finally gotten a taste of what it felt like to believe Kayla guilty. As she had held those scrap papers in her hand, she had believed without a shadow of a doubt that Kayla had written the note herself. It felt awful to think the worst of a child. Her own child.

She had no idea how any of them were going to get through the next twelve hours.

It had snowed all day, but the light, wet flakes were obliterated the moment they touched the ground. Kayla fretted about what the sleet would do to her hair. If she was this concerned over a rehearsal, Olivia knew that she'd be a ball of nerves and fears tomorrow night.

Zach drove them to the town hall. He barely said two words, except to remind Kayla to stay within their view at all times tonight.

The auditorium lights were on when they arrived, but the room was empty. Zach and Olivia sat in the front row. Kayla ran up to the stage and practiced walking on and off from the left and right.

The doors opened, and Colleen came hurrying down the aisle with her usual stack of papers and clipboard. Marnie and Brianna followed a few minutes later, then Cecily and Rorie. Kayla hurried off the stage and sat between Zach and Olivia, her expression nervous. It was as though she remembered that someone had made a terrible threat against her.

Colleen peered around the auditorium. "Deenie McCord? Are you here?" Colleen shook her head and glanced at her watch. "It's five after, so let's get started. If Deenie doesn't arrive in the next ten minutes, she will not be able to compete tomorrow night. That rule is stated clearly in the pamphlet handed out at our last meeting."

"And you said that at the last meeting," Brianna called out. "So it's totally fair."

"What a brown-noser," Kayla whispered.

Deenie arrived with one minute to spare. "Sorry I'm late," she said, in a low voice. "I had to wait for my mom to get home from work so I could drive here. I live at the other end of town."

"You're here now," Colleen said. "So, before we move on to why we're here—to go over the order and how you'll be introduced and stage directions— I would like to say on behalf of the town of Blueberry that you've all displayed a great deal of inner beauty in the face of some serious ugliness. As you know, the Abernathy twins have dropped out of the competition because of the threat against one of the girls. Brianna, Cecily and today, Kayla, were all the victims of vicious remarks and threats. The police are involved and are—"

"I haven't received any threats," Deenie said, standing up. "I don't understand."

"That's a good thing, Deenie," Brianna said, rolling her eyes. "You're lucky."

"But why?" the girl repeated. "Because I'm not a threat to anyone? Because I couldn't possibly beat any of you?"

"You could beat us to a pulp," Brianna said, laughing.

There was a gasp, and everyone turned around. Jacqueline McCord was standing, her face red. "How dare you, you little princess," she spat at Brianna.

"Don't you dare speak to my daughter," Marnie yelled, bolting up.

"Everyone, sit down this minute!" Colleen called. "This meeting will come to order!"

Jacqueline and Marnie sat.

"This is ridiculous," Zach whispered to Olivia. "Colleen should put us out of our misery and cancel the pageant."

"If there are no further outbursts," Colleen said, "we can continue on with rehearsal. Kayla, you'll be up first. You'll read your essay on what inner beauty means to you, and then you'll smile at the judges and the audience and take a seat in one of the chairs that will be lined up in front of the back curtain. When Kayla sits, I'll announce that our next contestant to share her essay will be Cecily. Cecily, you'll then do the same as Kayla. And so on."

"That sounds easy enough," Kayla said.

"You're going to do great," Olivia assured her.

"Creepy," Kayla whispered. "I feel like someone is staring at my back."

Olivia glanced behind her. Deenie McCord was

staring—no, glaring—at the back of Kayla's head. And Jacqueline was doing the same to Zach.

Then Marnie slid her cold gaze her way, and the hairs on the nape of Olivia's neck stood up.

When Colleen finally dismissed the meeting, Olivia couldn't wait to get out of the room, if only to breathe some clean air.

Zach stared at the drawing he was working on, the lines blurring into nothing. He might as well forget trying to work. Until tomorrow night, he wouldn't be able to concentrate.

The phone rang, and he braced himself, but it was only William Sedgwick's attorney for Olivia. He asked the man to hold on, then ran into the guest room to get Olivia, expecting her to be excited for the outcome. But she seemed barely interested in picking up the phone.

"I see. Yes. All right. I'll do that. Thank you, Mr. Harris." She hung up and stared at the receiver.

"And?" he prompted.

"And the cottage is mine," she said. She didn't turn around. "As is an undisclosed sum of money. I'm to receive another envelope no earlier than thirty days after I first arrived in Blueberry."

"Another envelope? Meaning a check?"

She shrugged. "I guess. At least my mom will be all right," she said, finally turning around. "Do you know that if it weren't for my mother, I might not have come to Blueberry in the first place? I didn't think I could face the cottage or the memories, but my mother manipulated me with her financial problems."

"Interesting how things work out, huh?" he said. Crazy was more like it.

He was about to ask her what her plans were for the cottage, what her plans were period, what she wanted, but the phone rang again.

Zach should have braced himself this time. It was Rorie Carle. She had received another threat. "I wish my husband weren't away on business. He'd know how to handle this. Cecily is beside herself. She won't come out of her room."

"Was it a note?" Zach asked.

"Yes. It said, 'Tell Miss Perfect to drop out of the pageant or what happened to her sponsor will happen to you.'"

"Her sponsor? The owner of the hair salon next to Johanna's shop?"

"Yes. I rushed over there with a police officer, and there was no sign of Taffy. That's Cecily's sponsor's name. Taffy Johnson. And there were definitely signs of a struggle. The shampoo display was over-turned, and one of Taffy's shoes was just lying in the middle of the mess. It's as though she was dragged away, kicking and screaming."

"What do the police think?" Zach asked.

"They're not saying. They assured me they went over the place with a fine-tooth comb."

Yeah. Sure they did.

"Cecily wants to drop out. She's scared out of her mind. She won't come out of her room."

"I can understand that," Zach said. "Her mother's been threatened. Her sponsor has disappeared in what looks like violent circumstances." He paused. "Maybe all the girls should drop out, Rorie. This is beyond dangerous now. I think we should suggest to Colleen that the damned pageant be cancelled."

She was silent for a moment. "That would be so unfair to the girls," she said finally. "Look, Zach, your Kayla seems like a nice girl and all, but let's be honest, Cecily is Cecily. She'll win the competition. It's a lot of prize money and a monthly column in the paper. This could help her get a scholarship to the ivy league. We just have to get through one more day."

Cecily is Cecily? She'll win the competition? Excuse me?

"We might not have one more day," Zach said.

"Do what you feel is right for your daughter," Rorie said. "I'll do the same."

Zach hung up and filled in Olivia.

"Oh my God, Zach," Olivia said, "I just realized something. That makes two sponsors who are missing. Taffy and Johanna. Who's Deenie McCord's sponsor?"

"I assume whoever owns the jewelry store that Jacqueline works for," Zach said, picking up the phone. "I'm calling the police to see if there's any news about Taffy."

A minute later, Zach hung up, more frustrated than he'd been before he'd called. Supposedly, Taffy Johnson was having a hot and heavy relationship with a guy with a temper. They'd had two huge arguments in the past month, both of which resulted in overturned displays. Once she went missing for two days and came back annoyed at all the hoopla; she'd been shacked up in a motel with her boyfriend.

"So they're not even conducting an investigation?" Olivia asked. "What did they say when you mentioned that the former coordinator of the pageant also just up and disappeared?"

"They claimed that Shelby did no such thing, that she left a note explaining she was moving to Florida for the weather."

"I don't know, Zach. Two weeks before the pageant? Why make such a big commitment, then? Shelby had signed on to the pageant just the week prior to leaving town."

"Do you know anything about her?" Zach asked.

"I think she was a teacher at the high school. Biology or chemistry, I forget which. I could do a little asking around. Namely of Pearl. She's been laying low about everything that's been going on. Perhaps it's time I paid her a little visit."

"I'll go with you. For all we know, she's the one."

Olivia tried to smile, but she didn't have one in her. "I'll be fine, Zach. Her office is on the ground floor of the town hall, right near the entrance. You need to stay with Kayla anyway. I'll be back in an hour."

Zach nodded. "There's no way any of this is a coincidence. The former coordinator disappears two weeks before the pageant. Threats start getting made. You've been targeted since you arrived. And two sponsors have disappeared into thin air."

"You know, Zach," Olivia said, grabbing her coat from the hall closet. "I just realized that maybe what was going on with me wasn't connected to the pageant. I had no connection to it the first day. And that first break-in at the house, the smashed figurines, that occurred on my *first* night in Blueberry."

"So maybe we're looking at two different situations, two different psychos. The more the merrier," Zach said, letting out a deep breath. "The only decent thing the officer said was that there would be an officer assigned to the pageant, given 'all the hijinx.'"

"One officer?" Olivia said. "I hope he carries a big gun."

Olivia wasn't the only pageant mom to want answers from Pearl. As the town's manager of recreation, the pageant was her responsibility, period. And Colleen, who liked bossing and barking orders more than dealing with the fears of concerned parents, had fled the building a half hour ago.

"I want to know what will be done to protect my daughter!" Marnie was shouting when Olivia arrived. "If the police think that one lousy officer stationed in the back of the room is good enough, then I call for the elimination of Kayla Archer from the pageant. We might not have proof that she's been responsible for what's been going on, but there is *evidence*. And that should be red flag enough for you people."

"We people don't eliminate contestants from the pageant because they *might* be guilty, Ms. Sweetser," Pearl responded wearily. Clearly Marnie had been at it for a while.

"I'm glad to hear that, Pearl," Olivia said, stepping inside the office.

Marnie turned around and glared at Olivia. "I'm glad you heard what I said. Everyone wants Kayla out. So why don't you do the right thing for once?"

"The right thing would be for me to wait outside until you've finished your business here," Olivia said, stepping back out.

Marnie jumped up. "I am through. And after tonight, your daughter will be through, too. As if there's a chance she could win or even come in second. She's got all the inner beauty of the devil."

Olivia gasped. It was one thing for Marnie to hurl insults at Olivia, quite another to say something so despicable about a child.

Marnie rushed past Olivia, knocking her against the door frame as she stormed out.

Olivia rubbed her shoulder. "Pearl, if you can spare me a few minutes, I want to ask you a few questions about Shelby Maxwell."

"Why, is she back? I have half a mind to—"

"No, Pearl, she's not back. As far as I know, anyway. You said she just up and left, leaving a note behind for you. Do you happen to still have that note?"

Pearl stood and walked over to the ancient stack of file cabinets on the wall. "I'm sure I put it in her personnel file. I wanted it on record that she left us completely in the lurch. I'm sure the high school did the same."

"So she sent a note to the principal too?"

"What's odd is that she sent the letter to me, but cc'd the principal, as though coordinating the pageant was more important than her full-time job as a biology teacher! That's how nutty she clearly was. Who runs off to Florida with a man she met on-line?"

As Pearl nattered on while searching through Shelby's file, Olivia was beginning to think that poor Shelby might be the victim of the nut. Or, for all anyone knew, the nut herself.

"Ah, here it is," Pearl said, handing Olivia a plain piece of paper, the kind anyone would use to print letters.

Ms. Pearl Putnam
Blueberry Town Hall
Blueberry Boulevard
Blueberry, ME 04000

cc: Principal Smith, Blueberry High School

Dear Pearl,
I regret to inform you that I will not be able to take on the coordinatorship of the Inner-Beauty Pageant, after all. I've decided to move to Florida to hopefully marry a man I met via the Internet on a dating site. I'm sure you'll understand, as will Principal Smith, that this is an opportunity I can't pass up.
Thank you.
Shelby Maxwell

Olivia flipped it over. Nothing written on the other side. Nothing unusual about the envelope, either. Pearl's name and address were typed neatly in the center of the envelope.

"She didn't even sign her name," Olivia said. "That's odd, isn't it? Usually people sign their name

to letters between the close and their typed name.
If they bother typing their name at all."

"The whole thing is odd," Pearl said. "I just know
that whoever she met has her brainwashed. That
letter doesn't even sound like Shelby. I've never
heard Shelby use an officious tone like that. She's
a real people person, bubbly."

Someone wrote the letter for her. Typed on plain
white paper, like all the notes.

Next time I'll tighten it. . . .

What the hell had happened to Shelby Maxwell?

"I'll bet the boyfriend wrote it for her," Pearl continued. "Something a controlling type would do.
And he's clearly a controlling type if he convinced
her to move to Florida and give up her entire life
here."

Olivia would bet quite a lot that a man had nothing to do with it at all.

Chapter 23

The Inner-Beauty Pageant was well attended. The controversy brought out practically the entire town. But while people sat buzzing in their seats about teenaged girls going for each other's throats, Zach sat seething. He wanted to jump up and tell the morons behind him—grown women—that there was nothing amusing about girls being vicious to each other. About anyone being vicious to each other.

What Olivia had told him about Shelby Maxwell had him on edge all day. He didn't know Shelby well; he'd only seen her in passing a few times. She hadn't lived in Blueberry. And he doubted she now lived in Florida. Something terrible had happened to her. And showing the police a polite resignation letter, copied to her place of employment and her volunteer position, would hardly constitute a threat against her. The police would tell him to get lost.

He'd have to see this through. The pageant. He had a sick, sick feeling in his gut that tonight the psycho behind everything would make some kind of final move to win this thing. His only consolation was that Kayla would be in view at all times. When it wasn't her turn to speak, she would be sitting down in a chair just a few feet behind the podium. Zach glanced at the back of the auditorium. The officer, in uniform, stood by the doors. That barely helped the knot in Zach's gut.

Kayla was nervous too, but she hadn't seemed nervous about the threat made against her or the fact that someone was working so hard to frame her. She'd tried on so many different outfits today, and Zach had never been more grateful that Kayla considered him hopeless at fashion. She'd only wanted Olivia in her room, helping her with her hair, her clothes, her make-up, which Zach had limited to only enough to cover up her imaginary pimple on her chin, and lip gloss.

The front row in the auditorium was reserved for parents. Zach sat on the far end, Olivia next to him. Rorie Carle sat beaming next to her, fussing with a video camera. Jacqueline McCord was late, which wasn't a surprise. Marnie was next to Rorie. Colleen, the assistant coordinator, sat at the very end, looking exhausted.

The four contestants sat in chairs behind the podium. Kayla was biting her lip and alternating between bursts of smiles and looking like she might throw up. Cecily, next to her, was a model of poise. Deenie slouched and reminded Zach of a deer caught in the headlights. Her eyes were wide open and she stared straight ahead, as though afraid to actually see how many people were in the audience.

"Welcome to the Thirty-First Annual Inner-Beauty Pageant!" Pearl Putnam announced from the stage. "The pageant celebrates and values our girls ages thirteen through seventeen who know that beauty is only skin-deep. Each girl will read an essay on what inner beauty means to her, and then she will give an oral presentation on the most influential person in her life. Finally, she will answer three questions, one from each judge. The judges will then tally their scores and a runner-up and the winner will be announced. The winner will receive two thousand five hundred dollars in cash, awarded by our sponsors, and she will also be given her own monthly column for an entire year on the subject of inner beauty in the *Maine Daily News.*" Pearl took a breath. "So without further ado, let me introduce our contestants!"

There was a round of applause. Pearl read each girl's name and age, and each girl stood up and smiled, then sat down. Deenie had chosen to wear such a long skirt that she stepped on the hem when she stood, and there was some obnoxious snickering from the teenagers in the audience. Red faced, she shot back down.

Zach glanced at the row of parents. Jacqueline still hadn't arrived. Deenie appeared to be looking for her, her gaze straight ahead over the audience.

Just as Pearl opened her mouth to speak, the auditorium doors swooshed open, and Jacqueline strode in. She took her time walking to the reserved row, smiled at Deenie, and took her seat.

"All rightie!" Pearl said. "Our first contestant is Kayla Archer."

Kayla smiled and walked to the podium. She cleared her throat, then began reading her essay.

If any of you asked my dad to describe me, he'd probably say that I'm quite a handful. That's how people have described me my whole life anyway. Teachers and counselors at camp. And I have been a handful. I've said things I regret. I've done things I regret. I've been mean. Rude. I've been suspended from school for smoking in the bathroom. I made my little neighbor—he's only five now—cry because I told him monsters were going to eat him. I've called girls fat. I've called boys stupid losers. I've cheated on tests. I could go on and on about the bad things I've done. The bad person I used to be. Used to be is the key phrase. The Inner-Beauty Pageant completely changed me. Changed how I think about things. My mother won the pageant when she was fifteen, and I want to make her proud of me. I want to be the kind of daughter that a winner of the Inner-Beauty Pageant would be proud to have. But having inner beauty isn't about being a good person so that other people will like you. It's about being a good person just because.

Zach's eyes filled with tears. He noticed Olivia dabbing away at her eyes, so he knew she was full-out crying. Olivia reached for his hand, and they both squeezed.

Kayla read on, each word, each sentence making him prouder, making his heart move in his chest. Finally, she smiled and then walked back to her chair, and the audience burst into applause. None of the other contestants were smiling.

He shot Kayla a thumbs-up, and she grinned. He wanted to rush up to the stage and grab her into a hug, but he couldn't do that. And besides, Cecily was already at the podium. Her essay sounded a bit canned, in his biased opinion. Kayla's had been much more from the heart, much more honest and real. Cecily finished and also received hearty applause, and then Pearl called Deenie's name.

She didn't move. She stared, deer caught in the headlights, above the audience members' heads.

"Deenie, whenever you're ready, dear," Pearl prompted.

She still didn't move. Cecily gave her a gentle tap on the shoulder, and Deenie almost jumped.

She stood, looked at the audience, her face getting paler and paler. Zach glanced at Olivia; her expression told him she felt for the girl. This was painful. Zach eyed Jacqueline, who seemed to be mouthing, "Go ahead, it's okay," to Deenie. But Deenie only stood there. Finally, she took a step and then said, "I can't! I just can't!" and fumbled with the curtain behind her, disappearing backstage.

"All rightie!" Pearl said. "Let's take a moment's break and we'll be right back with our next contestant." Pearl hurried through the curtain. The audience was buzzing, clearly delighted by this turn of events. In a moment, Pearl was back. "Attention, please. Unfortunately, Deenie McCord isn't feeling well and will not be competing. Our final contestant is Brianna Sweetser."

Marnie jumped up and clapped. "Go, Bri!" she shouted.

Brianna's essay was good. Not canned or too perfect, like Cecily's. Not quite as down home as Kayla's. She talked about being from a broken home, and how that made her stronger, more independent, made her value the importance of relying on herself to attain her dreams. Her round of applause was the loudest, and she beamed all the way back to her seat.

Next, Pearl announced the start of the oral presentations. Zach had no idea what the difference was between reading an essay and giving an oral presentation of an essay, but he was in pageant land. Just as Pearl announced Kayla's name, Brianna let out a moan and gripped her stomach.

"Uhhhhhhhhhh," Brianna groaned, falling from the chair to the floor. "Mom!"

Marnie ran up on stage. "Bri? Honey, what is it?"

"My stomach. Owwwwwww!" She writhed on the floor in pain, the kind of pain Zach had once seen Kayla in when she had food poisoning after eating potato salad at the Blueberry Summer Carnival. Brianna continued to writhe and groan, and then she vomited all over her mother's feet.

Pearl called for the janitor, and a young man came lumbering up the stage with a mop and bucket.

"Can you continue on?" Marnie asked Brianna. "Do you feel better now that you've thrown up?"

Brianna's response was to vomit again. This time Marnie jumped out of the way. "Can someone help me carry Brianna to my car? I need to get her to the emergency room!"

At least ten men ran up onstage, their eyes more on Marnie's low-cut dress than on the girl in pain on the floor.

Marnie slid Kayla, then Zach and Olivia the dirtiest look she seemed capable of, then left through a side door, with one of the men carrying Brianna in his arms.

"Poor Brianna," Olivia whispered. "That looks like food poisoning."

"I think so too," Zach whispered back. "Coincidence?"

Olivia's face fell. "I hope so," she said. "I really hope so."

And then there were two. Kayla and her friend Cecily. Which told Zach that the guilty girl was either his daughter or her mentor, a girl Kayla looked up to. Cecily had had a lot to do with Kayla's turnaround these last couple of weeks.

But there was nothing remotely off about Cecily. And there was history, which Kayla had shared with just about the entire town, of off behavior from his daughter.

But Kayla was not a bad person. He knew that in his heart, in his gut. He knew it as Olivia seemed to know it. Kayla wasn't responsible for the vicious threats and attacks.

Which left Cecily Carle. He stared at her, taking in her concerned expression. He saw her say, "I hope Bri's all right" to Kayla. And then she turned to the audience and smiled, her hands folded in her lap, her expression changing on a dime.

He continued to stare at her, but all he saw was a girl smiling demurely. Great. Now he was wishing a perfectly nice girl who'd been nothing but helpful to his daughter was some kind of demon, just so it would make sense that it wasn't Kayla.

Pearl took to the podium. "Due to the sudden onset of illness, Brianna Sweetser is no longer competing. I would like to take a short recess, just five minutes, to give our remaining two contestants a moment to gather their thoughts and for our janitor to give the stage a final cleaning."

A curtain between the podium and where Kayla and Cecily sat was drawn closed so fast that Kayla was gone from his sight before he could jump up.

"Why did they close the curtain?" Olivia asked. "I want both girls in full view at all times. She ran over to where Pearl was sitting, in the first row of the aisle of seats on the left.

Zach saw Pearl say, "Oh, dear," then rush up to the stage and pull the heavy rope. The red velvet curtains parted.

The chairs were empty. Both girls were gone.

Chapter 24

"Where the hell are they?" Zach demanded, racing around backstage. He threw open the side door and looked, straining his neck to see beyond the hill, but it was dark, and the lack of street lamps didn't help. He hoped he'd catch a flash of Kayla's light blond hair, but he saw nothing.

"I want them arrested!" Rorie Carle screamed as Zach ran down the steps to where Olivia stood with Pearl and the police officer. "I knew Kayla was behind everything that's been happening, and now she's made off with my daughter! I want Zach and Olivia arrested right now!"

"And the charge is?" the officer asked, as though he'd rather deal with the inane Rorie than where two missing teenagers were in the midst of all the earlier threats of violence.

"They didn't raise her right!" Rorie screamed, then broke down in tears. "Oh, God, where's my baby? Why aren't you out there finding Cecily?" she screamed at the officer.

Zach grabbed Olivia's hand. "Let's go find Kayla."

They rushed outside, both looking in every direction. "Zach!" Olivia shouted. "Look! That's Kayla's watch!" They ran over to where the silver edges of her Hello Kitty wristwatch glinted. Olivia picked it up and squeezed it in her palm. "She must have dropped it on purpose, as a clue to where she was being taken. There's no way this clasp would come undone by itself."

"Did whoever closed the curtain pull a gun on Kayla and Cecily and drag them off?" Olivia asked. She froze. "Oh my God."

Zach felt his blood freeze. He gripped Olivia's shoulders. "What?"

"It's beginning to add up, Zach. Cecily. She was at your house the day before Kayla found that note slipped under the door. She could have planted those notes in the trash. And then slipped the note under the door early in the morning. She was in the house, Zach. And Kayla was over at Cecily's house the day before those markers were found in Kayla's backpack. Cecily made those posters about Brianna, then put the markers in Kayla's backpack!"

Zach closed his eyes. "Where the hell are they?" he said, his heart beating a mile a minute. If Cecily was that unhinged, who knew what she'd do to Kayla.

"Zach, if it's any help while we're searching," Olivia said, "Cecily has only resorted to threats and dead rodents. The noose on my bed. She hasn't hurt anyone physically."

"What about Brianna's sudden case of food poisoning?" Zach asked. "I'm sure we'll hear later that

Brianna had breakfast at Cecily's this morning. And where is Shelby Maxwell?"

Olivia's hand trembled around the watch. Zach steadied it. "We'll find Kayla," he assured her. "We'll check Cecily's house and the high school."

A crowd had formed outside the town hall. Two police cars pulled up, and Zach ran over to talk to the officers. One set of cops would follow Zach and Olivia to the Carle house; the other would check out both the middle school and high school.

Zach and Olivia got into his truck and sped down Blueberry Boulevard. He was about to turn left for the Carle house when he stopped short, then turned on his blinker and turned right instead. *Follow me,* he willed the police car. It did.

The drugstore's lights were on. Cecily Carle's mother managed the drugstore. And it closed at seven-thirty.

His heart beating so loud he could barely hear the officers shouting something about staying back, Zach ran to the front door. Locked. He ran around to the back, where a sign indicated, "Employees and Deliveries Only."

He tried the door.

Open.

"Kayla!" he called out, straining for a response, a whimper, anything.

"Zach, I think I heard something down those stairs," Olivia said, rushing to the top of the stairwell. "Like something skittering across a floor."

They rushed downstairs, the officers yelling at them to stay back. But Zach paid them no attention. There was a locked door in the basement behind the boiler.

"Stand back!" an officer shouted at Zach; then both cops kicked open the door.

Shelby Maxwell, her face crumpling in relief, was tied up to a pole in the back of the closet, a gag in her mouth. A tray of half-eaten food was on the floor by her feet. Empty water bottles littered the room. Her face was bruised, some patches black and blue, others bright red and brand new. One of her legs was twisted at an odd angle.

And Taffy, Cecily's sponsor, lay curled in a fetal position, her arm handcuffed to a pole. She was unconscious, the side of her face purple and black and swollen.

"Oh, God," one of the officers said, then radioed for help and an ambulance. After Shelby was untied, she rubbed her jaw, trying to open her mouth to speak.

"Ce . . . ly," she managed to say. "Cec-ly." And then she passed out.

Zach heard the sirens, which meant Cecily heard them too. He had to find Kayla. Had to.

"Zach, listen!" Olivia said. "I think I hear singing."

They strained to listen. Olivia was right. It was singing. Beautiful, melodic singing coming from another closed door at the far end of the basement.

Zach and an officer stepped over, the officer's gun drawn. The officer tried the doorknob. The door swung open easily.

Kayla sat handcuffed to a desk, a gag in her mouth, her eyes terrified. Cecily sat atop the desk, which was full of cosmetics. She held a tube of lipstick in her hand, which she applied to Kayla's chin. Kayla's face was already a rainbow of colors, her eyes lined in black and brown.

Cecily smiled. "Hi, Mr. Archer, Ms. Sedgwick," she said. "I thought that I'd give Kayla a makeover during the break. Ugly girls always have the edge in this competition. So now we're even."

"Cecily Carle," the officer said, "please step away from Kayla."

Cecily smiled. "Of course, officer. Anything to help." She moved toward the police, then screamed at the top of her lungs and reached for a large purse on the floor.

"Don't hurt my baby!" Rorie Carle cried, pushing Olivia out of the way. "Cecily! What have they done to you!"

"I couldn't let her win, Mom," Cecily said calmly, as though she hadn't just screamed like a banshee or lunged for the knife in her purse. The police officer had grabbed the bag first. "I couldn't let any of them win. And that bitch Maxwell told me to my face that I shouldn't even enter the pageant because she caught me cheating on my biology midterm. She was going to tell you, Mom! So I had to make her go away. I had to, right? I'm the best at everything. I'm Harvard material. You said so."

"Cecily?" Rorie said, staring at her as though she was an alien with four heads. "What did you do, baby? What did you do?"

Cecily smiled; then the murderous glint was back in her eyes. "I had to, Mom. Everything was spiraling out of control."

"What was, baby?" Rorie asked, clearly trying to hold it together.

"Everything, Mom," Cecily said, tears welling in her eyes. All of a sudden, the tears were gone and the demure, polite, smiling Cecily was back. Until her expression changed again. "And that bitch Taffy said she wasn't going to sponsor me. Said she was going to tell Pearl that there was something seriously wrong with me. All because I told her that if she didn't make my hair look like Reese Witherspoon's in *Legally Blonde,* I'd shove a hot curling iron up her ass and then down her throat. Do you know what she said to me, Mom?"

Rorie swallowed. She glanced at Zach and Olivia, then closed her eyes for a moment. "What, honey?" she finally managed.

Cecily pouted. "She told me my hair was too thick to look like Reese Witherspoon's. She said that only hair like Kayla Archer's could be cut and styled that way to look good. Do you know what else she said?"

"What, sweetheart?" Rorie asked, her voice cracking.

"She said my hair had the texture of straw from too much processing." She narrowed her eyes. "As if she wasn't the one who'd been processing my hair for the last year!"

"Cecily Carle, you are under arrest for the kidnapping of Shelby Maxwell and Taffy Johnson and Kayla Archer," a police officer said. "You have the right to remain silent. . . ."

Rorie stared at her daughter as Cecily was read her rights, then began to shake. The police led Cecily away, and another officer helped Rorie follow.

Zach and Olivia rushed over to Kayla and removed the gag from her mouth. She immediately began to sob hysterically. He frantically searched the desk drawers for a key, then saw it shining right on the desk where Cecily had been sitting. He turned the key in the handcuffs. They opened. His daughter fell limp into his arms. He picked her up. "Let's get her the hell out of here," he said to Olivia, then headed for the steps.

It was over. Finally, blessedly over.

Chapter 25

The children were running in circles around a large green meadow, the boy flying a kite in the shape of an octopus, the girl blowing bubbles from a wand. They were young, maybe four or five. And they were different children from the last different children. Entirely different from the original ones. The boy and girl were laughing. They were happy. Olivia was running after them, her arms outstretched like an airplane. She was laughing too. Happy too.

And then the girl and boy stopped short. Just stopped and looked at her, waiting.

"What?" she asked them. "Do you want some pineapple?"

They said nothing. Just waited. Watched her. No expression on their faces.

Were they shaking her? Why were they shaking her? How were they shaking her from three feet away?

"Olivia?"

She jerked up and realized she'd been asleep.

Dreaming. She'd curled up on a chair in the hospital lounge. Kayla's Hello Kitty watch was still clenched in her fist, so tightly it left an imprint. She glanced at it; it was almost 2 A.M.

Zach stood in front of her, pale and weary. He ran a hand through his hair. "She's okay," he said. "She's in a kind of shock and will need to stay a couple of days for observation. But she'll be okay. Physically anyway."

"She'll need some time to heal emotionally," Olivia said. "That was some ordeal. Especially with two adults beaten and bruised and handcuffed on the floor." Olivia shook her head, tears threatening. "She must have been beyond terrified."

He squeezed her hand. "It's all over now."

She glanced up at him, afraid that it was over for her as well.

"How do you think she'll feel about the pageant?" Olivia asked. Pearl and Colleen had come by the hospital to see Kayla, and they'd announced that after a committee meeting with the town council, this year's pageant would be considered officially cancelled due to unforeseen circumstances interfering with the contestants' ability to compete. "All that hard work ruined by a girl with serious mental problems."

"I think she just might start understanding something about process," Zach said. "How it's the doing of something that provides the real reward, not the prize."

Olivia nodded. "You're right." She let out a deep breath. "Cecily was behind everything? How could one girl do all that? How could she be so seemingly normal, yet—" She let out a breath. She barely had the energy to speak the words.

"A detective was trying to explain it to me a couple of hours ago," Zach said. "Something about psychopaths being highly functioning. I was so worried about Kayla I barely paid attention."

"Are Taffy and Shelby going to be okay?" Olivia asked.

He nodded. "They both have broken ribs. Shelby's leg is broken, and Taffy's jaw is broken. Cecily had Shelby locked up in that room for a little over two weeks."

"And her mother had no idea any of this was going on? That her daughter was completely insane?" Olivia asked. "It's so hard to believe."

Zach sat down next to her. "Cecily had a lot of people fooled."

Olivia twisted her hair up into a knot atop her head. "What I don't get is the timing. Cecily trashed the cottage the day I moved in? That makes no sense. She didn't know of my connection to Kayla. All of those early incidents—why would Cecily have targeted me then?"

"That stuff might have been the work of Johanna or Marnie," Zach said. "We may never know."

"Where is Johanna?" she asked. "What do you think Marnie did to her?"

"Maybe sent her away?" he suggested. "Maybe has her body stuffed in a bag in a closet? I have no idea. No idea if she's capable of that. I have no idea of anything anymore."

She reached over for his hand and held it. He

slipped it away and then stood up. "I'm going for more coffee. Should I bring you back a cup?"

She nodded and watched him go, so worried about his state of mind. He was very likely in a state of shock himself.

I love you, she whispered softly after him.

Olivia put the cottage on the market. She'd spoken to her sisters, and they both were glad to see it for sale. Neither of them had good memories of that house, they'd told her. They'd be as happy as Olivia to know it was out of the family, irrevocably changed into someone else's home.

She stood on a patch of yellow grass across the road from the house, staring up at it, comforted by the "For Sale" sign on the front lawn. She'd come to say good-bye to a chapter in her life.

Her cell phone rang, and she hoped it was Zach telling her to come home.

Home. She had no idea where that would be. What that even was. Home felt like Zach's house, but even that would soon be no more. Zach had also put his house on the market. He'd told her he wanted to be out of Blueberry within the week, as soon as he could secure movers.

He said nothing about her coming with them. Him and Kayla.

It had been four days since the night of the pageant. Since Cecily's arrest. Since Kayla had been discharged from the hospital, in good health but shaky, scared. Emotionally scarred. Zach had told Olivia he was taking a solid month off from work.

He'd recently finished a project for a client and wouldn't be leaving anyone in the lurch.

What about me? she wanted to scream from the rooftops. What about us? But she didn't want to add to his pressures. He was still in a state of shock over what could have happened to Kayla. If he wanted Olivia to join them in Marbury, he would ask. Perhaps he wanted her to go back to New York, to let him and Kayla be. They had been safe until she had arrived.

A car honked, and Olivia turned, surprised to see Johanna's little red car pulling over in front of the house. Johanna got out of the car, her expression grim. She was oddly dressed, as though she forgot it was winter. She wore a sundress with a light cardigan over it and high-heeled sandals, her feet encased in white peds with pink pompoms. She also wore red earmuffs and orange wool gloves.

"Johanna, aren't you freezing?" Olivia asked, hoping her voice sounded natural. From the way the woman was dressed, and her expression, plus the fact that she'd been who knew where for a week, Olivia didn't want to take any chances on making her angry. They were alone out here; the nearest neighbors were a quarter mile down the road.

"I don't feel a thing," Johanna said, walking toward where Olivia stood across the road. She sat down next to her on the cold, hard, yellow grass, leaning back against the rocky hillside, and stared up at the house. "I like this view of the place," she said. "I often sat here in the past month, just looking at it. Before you came, I would sit here and imagine it was mine.

I was so sure it would be too. But then William left it to you."

"Johanna, are you cold? I have a blanket in my car," Olivia said.

"I don't feel a thing," she repeated. She glanced at Olivia. "Will you sell the cottage to me?"

"Sure," she said. "You can put an offer in through your broker or through mine."

"A broker? Olivia, don't be silly. I don't have any money."

"Then how will you buy the cottage?" Olivia asked.

"You'll give me a good deal. Say, four hundred? That's what I have in my checking account. I would have had more, but I finally paid February's rent."

"Let me talk to my broker," Olivia said, hoping that Johanna didn't have a knife or a gun hidden on her somewhere. The woman was oddly calm, but there was a maniacal quality to her serenity.

"I shouldn't have trashed the house," she said, kicking a mound of dirt with the heel of her sandal. "Now I'll have to spend a fortune renovating."

"Why'd you do it?" Olivia asked.

"Because you didn't deserve it," Johanna said, glancing at her. "You're an ungrateful slutty opportunist, just like Marnie said. You were a bad daughter; then when your father died you came up here to take your inheritance. And Marnie's boyfriend too. You deserve to die, Olivia."

Johanna didn't move. She sat there calmly, then began kicking the mound of dirt again. "If you'd been in the house the night I trashed it, I would have trashed you too. Slit you open with a butcher knife, maybe."

"I loved my father, Johanna. I really did," she said, but she finally knew it wasn't true. She had loved him once, when she was very, very young. But she'd stopped loving him, stopped liking him, stopped expecting any kind of love from him when she was a girl, way before she'd gotten pregnant. He'd been a terrible father, plain and simple, to her and to her sisters, and whatever his reason for manipulating so many lives so that she would think her baby had been born dead, he'd had no right. The anger and bitterness she'd felt when she'd first learned what he'd done had been replaced by acceptance of her father for the man he was.

"Well, he didn't love you," Johanna said. "You were a big disappointment to him. Yet here you are, inheriting his house and just selling it when it should be mine."

"If you didn't want me to have it, why did you leave?" Olivia asked. "Because you left and didn't collect the receipts, I got the cottage—and before the thirty days were even up."

"That bitch Marnie threatened me," Johanna explained. "She said I had a big mouth because I told you too much. She's such an ass. Like if it was such a big deal, I wouldn't have told her I told you what I told you."

"So Marnie was angry because she was in on everything with you?" Olivia asked.

"I'm not allowed to talk about Marnie behind her back," she responded, getting up. "You're like the devil, Olivia. You get me to talk about things I'm not supposed to. Did you know that I've spent some time in mental hospitals? Marnie said she might have me committed again. That's why I agreed to leave. Do you believe that she thinks I'm a bad influence on Brianna? She's my niece! I love her!"

Olivia started to back away, but there was nowhere to go, nowhere to run. The hillside stretched in both directions for miles. And across the road was the cottage and forest on either side, the beach in back. She'd never make it to her car, even with Johanna in those sandals.

"I'm going now," Johanna said. "I just wanted to come see the house one last time. Of course you had to be here to ruin it for me. Now I'll think of you every time I think about the last time I saw the cottage. And I hate your guts." She blinked a few times, as if to get rid of Olivia's image. She cocked her head to one side. "You have his eyes, did you know that? Your dad's eyes. The color, not the shape."

And then she walked away, as calmly as she'd come over. Olivia stood frozen, waiting to see the glint of a knife or the barrel of a gun. But Johanna walked to the car and got in, turned on the ignition, and rolled down the windows as though it were spring and not, say, thirty-six degrees. "Bye, Olivia. I hope you rot in hell."

And then she jammed on the gas and turned the car in Olivia's direction.

"Oh, God, no," Olivia screamed as she ran. She could only run parallel to the hillside. There was nowhere to go.

Another car horn blared, and Johanna stopped

short. Stopped short of pinning Olivia against the rocky hill.

Marnie and Brianna. Marnie shouted something to Brianna, then raced out of the car toward Johanna.

"What the hell are you doing?" Marnie screamed at Johanna.

"Taking care of what I should have before you blackmailed me into leaving," Johanna said. "I should have strangled her when I had the chance—when I left the noose."

"Jo, come on with us," Marnie said slowly. "We'll go back to my house and talk, okay? She's not worth it."

"He should have left the house to me!" Johanna yelled, breaking down in sobs. "Why did he leave it to her? And look—she doesn't even want it. She's selling it. I could never afford to buy it. I should have killed the bitch when I had the chance!"

"Not in front of Bri," Marnie hissed.

"Shut up," Johanna said. "You're a wuss. You couldn't go through with any of our plans. You were just all talk. Well, I'm *not*."

Johanna backed up the car, and in that instant, Olivia dove out of the way, falling on a shard of rock on the hillside. She tried to get up, but the pain was so intense, and her leg wouldn't listen to her brain. It was broken, she knew. And she was trapped. She inched as best as she could out of the way. Marnie screamed, "No!" and raced over to Olivia and began pulling her by the arms out of the way as Johanna slammed on the gas and drove at least fifty miles an hour toward Olivia as she half crawled, half let Marnie pull her out of the way.

Johanna's car crashed into the hillside, the left wheel a foot away from Olivia's leg. Marnie collapsed next to Olivia, her breathing ragged.

"Mom!" Brianna screamed, racing over.

"We're okay," Marnie told her daughter. "It's over. She can't hurt anyone anymore."

"Just like Cecily," Brianna said.

Marnie nodded. "Call the police, honey," she told her daughter. "And call Zach Archer."

"Thank you," Olivia said. And then everything faded to black.

The dream boy and girl were still waiting. They stood in the meadow, wildflowers at their feet. The boy held a coconut. The girl was eating a chocolate bar.

"What is it?" she asked them. "Do you need something?"

They said nothing. Only stood and waited. But for what?

The girl held out the chocolate bar, and Olivia wanted it, wanted it so badly. She never craved chocolate. The only time she'd ever craved chocolate had been when she was pregnant.

She reached for it, but though the girl didn't move back, the chocolate remained out of reach.

"Chocolate," she said. "Chocolate."

"Olivia," a voice called. Unfamilar. "Olivia? Are you dreaming about chocolate?"

"Chocolate," she said, her eyes fluttering open. "I

was dreaming." She had dreamed of the boy and girl again, the different ones. She suddenly wanted chocolate. She tried to sit up, but she couldn't. She opened her eyes.

"Olivia, you're in the hospital. Your leg is broken, but you're fine. Can you hear me? Did you hear what I said?"

"My leg is broken, but I'm fine," she repeated.

"Olivia, my name is Dr. Fielding. You're also pregnant."

Olivia's eyes opened wide. She stared at the doctor. A young woman with a pen behind her ear. A white coat. She looked nothing like the staffers at Pixford. Olivia relaxed. Pregnant? She was pregnant? She moved her hand down to her belly, a peace she hadn't felt in years settling over her, along with a new kind of happiness. "I'm pregnant," she repeated, the words like magic. "Pregnant."

"Good thing?" the doctor asked.

"Very good," Olivia said, smiling. "By any chance is it twins?"

The doctor smiled. "It's a bit too early to tell."

Olivia smiled. She'd dream about the boy and girl until she gave birth. Maybe in the next dream they'd continue running and laughing. They could stop waiting. She knew that she was pregnant now.

"Doctor," Olivia said, "what happened to Johanna Cole and Marnie Sweetser. Are they all right? And Marnie's daughter, Brianna?"

Dr. Fielding's expression changed. "Marnie Sweetser and her daughter are fine. Johanna didn't make it. She died on impact."

Olivia took a deep breath and nodded.

"There are two people waiting very anxiously to see you," the doctor said. "Zach and Kayla Archer. Shall I send them in?"

"Yes," Olivia said, desperate to see both of them. "Yes, yes, yes."

The doctor smiled and opened the door, and the two great loves of her life came in. She had big news to tell them both. But perhaps she would wait, give Zach a chance to make some decisions on his own before she sprung news of the baby on him. She didn't want the pregnancy to dictate his choices. She wanted him to choose her or not.

And so she let them hug her and kiss her, and she responded to all their questions about how she felt, which was more than fine, now.

Like the dream children, she would wait.

The next day, Olivia was released from the hospital on crutches. Zach wheeled her to the truck and helped her inside, Kayla silent at her side.

"Honey? You okay?" Olivia asked her.

Kayla's face crumpled and she burst into tears, then turned and ran across the parking lot to a bench at a bus stop.

"What the—" Zach said, staring after Kayla.

Olivia inched back out. "Help me back into the wheelchair. I think I might know what's wrong."

"Do you think she's overwhelmed by everything that's happened?" he asked as he helped her into the wheelchair.

Olivia nodded. She'd been through hell for one thirteen-year-old. She'd learned of Johanna's death from Brianna, who'd come to see Kayla at the hospital. The girl had apologized for not believing Kayla, for being so mean, and she'd broken down in tears about her aunt trying to kill Olivia. Kayla and Brianna had hugged and talked for hours, and the therapist who would be meeting with Kayla twice weekly had told Olivia and Zach that the new friendship between Kayla and Brianna would help both girls tremendously.

After a long session with detectives, Marnie had confessed to beginning her relationship with Zach after learning from her cousin that Zach's daughter was the daughter of William Sedgwick's estranged daughter, and that he was on his deathbed. Marnie told police that she really didn't know if Johanna loved William or not; her cousin had never been "quite right" and had spent time in mental hospitals from the time she was in high school. Apparently, Marnie knew Johanna had broken in that first night and warned her cousin to never do it again, especially because another cousin of theirs was on the force and it would be an embarrassment to him if Johanna was caught. Johanna admitted to Marnie that she'd been responsible for trashing the house and leaving the noose on Olivia's chest.

All the other incidents and threats had been the work of Cecily, who was currently under observation in a psychiatric ward in a mental hospital.

Marnie had been responsible for one thing: the photograph of the castrated man left on the guest bed after Olivia and Zach had made love for the first time. Marnie confessed that she'd suspected Zach had cheated on her with Olivia that night. The next morning, when she'd come over, she'd left the photograph and scribbled the note on the guest bed when Zach had been in the shower. It had been a test, to see if he'd react as she thought he would. By admitting to sleeping with Olivia. And he had.

Olivia closed her eyes for a moment, willing the images of all that had transpired away. Marnie had come to see her in the hospital yesterday and had apologized for how horribly out of hand everything had gotten. Olivia thanked her for saving her life, and a truce was formed. Marnie also mentioned that she and Brianna would be moving far away for a fresh start. Olivia thought that was a good idea.

"You okay, Liv?" Zach asked, his hands on her wheelchair. "You seem a million miles away."

"Just thinking about everything that has happened," she said, taking a deep breath. "I'm okay. I'll go try to make things as okay as I can for Kayla."

Zach nodded and wheeled her over to where Kayla sat, her knees up against her chest, her face buried in her hands. Zach walked back to the truck, and Olivia wheeled herself closer to Kayla.

"Kay," she said. "I think I know why you're so upset."

The girl sniffled. "It's not because of the pageant. I don't care about that anymore."

"Because you don't need a sash around you to tell you you have inner beauty?"

"Because nothing matters," Kayla said, breaking into sobs again. "You could have *died*, Mom."

Olivia's heart moved in her chest, and her own eyes filled with tears. That was exactly what she thought was troubling Kayla. The girl had just gotten her mother back and she'd almost lost Olivia again.

"Come here, sweetheart," Olivia said, stretching out her arms.

Kayla flew off the bench and snuggled against her, wrapping her arms around Olivia. "I love you so much, Mom," she said in broken sobs against Olivia's coat.

Olivia lifted up Kayla's chin. "I love you too, Kayla. I always have and I always will."

"No matter what?"

"No matter what," she assured Kayla.

"So why did Daddy say he didn't know if you were coming with us to Marbury?" Kayla asked, the tears returning. "If you love me and want to be my mother, why aren't you coming?"

Olivia's heart sank. Kayla must have asked if Olivia was moving with them, and Zach must have answered honestly with an "I don't know." Because he hadn't yet decided if he wanted her to live with him, if he wanted her in *his* life.

"Honey, I want to assure you of something. Even if I don't live in your house, I'll live within walking distance. I promise you that."

Kayla brightened. "Okay, that sounds good. But I'd rather you lived with us. Do you want to know why?"

Olivia nodded.

Kayla opened the backpack that was slung over her shoulder and took out her pink Inner-Beauty Pageant folder. She withdrew two pages and handed them to Olivia.

Olivia smiled. It was Kayla's oral presentation, titled "The Most Influential Person in My Life."

A long time ago, my mother, Olivia Sedgwick, won this pageant. I went to the town hall and asked Mrs. Putnam if I could see copies of my mother's winning essay and oral presentation. Not so I could copy it or anything, but so I could just learn more about her. You see, my mother and I were separated from the time I was born until just recently. I don't want to get into all the details, because if there's one thing I've learned lately, it's that some things are private. Anyway, I'm just getting to know my mom, and I thought that reading her essays would help me get to know her even better or maybe even faster. It turned out that my mom's oral presentation about the most influential person in her life was about two people: her half sisters. My aunts Amanda and Ivy, whom I met for the first time just this past week. My mom wrote that there was no way she could choose between them, that even though they were her half sisters, they made a whole in terms of influencing her the most. The judges said they agreed with exactly that phrase.

So I'm using that phrase too. The most influential person in my life is my father and my mother. Because they are two halves of a whole for me, and now our family is complete.

"Oh, Kayla," Olivia said as she finished reading. "This is absolutely beautiful. I'm so touched. And so honored. And I know your dad will be too. Will you share it with him?"

She nodded, then flew into Olivia's arms for a hug. "Can I wheel you back to Daddy?"

Olivia smiled, and Kayla gently pushed her chair back to the truck. Once they were on the road to Zach's house, Olivia rested her hands on her stomach. *Everything's going to be okay,* she said silently to the baby growing inside her. *Zach and I are two halves of a whole. Neither of us is quite complete without the other. I just hope your daddy feels the same way.*

Olivia glanced out the window at the light snow falling, at the moving scenery. She slept most of the way back to Zach's house. She thought he'd said something about having called her mother, that Candace was flying up this afternoon. The next thing she knew, she was lying on the guest bed, the blankets pulled up to her waist. Her medicine and a glass of water were on the table next to her. And a "Get Well" card from Kayla and a vase of tulips were next to the lamp.

"Hi, how are you feeling?"

Olivia tried to sit up, but she felt so dizzy. That was her mother's voice, she was sure of it. She blinked a few times, and yes, there her mother was, her face full of concern.

"Kayla is so beautiful," her mother said. "She has your hair."

Olivia nodded. "Hi, mom. I'm glad you're here."

"And Zach seems absolutely wonderful," her mother continued. "So handsome. And clearly wealthy!"

It was almost a relief to know that some things never changed—like her mother. Olivia, Zach, and Kayla would never be the same.

"And here he is now," her mother said, beaming at Zach, who did indeed look gorgeous, as always.

"So, your mom and I have been talking," Zach said. "I thought that since the new house in Marbury is so big, your mom could have her own wing. A big bedroom and bathroom. Her own Jacuzzi too."

Candace beamed.

"Of course, I mentioned to her that since I was setting up shop in Marbury, I really would need a new part-time secretary. And your mom informed me that she used to be a secretary, albeit for a few weeks before she met William. And guess what, Olivia?"

Olivia couldn't help smiling. Zach was good, that was for sure.

"Your mother suggested that she take the job," Zach said. "Isn't that wonderful? Kayla will have her grandmother right in her new home."

"I'd like that," her mother said, tears welling up in her eyes. "Say yes, Livvy."

"Of course, Mom," she said, squeezing her mother's hand.

"Now where did that gorgeous grandchild of mine get to?" Candace asked, leaving the room.

"I thought that would make you happy," Zach said, sitting down on the edge of the bed.

"It did. Very." She waited on pins and needles, the hope making her chest hurt.

"I took a risk on calling your mom and inviting her up," Zach said. "But I believed in here," he added, patting his chest, "that she was as in the dark about Kayla as you were. When I called her, she broke down on the phone, sobbing that she hadn't known, that she was terrified you wouldn't believe her, that you'd never speak to her again, that she wouldn't ever know her grandchild. We talked for a good hour."

"I can't tell you how much that means to me, Zach," she said. "I'll always have some issues with my mom, but I love her. And I've been so worried about her. Now I'll know she's secure and safe—and working. I think she'll love it. And I know she'll love getting to know Kayla. She'll spoil the girl rotten."

Zach laughed. "So, until we move to the new house, I thought we'd put your mom in the guest room. She'll be comfortable here, won't she?"

Olivia nodded. "I'm sure she will be. And I'll be fine on the living room couch. It's so big and comfy."

He laughed. "Silly, I was hoping you'd move into my bedroom. *Our* bedroom." He lay down beside her, gently stroking her cheek.

She stared at him, the words slowly sinking in. "Oh, Zach," she said, so happy that the tears just started pouring. "I thought you'd never ask. I wasn't *sure* you'd ask."

He held her gaze, his fingers caressing her cheek. "I love you, Olivia Sedgwick. I've loved you from the moment I met you."

She wrapped her arms around his neck. "I love you too. And the same for me."

"Will you marry me?" he asked. "Make our family complete?"

"Yes," she whispered into his ear. "Yes, yes, yes. I've wanted to marry you since I was sixteen. Olivia Archer," she said, trying out the new name she'd adopt. "Has a beautiful ring to it, don't you think?"

He nodded. "How's this for a beautiful ring?" he said, reaching into his pocket and handing her a small black box. He opened it, and she gasped. The round diamond sparkled. He slipped it on her finger, and for a moment, they lay there, admiring it. "Thank you, Zach," she said. "I love it. And I love you." There was so much more she had to tell him, but for this moment, she just wanted to let his declaration of love, his marriage proposal and her acceptance, linger in the air, in her mind, her heart.

He leaned over for a kiss, so soft and gentle. "Ah, I almost forgot." He reached over to the bedside table and pulled out an envelope from the drawer. "A letter from your father's attorney arrived for Kayla. The envelope says, 'For Kayla Archer, to be read at the discretion of her mother or father.' Let's open it. Maybe it will explain a few things."

Olivia slid out the single piece of paper and read aloud, "Dear Kayla, I wanted to give you the best life I could. I made some mistakes, yes, but I have no doubt I did the right thing, albeit the wrong way. I hope one day you'll forgive me. Your grandfather."

Zach took the letter and slid it back inside the envelope, then set it on the table. "Short and sweet, but I think this will mean a lot to Kayla. She's ready for it. It may help her forgive him."

"Forgiveness," Olivia repeated. "It's funny—I don't even think in those terms anymore. My heart is so full, there's no room for anything but love." She smiled at him. "Oh, and one more thing, Zach."

"What's that?" he asked, holding her hand.

She took their entwined hands and placed it on her belly. "We're going to have a baby," she whispered. "I was told in the hospital. Kayla is going to have a little brother or sister." As she said the words, she realized that she would never again be haunted by the dream children. She would dream of them, she was sure, but they would continue running and laughing, singing and dancing, playing with their frogs and bubbles. The waiting was over. A family was complete.

As he smiled that beautiful smile and kissed her again, absolute joy in his eyes, she had to concede that her father had been right about one thing. All her dreams *had* come true.